I0655721

Of Sentimental Value

FUMI HANCOCK
Bestselling Author, Nollywood & African
Film Critics Association (NAFCA)~African
Oscar Peoples' Choice 2014 Favorite
Screenwriter Award Winner

http://www.worldoffumihancock.com   http://about.me/fumihancock
http://www.facebook.com/ofsentimentalvalue
http://www.twitter.com/cambiumbreakpix
http://www.ofsentimentalvaluenovel.com

Online TV Show: Your Vision Torch™:
The Princess in Suburbia™ Lifestyle TV Show~2014 NAFCA African Oscar nominated ~Best Talk Show www.princessinsuburbia.com

The Movie: Of Sentimental Value~ A Dramatic Suspense where Hollywood, Nollywood, Bollywood Ghollywood Collide!
http://www.ofsentimentalvalue.com
http://www.cambiumbreakpictures.com
http://www.ofsentimentalvaluemovie.com
Nominated for 2014 NAFCA African Oscar Peoples' Choice Awards" Best trailer, Best Original Scoring. It was also nominated for Best Drama in the foreign films category and Best Make Up.
Cover design by Phatpuppy Art

Printed in the United States of America. All rights reserved.
223 Towncenter Parkway, #2071, Spring Hill, TN 37174

Copyright © 2014 Fumi Stephanie Hancock - Princess in Suburbia® Brand
Library of Congress Control Number: 2014912625
ISBN: 0990584801
ISBN-13: 978-09905848-0-3

DEDICATION

To my wonderful husband, Dr. David Allen Hancock; my terrific children, Bola, Demola,; incredible step-daughters, Holly & Marlee; and my extended family, mom & dad, Prince & Princess T.A. Ogunleye, you are all loved and greatly cherished. Without your support, I could not have finished yet another great storytelling adventure. David Allen Hancock, you are my rock! Thank you. I salute my royal family, the Adumori Nigerian Ruling House, both in Emure Kingdom and in Diaspora. King Emmanuel Adebayo my royal father, thank you for believing in me.

To all the previous readers, reviewers and fellow authors of my first crack at fiction, The Adventures of Jewel Cardwell: HYDRA'S NEST; I thank you for pushing it to a bestseller list. Now, let's make it happen again alongside the movie, *Of Sentimental Value.*

A big thank you to my cover art designer, Phatpuppy Art, Claudia McKinney & Catie Crahan who rocked my world with their ingenuity. To Ese Morrison, who daily surprises me with his expertise in photography and video /film production, thank you. And to all of my cast members and crew/producer (Chichi Njoku) on Of Sentimental Value, the movie. Thank you for hanging in there and making the movie the best it could be.
To DStreet Films team, Demetrius Navarro, Matt Pavlo, Enrico Natale who helped in safely delivering the finished product ~ the movie. THANK YOU.

"Come, come Si-be-ria. Yes, that's right, come to me now!"

Her resounding evil laughter increases with the anticipation of doom lurking in the murky night. Suddenly, her phantomlike image is swallowed by the dusk. Just when I am about to breathe a sigh of relief, Yemoji's face reappears! Only this time, her limpid brown eyes begin to blink rapidly; morphing into a grayish set of eyes in distress, with the different, yet familiar, face of Naiya, you know her by now… that's right, my older sister! How could this be, thinking out loud? But then again, stranger things have been known to happen in my village. Before I could figure out if it was really my sister's face, the alarming tick-tock sound began yet again, the disconcerting image of Naiya abruptly disappearing. I am now left in the pitch black!

FUMI HANCOCK

DISCOVER
The Sorcerer's Purgatory

A Sequel to Bestselling Young Adult Fantasy
Novel~ The Adventures of Jewel Cardwell:
HYDRA'S NEST

COMING SOON TO BOOKSTORES
NEAR YOU!

FUMI HANCOCK

BESTSELLING BOOK

The Adventures of Jewel Cardwell: HYDRA'S NEST

AVAILABLE AT ALL BOOKSTORES (BRICK & MORTAR AND ONLINE STORES)

PRAISES FOR
Of SENTIMENTAL VALUE

A sentimental tale of family and the traditions that make us who we are, Of Sentimental Value will thrill and entertain you with its colorful mix of characters and intriguing story line. Bringing this story to life is an eclectic mix of actors and actresses that are well known to the big to the acting community. Of Sentimental Value is a must see and can be thoroughly enjoyed by the entire family.
LACHELLE REED, Author of When Angels Fall....

Hancock has no rivals for her writing on the mysteries of Africa! A gripping adventure, prepare for the ride of your life through the challenges, both in the physical and spiritual plane, of a teenage girl in deepest, darkest Africa!
NA~TIMES

I don't know if I'm cold but after watching the trailer, it gave me goose bumps. I love the fact that this author didn't show the face of the mystery lady and that gave it even more mystery....I can't wait to see the movie and finish the novel itself to find out about the stone and it's mysterious power and why everyone is looking for it....thank you for allowing me to be a part of this experience.
RUTH BROWN, Little Feather Brown

I absolutely loved the story and its' compelling trailer. I loved how it began and ended. The mystery woman certainly evokes a great deal of curiosity and then there is the Silleri stone... I really want to know more about that. It has the fantasy mystery about it. I showed it to my son and he loved it as well. The background music in the trailer is just awesome and adds to the mysterious effect. Congratulations.
CLARRISA CARTHARN, Author of Red Collar, Winter's End, Scents of Roses

This is a masterpiece depicting a mix of the very best from Hollywood, Bollywood and Nollywood characters. A foretaste of the trailer leaves no doubt whatsoever in the mind of the beholder that the genre of this work might have been predicated on a first class imagination of a literary expert but which ended as a hilarious dramatization of what ordinary African immigrants experience first hand in America. The introduction of the percussion with the unmistakable sounds of African drum beats (in the accompanying movie and trailer) set the pace for a pleasant and enjoyable evening out after dinner or a never-to-be-forgotten movie event at any time of the day.
THEODORE LEYE, Avid Reader & Movie Goer

CONTENTS

SIBERIA TONKA (Aleta Myles) THE MAIN FEMALE LEAD IN THE MOVIE PLAYS WITH THE CAMERA, WHICH WILL CHANGE HER LIFE FOREVER!

AUTHOR & FILMMAKER, PRINCESS
FUMI HANCOCK DOING HER THING
ON THE SET OF, OF SENTIMENTAL
VALUE.

It is during our darkest moments that we must focus to see the light.

Aristotle Onassis

"The Thing I fear the most has come upon me...."
Job 3:25

FUMI HANCOCK

1 MURKY HAZE

COME...LET ME TAKE YOU TO A LAND. A land of deep rich forest... a land where knowledge is our clothing and unconditional love our way of life. There is a river which runs deep in the heart of this land... come, drink from the river of wisdom. Our destination is Africa.

@@@@@

Spiraling through the murky haze is a stream of white smoke; Africa's humid and gloomy weather punctuated the striking of an African "bata" drum; a sign of impending doom in this Never-never land called Oyo, set majestically in the flat plain fields of West Africa.

Wrapped in ruffled white sheets and face painted with pungent white chalk, distinct tribal marks from Oyo; she chuckles and giggles out loud, sometimes overpowering the African "bata" beats rippling the air. This enigma of a mystery woman's deep tones carries with it an air of danger and magic. Her fiendish chuckles are exaggerated by her threatening mannerisms. She adds to the mystery in the air by thrusting out her spectacularly painted arms, holding a uniquely designed African clay pot filled with bubbling steaming water. The steam spiraling out of the magical pot is hypnotic. She begins to laugh again as the rhythmic African beat gently fades, instantly replaced by an urgent tick-tock sound, intensifying the anxiety. Seeing my clandestine woman's animated and daunting striking face, Yemoji becomes boisterous as she squints her overpowering eyes; eyeballs fiercely protruding, eliciting intense fear in those who behold the strange sight.

As the tick-tock sound gets louder, Yemoji abruptly clutches her magical pot to her bosom. Her arms stretch out with purpose, displaying her remarkably long claw-like nails. She beckons me closer. Yemoji welcomes hushes me into undeniably captivating presence, placing one finger to her sultry lips.

"Sshh! Sshh!"

Suddenly, the tick-tock sound intensifies yet again as Yemoji's thunderous and wickedly cold laughter reverberates into the atmosphere.

"Did you hear me? I said.... Sshh! Sshh! Siberia! Si-be-ria!"

Her voice echoes into the darkness of the night in my village, a place I'd called home all of my life… a place where I would sit under the gargantuan iroko tree… my village's popular meeting spot for the village youths. Of everything we prided ourselves on in this neck of the woods, first would be our iroko tree… a large hardwood majestically poised in the middle of the community, it's brownish color distinct. This is an enchanted place where I would scribble all of my innermost thoughts, my dreams… good, bad or indifferent. I would jot them all down on some stacks of crinkled paper.

This popular meeting spot carries with it an air of magic as the rumor permeating the slim and dusty streets of the village is that everyone who'd dare to sit under the tree would have all of their dreams come true, if you offered the right sacrifice! So every year during the summer season, the villagers would gather round and offer sacrifices to the spirit believed to live in the tree. While mama and papa warned me about believing such rumors, they were not taking any chances either with any of their children! They once called us in and reminded us what we'd heard growing up about the iroko tree... that the day you see the spirit come out, that is the day you become insane and die a miserable death! And whoever might choose to cut down that tree, just dumped a slew of misfortune upon his own head and that of generations of his family! With all of these rumors flying around, the tree had been sitting in the center of the village for over 200 years! Through it all, I was most enamored at the thought of my dreams coming to pass... and I was undaunted by the rumors. This was the chance of a lifetime and I was willing to take it!

At the setting of the moon, when mama and papa had said their good nights, I ran out and sat right beneath the tree, watching the sparkling stars and wishing my innermost dreams would quickly come true. Some time later, I was awoken from my dream by the rattling sounds of an airplane zooming through the often dark and murky skies of Oyo, my motherland.

While others had dreams of becoming the village's most popular caterer, or a plumber, or perhaps a teacher like both my parents, who were now retired, many others had more simple dreams... to be married at the expected age of nineteen. Mine? I would watch the airplanes fly by and wished one day I would be in it, jetting away to a land I'd heard of… a land where we'd gather in the village hall and, through the television, watched the white and black folks walk around like they are going somewhere….a land they'd told me was flowing with milk and honey. It was a land with a Midas touch; you had no choice but to succeed. America … a free country they say, is a land of opportunity with streets inlaid with gold that bedazzle everyone on that part of the planet. This wonderful dream is where the daily hunger most experience here in my home village is non-existent! If you ask me, it reads like heaven! And one day, I will ride in one of those powerful jumbo jets and fly away from a place I'd called home for all of my twenty years and venture into a world where all of my hopes and aspirations of becoming a bestselling author are just waiting for me! The thought of one day accomplishing all of this fuels my pen and I find myself ignoring the strange noises coming from within the iroko tree. The noise the young villagers have been warned to stay away from. Whatever that strange and evil spitting noise was, it was inconsequential to my big dream. If sitting through the scary noise meant my dream of flying away and being all I'd prayed for would be accomplished; then no evil scare could deter me away from sitting under the tree…. Well, except for my parents who I knew would be livid if they knew what their youngest daughter was doing every night when the whole village was asleep.

Of all of my parent's children, Naiya Tonka and myself, I was the one they'd always referred to as the one who would probably kill them from worrying. Mother calls me the daredevil amongst the clan, while Naiya, the oldest, was the quiet home-body type. Naiya, in her early twenties, is content with living the village life; a desire she took from mama and papa who'd spent most of their lives in the village. Naiya hopes to one day get married and settle down as a primary school teacher. Her wish to become a teacher finally came true and now she awaits the suitors… the right one, at least. The one mama and papa believe would take good care of their daughter. Though the clock has long passed her over, as other youths in the village rudely remind her, she is nervous at the thought of no one coming to seek her hand in marriage. Mother, on the other hand, a secret rebel herself, rests on that issue, fervently reminding Naiya that she has a home with them and should wait for the right man to show up, a concept totally strange to papa. They married when mama was exactly nineteen years of age.

@@@@@

"Come, come Si-be-ria. Yes, that's right, come to me now!"
Her resounding evil laughter increases with the anticipation of doom lurking in the murky night. Suddenly, her phantomlike image is swallowed by the dusk. Just when I am about to breathe a sigh of relief, Yemoji's face reappears! Only this time, her limpid brown eyes begin to blink rapidly; morphing into a grayish set of eyes in distress, a yet familiar, face of Naiya, you know her by now… that's right, my older sister! How could this be, thinking out loud? But then again, stranger things have been known to happen in my village. Before I could figure out if it was really my sister's face, the alarming tick-tock sound began yet again, the disconcerting image of Naiya abruptly disappearing. I am now left in the pitch black!
Dear diary, my name is Siberia Tonka and this is my

story. Born in the heart of Oyo, a land though riddled with poverty yet rich in colorful culture and fierce tradition; a place I hope to one day return; fortified with wealth and notoriety as Africa's biggest superstar! When you read my story, some of you may love me; others... well. Here is my story.

2 A LAND OF HORRID DREAMS?

LYING COMFORTABLY UNDER MY RUFFLED SHEETS ON MY SOFA BED in my brightly colored living room, I wake from an unsettling dream… literally jumping out of my skin! Thanking the heavens that I woke up from the nightmare, I quickly roll my hot, sweaty body out of the bed. I take my seat quietly, attempting to pull my sweat-stained nightshirt off of my skinny body, replacing the gown with a long t-shirt and sweat pants and begin pacing around the room, worried about the horrible dream I just had. If this is what America is all about, then I'd gotten it all wrong! My people back in Oyo had gotten it all wrong! Since my arrival to this land of milk and honey, nothing has worked out for me. All the fantastic stories I'd read in papers back home in Africa seemed so far off now. Instead of meeting with a wealthy and plush lifestyle, it seems I am getting more and more into debt… I am being swallowed by the darkness that I thought I'd left behind in Africa. The harder I try to push my writing, the deeper and farther away I seem to be living from my elaborate dream life. The only hope I am hanging onto is waking up to the sound of my TV idol, The Princess of Suburbia, an icon I'd admired most of my adult life. She was my inspiration for packing up and leaving, convincing my parents that I was better off attending a college here in America. After many agonizing discussions and making their lives as miserable as I could, mama and papa finally gave in to my ranting and raving… it was time for me to venture into the world I'd so admired from afar.

Winning the last African beauty pageant was the opportunity I'd been waiting for all of my life. As part of the benefits of winning, I'd won a scholarship to attend a college in Nashville, Tennessee, a place I'd never even thought to look up on the map. I was familiar with the Big Apple… New York City and I'd hope to one day land there. I settled for Nashville, Tennessee and desperately prayed the abundant rain of blessing from the Big Apple would overshadow me in the music city. Either way, I was better off being here… as I was closer to my dream to be a celebrated writer! I was closer, or so I thought!

Framing the sides of the beaten up looking laptop on my study table are THE PRINCESS OF SUBURBIA's inspirational books. Her latest book, the Adventures of Jewel Cardwell, a young adult fantasy novel, is displayed face up on the much disorganized and completely overloaded study table. I aimlessly reach out to my laptop, hit the play button and turn up the volume. There was my hero; my reason for being in the United States of America… The Princess of Suburbia, a woman I considered my imaginary personal mentor. I was suddenly drawn to the image of this elegant looking African Princess, making it big in America. I slowly settled at the edge of my bed, listening attentively and taking notes for my next steps in seeking my elusive stardom.

@@@@@

"That's right; I said it again and again! This is your day to get up from underneath that slumber! You can do it. You can make a difference if you put your mind to it," her voice echoes through my room. I quickly mumble those affirmations, repeating after the Princess.

"Stop believing the hype that you are a failure! You can't quit now. You too can be a bestselling author, if you desire it enough and if you are willing to do the work... I want you to say this after me," she continues amiably and with both of our voices in sync.

"Being my authentic self is the beginning of success. I can achieve it if I believe it. I will only receive what I believe. Today, I choose to be a winner and not a failure!" I desperately echo her voice like my life is dependent on it and certainly very soon, I too would have a success story to share with the world. In the midst of my dangling fear of failure, I can always count on the Princess to pump blood back into my heart again, with her inspirational words. My aching, tired heart melts as she begins to blow her usual love kisses into the screen and straight into my room. Just when I think my day could get no better, the unimaginable happens! The Princess of Suburbia announces that she is coming to a book club near my house! If this is not fate, then I don't know what it is! The odds of her choosing to come to an event in my small town were very slim. But there it is, an opportunity is finally here, when I will get to meet her one-on-one! Perhaps a joyous moment has finally come upon me. Either way, I am not going to miss this for anything in the world. Whatever great favor she has going for her, I will get close enough to tap into it.

@@@@@

Piti-pat! Piti-pat, piti-pat"… the sound jars my mid-day fantasy. It is light footsteps from behind my room window. I have lived in this neighborhood long enough to know exactly whose footsteps they are. Jessica and, argh, yes, Josie her sister. These two Hispanic ladies are the nosiest people in town. They are sometimes obnoxious and intrusive yet one could be captivated by their caring attitude towards others, especially Jessica. Her slightly accented Spanglish is blossoming every day while Josie's thick Spanish accent often drives me crazy. Whoever says my accent is too strong to understand; I now know the cure… Josie!

No woman is an island, as Jessica would always say to me, as she accosts me on my way out of the my home. She has an uncanny way of always knowing when I sneak out of my house… I could swear that she has a "bug" in my house to watch my every move. With their steps getting louder and closer, I quickly pull back my curtains, in time to see Jessica and Josie panting; looking out of breath. I hid behind my curtains and watched them argue with each other, an event all too familiar to me as their neighbor. When Jessica and Josie get irate, no one hears what they are saying, especially Josie who turns into a bull dog, ranting and raving in her mother tongue, wild enough for anyone to guess she is angry….

"Hold up mama I'm out of breath" Jessica gasping for air even more visibly.

"We are out of time. Come on," Josie replies, still attempting to take few more steps towards their house, a little bungalow cushioned behind some oak trees across from my residence. As soon as Jessica looks in my direction, I withdraw further behind the curtains. I was not ready to start my day yapping with her. After my little unsettling dream and my recent cozy moment with the Princess of Suburbia to wind me down, I was not ready to be excited again with those two. I found my way back to my sofa, picked up my remote and slid into yet another inspirational message from my heroine. With all the problems I have encountered in America, not being able to pay my bills on time, not finding any job to help with my bills and my rent overdue; the Princess of Suburbia was my temporary respite from the hard realities of life.

"Gosh, I love this woman. What an inspiration she is and she is actually coming here. I don't care what it takes, I have to meet her," mumbling then sighing in pure elation. Just as I was settling into yet another episode of the Princess of Suburbia's talk show, an intense hammering noise interrupts my temporary bliss. With all of my attempts to ignore the horrendous banging at the door, Jessica's rattling voice comes crashing through the delicately hinged door, her sister's heavily laced Hispanic-accented voice follows suit. Suddenly, all my attempts to avoid them fail. Raising her voice in an extremely high pitch, Jessica blasts out ignoring the discomfort this may be causing the rest of the neighbors on the street, "Mama! Are you there mama?" She continues banging away at my door. Then and there, I knew I had two options; ignore her and hope when she got tired of knocking on hard wood she'd quit and leave or should I just bite the bullet, open the door and shed of my privacy. The minutes of constant banging seemed like eternity, my head pounding to the rhythm. There was no end in sight to their noise, so I got up and sluggishly and reluctantly found my way to the door. Jessica's hand was poised mid-bang, hanging in the air, when I pulled my door open.

"What is it Jessica? I am really tired. What do you want?"

"Me? Want something? No mama. This is your problem mama. Just trying to help" she replies, guardedly.

"What do you mean my problem Jessica? What is going on?" I inquired in haste, scanning from Jessica's position to Josie who is half on the street with worry written all over her face.

"If I hear any bad news, I don't know if I can take it... But here we go, what is wrong Jessica? Spit it out please. Don't keep me in suspense."

"Look... Josie and I have been trying to get you to come out..." Jessica rambles on.

"Yeah... yeah.... Yeah. I am out now Jessica, let's have it."

"Well mama, there is no time to waste," she continues.

"For what Jessica... Josie?"

"Come on Jessica, do your thing and let's be out of here quick!"

"We need to leave now!" with much anxiety.

"And why would I want to do that Jessica? When was the last time I went anywhere with you?" I added.

"True.."

"Detour Jessica! Don't detour from the truth! Spit it out please unless you want me to! After all, you are the soft , gentle and kinder one, right Jess?" she yells from across the lawn.   "Hush your mouth girl!," Jessica lashes out at Josie.

"Then quit wasting time!" Josie replies, anger rising in her tone.

"Your car is being repossessed!" Jessica blurted out.

"What? I parked it where you told me to... blocks away from your house."

"I know, that's why I ran over to let you know. The repo guy is now handling his business. We need to go quickly. Come on Siberia," Jessica adds to my misery.

"You said no one would find it there. What is this nonsense Jessica! How could they have found it there?"

"Well I don't know what to tell you sister, someone did! The tow company did mama," she replies forcefully pulling one of my arms towards the street.

"I can't believe this Jessica. After all of my efforts to keep this car out of sight!

"So sorry mama, I really thought it was safe there. I didn't think anyone would go out there," Jessica continues apologetically.

"Jessica, is this a cock-a-bull story! Seriously girl! The place is supposed to be safe. Right?" lashing out at her, ready to pound on anyone who would give my anger audience.

"But why are you blaming me for this mama? I didn't call the repo man," Jessica responds, completely nonplussed by my reaction.

"I was only trying to help you mama. Is this the thanks I get?" Jessica increasing upset at my ingratitude.

"Look I am just exhausted from waking up to one drama or the other. This America thing... don't know how long I can hang in here," reacting to Jessica's words.

"Okay sister, you've got two choices... stay here and continue to yell at my sister; or we run down the street and see what we can do with the tow truck man.

Choose your poison. What will it be?" Josie yelled in support of her sister. Astounded that Josie would even support her sister, they both stared me down, waiting for my response.

"Well then, perhaps you have made your decision. Don't you dare say we didn't warn you later!" Josie begins walking away from Jessica.

"Hold up. Did I say I was not coming? After all it is my car, right?"

"Well then, let's go! We have wasted enough time as is. Hopefully, he is still there…" Josie replies as she steps out to begin her run.

"Well, are you coming or are you going to stand there being mad at me?" Jessica inquires as she follows her sister.

"Okay Jessica, run along. I am behind you. I need to bring some papers along… Please hurry… go now… so someone is at least is there before I get there.

"Alright then… I will follow Josie," Jessica replies smiling in my direction breaking the ice between us.

"Hey Jessica, sorry I yelled at you. I am just upset that anyone saw the car there. I thought it was nicely tucked away," reaching out to her and hugging her.

"How warm and cozy! Now, can we go people before this man leaves with the car?" Josie interrupts our moment of reconciliation.

"Don't be jealous sister; we are just making up," Jessica replies, laughing at Josie's surly manners.

"Jealous of you two? God forbid such a thing. One minute you are best buddies, the next you want to choke each other! Who wants to be jealous of that? Besides, I think I have enough of you as my blood sister! Let's move people!," she replies sharply.

"Whatever you say sister. I know what I see!,"
Jessica replies.

"Josie, we heard you. Okay, let's go... quickly!"
Jessica follows Josie out into the street
"Don't be late Siberia" Jessica yells as she
makes her way down across the street.

Soon I follow them and we all run into the street, then
galloping across the greenery towards Jessica's cozy little
ranch house located across from Siberia's rented house. The
car had been on a street behind the house. Josie is in the front
row, followed by Jessica with me dragging along.... At a
distance.

@@@@@

ALAN HAMILTON, a forty-something year old, rugged
looking, 6 ft African immigrant and a high end art collector is
cruising along the road in his black Escalade. Alan' parents
had immigrated to the US when he was 5 years old. America
is where he'd call home though his South African accent was
still audible as his parents spoke Zulu (Afrikaans is the
language of the white oppressors) at home when he was
growing up. His parents always believed in keeping their
culture pure and alive with their family. However, they also
believed in taking the best of both worlds and taking
advantage of it. They worked hard as scientists, sending all
three of their children, Alan included, to the best schools.
Alan graduated from Harvard with a degree in Architectural
design and has since taken his love for everything
architecturally sound and beautiful and adapted it to his first
love, the Arts. His gallery is the talk of the town, elegantly

displayed on top of a hilly road in a back woods area of Nolensville in Middle Tennessee. His showings attract the who's who of the Nashville scene, political and entertainment mavens, causing a constant buzz around town. Some call him cocky, others see him has just confident in his craft of fishing out the rare gems others could not find. Alan gently lowers the volume of classical music melodically pulsing out of his over-priced stereo as he aligns his wheels with the curves of the back road on the way to his gallery. As usual, he is not doing anything out of the ordinary in picking up a call while driving. This morning, he is attempting to hold a conversation with his assistant over his cell phone, a very common habit his assistant had often warned him about. His childhood friend, JACK RUBEAU, a modern day, self-proclaimed forty something 5ft 11 ladies' man just landed in the USA from South Africa. Jack is enjoying the classical music while Alan is shifting between paying attention to the road and engaging in a heated debate on the phone. In the middle of the intense dialog, Alan slows down as he approaches a curvy section of the road.

"Tell him that is not acceptable, Sue. $1 million and that is my final offer!" he yells into the cell phone. Jack, unsettled at Alan's irate posture while driving, he attempts to catch Alan's attention in an easy-going and calm voice.

"Old boy, you and your wheeling and dealing while driving... One of these days, you will hit someone with your car. Just make sure she is a fine broad", he says jestingly.

"It's been two years since I last saw you. You have not changed a bit." He pauses to listen to Sue at the other side of the line. "Yes, I am here Sue".

"That's me Alan. I have absolutely nothing to

change brother. Life's been great. I can't complain." Jack replies with his usual alluring grin.

"You see what I mean, you and your killer grin!"

"Old boy, get your own grin. Whatever works man... Whatever works on my ladies."

"Yes, right. And your women out there in South Africa?"

"What about them?"

"Well, are they treating you right, or should I say are you treating them right?"

"Of course, I treat them well. That is why they can never get enough of good old Jack Rubeau," he sneers, his confidence radiating. "That's right Jack. That's why you are not married yet, right brother!" Alan becomes cynical.

"Whatever brother. The grass is too green to settle on just one for now. I have too much to do!" Jack replies.

"Really?"

"Yes, really Alan! But wait a minute, why are you on my case? When there may be fire burning down your own home," Jack replies with a curious look.

"I don't know what you mean Jack," Alan responds, avoiding the question.

"That's right. Of course you won't know when it comes to your dirt."

"You are impossible pal... absolutely impossible... Yes Sue, I am not changing my stance on that, okay Sue" Alan speaks into the phone.

"Anyhow, I'm here now. Another day man... more time for relaxation." Jack interjects.

Suddenly, Sue comes back on over the phone with Alan

again, this time with Alan covering a piece of the cell phone, avoiding Jack's words from being heard by Sue. He opens up the line again....

"Look Sue, I don't have time to be jerked around on this deal. He either takes the money or I pull out and go somewhere else" Alan continues in his elevated tenor, then soon turns in Jack's direction as he awaits a response from Sue.

"Look, are you going to get off the phone before you get us both killed? Or do I have to haul that away from your ear?" Jack warns.

"You are not serious partner. Anyways, this is how we do it here in the states bro'. No work , no play... no enjoyment of the finer things in life... It's as simple as that!

"Look old boy, I could take offense at your tone. We work in South Africa too. We just do it in a smart way. If you know what I mean," Jack replies.
Alan nods at him, unconvincingly. Jack winds down his side window and breathes fresh air in. He sighs in total contentment.

"Mmm! America. Ready or not, here I come!" Alan continues to juggle between the conversation he is holding over the phone with Sue and the animated tête-à-tête with Jack in the truck. Jack looks ahead as Alan's truck winds through the curvy terrain.

"Listen, I know everyone wants that baby... but here is the deal, I know I have the upper hand here. He either takes $1 million or the deal is off... right now! I mean it Sue, I've had enough of the jerking around." He pauses for a response, then continues raining his anger at Sue over the phone.

"I don't know why that broad takes your

junk!" Jack undertone.

"S-s-s-h! Don't go there," Alan warns Jack.

"Alright then, get me his number. I need to speak with him directly. Want to put an end to this," he added in a frustrated manner. Alan quickly returns back to his discussion with Jack as he waits for Sue with the number he'd requested.

"Heavens help the women who fall prey to your charming smirk this time."

"What are you trying to do. Please leave heaven out of this man."

"What? You are afraid of heaven pal?"

"No. I just say leave it out of our woman discussion. From where I am standing, may God spare the man who gets in my way of finding happiness. Time to party friend… it's time to really have some fun," attempting to close the discourse.

"Does that mean you are ready to settle down?" Alan asks emphatically. "Right man, you are ready to settle down?" Alan asks again. Jack pauses, smiles with no definite answer and begins swirling to the rhythm of the classical music in the background as his whistles accentuates the lyrics.

"This much I know, a thunderous hurricane will sweep this country when you get married. Lord, all the female casualties you'll be leaving behind." Alan says cynically.

"Na you sa be… That is your headache man. Not mine… what casualties? Everyone knew what they were getting into." Jack replies.

"I see you still break out in that pidgin English once a while," Alan inquires.

"I live in South Africa now, old boy, you

didn't think I was leaving that behind me, right?"

"I suppose," Alan replies.

"It keeps me grounded." Jack adds.

"Whatever floats your boat."

"Well then, I thank his royal highness for concurring…" Jack replies jokingly.

"At any rate, I can only imagine the pool of women who will raise war against you when that happens."

"Look ol' boy, leave that alone. I have long ways to go… Not in a rush," Jack trying to avoid the tensed up conversation. "You are killing my buzz here pal, come on. Lay off this… seriously."

Alan slows down, and pulls over into a street. He pulls his pen from his shirt pocket, attempting to jot down whatever Sue was sharing on the other end of the conversation.

"Typical for you to digress when we are talking about your escapades!"

"From where I am standing, you are no saint either bro"

"Not sure what you've been hearing but I've been good… "

"Yeah… right! Tell that to the pope when he comes around."

"Seriously… really been good. Really shocked me too," Alan grins with an air of arrogance and gratification.

"You can fool everyone else, not me Jack. Not me…Remember how we used to run around together? Yeah, please…"

"That's been a long time ago brother. This old guy has changed."

"Yes Sue, I am still here. Oh, please don't let

my assistant hear all that stuff," Alan whispers in his direction.

"You are the one talking too much about it. From where I am sitting, she probably has a bucket full of stuff on you already," Jack adds. "Leopards do not change their spots... old or not," Jacks continues. "And as for me, oh well, se la vie! It's just one of me, I can't marry them all." Jack speaks sarcastically.

"Hey, hey, hey, you are not in Africa where you can commit such acts. Unless you are ready to go to prison for it." Alan exclaims.

"How is Fanta by the way?" He awaits Alan's response. His question met by a firm stare that says more than words.

"You just proved my point. Reason why I am taking my time right now, and just enjoying the company of women. Enough said on that." Jack watches Alan struggle to jot down the address being given to him over the phone, while maneuvering the steering, all at the same time.

"Don't know what you guys are doing... married... living together ... what is it?" He continues.

"When I figure it out, you'll be the first to know," Alan shuts the discussion down with a cold stare; struggling with the phone and the pen.

"Hand me that, my friend. What are you doing? Trying to get both of us killed?" Jack finally snatches the pen and paper from Alan

"Oh knock it off Jack" He replies, not paying much attention to anything else around him. but focusing on Jack writing the number as he dictates it. Alan keeps his eyes on the pad instead of the road.

"Okay, let's have it... 5 -5 -5 –9 -8 -9 -6...yes

Sue?" Alan continues. Jack hands over the paper to Alan as soon as he'd finishes writing the number.

"Okay Sue. Thanks doll." Alan concludes his phone call and steps on the gas.

"Hey! You be careful with stepping on those pedals, you are carrying a special person here!"
Alan gazes in Jack's direction, then proceeds to step on the gas again, revving his engine as he drives along.

@@@@@

Jessica and Josie run through the intersection and keep running towards where my car is about to be high-jacked, with me lagging behind. Alan looks on as he proceeds into the intersection. We arrive at the same time.

"Whoa…whoa… Alan, stop quick!' Jack yells, looking like a deer in the headlights, only it was already too late. Before he could turn his head away from Jack's direction, he hears a loud scream, a thump sound and a screech his front tires. He had just had an accident; the one Jack had forewarned him of. Alan and Jack look in the direction of the screaming.

"Oh no!" Alan horrified.

"I know that's right!," Jack belts out in an anxious tone, as they both jump out of the truck.

3 THE CHEETAH STRIKES

THE SOUND OF A RACING HEART
EXPLODES INTO THE ATMOPSPHERE. Yemoji,
the mystery woman strikes again! Only this time, it is
in the heart of Africa! She laughs wickedly into the air
as darkness surrounds her. The force of her voice
echoes through the air in the green lands of Oyo,
clashing with her racing heartbeat. Suddenly, the
taunting sound stops! Naiya Tonka, Siberia's sister
jumps off her mat from her seemingly disturbed sleep;
looking like she'd seen a ghost. She grabs her chest;
then starts to scream! Dade, her robust looking mother
rushes to her side in total panic. Frustrated and
helpless, she watches her daughter's arms wrap around
her head, as she complains of a blinding headache.
    "Naiya, what is wrong? What
happened?" mama asks with an unshakable dread,

25

staring in Naiya's direction. Naiya's hands shake profusely, moving from her head, her protruding and rolling eyes, her severe pain and her nauseous stomach.

"Mama, my head ache is getting worse," Naiya replies in excruciating pain. Her cry escalates as sweat rolls copiously down her face as she rolls across her mat. Her father, Lani, rushes into the room alongside his wife.

"You this girl, you won't kill your mother and I. What happened this time?" looking completely perturbed by Naiya's health.

"Baba Naiya, what kind of questions are these? Eih? Look at your daughter! Don't you believe she is sick?" She lambasts her husband in anger.

"Look woman, don't misunderstand me. Who says I don't believe her! I am just frustrated, that's all," He replies to his angry and defensive wife.

"I am really worried oh. Since Siberia left, this girl's headache has not let up. The doctor can't find anything wrong. Even all the medicine… none has worked. Now she is beginning to run temperature too." Mama exclaims. Naiya's moaning and groaning intensifies as her father proceeds to examine her. He plants the back of his right hand against her forehead.

"What are you doing Baba Naiya? Are you the doctor now?"

"Be quiet woman, let me feel her head a

little," he replies.

"And what is that going to do? We need a quick and permanent solution and all you are doing is feeling her head! Will that cure her? Eih, tell me Baba Naiya," her anxiety increases along with Naiya's powerful screams. Naiya suddenly grabs her stomach, squints her eyes and continues to roll across the mat.

"My stomach mama… Mama, am I dying?"

"S-s-sh! Be quiet, don't say such a thing. Die? No way!" She looks in papa's direction as if wanting a promise that her daughter will not die.

"Right Baba Naiya, please tell your daughter she won't die! Right Baba Naiya?" Dade looks in her husband's direction with intensity.

"You heard your mother, you won't die," he responds with less conviction as Naiya's pain appears to have heightened.

"What do we do now?" Naiya's mother asked. "What are you going to do Baba Naiya?" she adds.

"Me? I am not God. What do you mean what am I going to do?" He answers defending his stance.

"You are her father, shouldn't I ask you what you will do?"

"All well and good. I am equally upset right now with all of her screaming." He replies.

"We don't have time… you have to think of something. I am tired of watching her in this much pain." She belts out. "Baba Naiya! Baba Naiya!" she

27

yells, perceiving him to be in profound thought.

"Are you hearing me?" She repeats.

"Go get me the boys. We need to get her to the native doctor quick!" He adds.

"The native doctor? Haba Baba Naiya, did you say native doctor?" She asks.

"Yes. Since the English doctor cannot find anything, I know Baba doctor will tell us what is wrong, once and for all." He responds with confidence.

He watches mama's body movement. She sits still, not responding to papa's instructions.

"Well, are you just going to sit there and contend with my instructions or are you going to do something to save your daughter?" He says.

"Now she is my daughter! She is yours too!"

"Look woman, quit arguing with me. Just do as I say!" Papa laments.

"I don't know Baba Naiya." She replies looking puzzled.

"Well, that is the only suggestion I have now. Please Mama Naiya, run along and get me the boys...please!" He adds, making his way to his daughter's side. Papa, taking his place by Naiya's side; mama makes her exit, screaming, with her arms struggling to hold on to the loose rolls of cloth wrapped around her from the waist down.

"Mama Naiya, handle yourself please.

You are not going to unrobe yourself and go naked in front of your daughter," papa observing his wife's struggle with the traditional African wrap.

"Leave me alone, Baba Naiya. I will do whatever I like. Even go naked, if I know it will heal my daughter." She adds.

"That is beside the point now. Just hurry back with the boys." She finally exits the hut.

"What is wrong with me papa? Why am I in so much pain?" Naiya looks into her father's eyes.

"We will soon find out. In the meantime, you need to conserve your strength. No more yelling."

"It's the pain papa…"

"I know but you must conserve your strength and don't shout too much. You hear me."

"Yes papa," she continues squinting her eyes, groaning in pain.

Mama storms back into the hut and heads straight to her daughter's side. Onye & Onka Tonka, Naiya's clownish-looking first cousins follow her into the sparsely lighted room. Dressed in their signature style, Onka, who identifies himself as the book worm of the Tonka clan and Onye, the sneaky and often conniving smooth operator. Their combined talents are lethal to the harmony of their community and they are habitually in trouble. When Onye is not busy duping people out of their hard earned money, Onka is busy accosting the young girls in the community. The word on the streets is that when Onye and Onka are on the road, even the animals in the community run and hide. Lately, they have been subdued; since their parents sent them to papa and mama to live there until further notice. They figured what better way to train them than to send them to two retired teachers who had obviously done well with their own children.

"Baba, what is wrong with Naiya?" Onka inquires as he moves into position.

"You two have eyes, use them! Now, please support her on each side. We need to take her to Baba, the herbalist."

"Quick! Carry her on that side." He says, watching Naiya being moved off the mat. They swiftly rush Naiya out of the room just in time for another bout of crying.

@@@@@

Back in the Nashville, Tennessee, Alan and Jack look ahead as they make their way out of the car with Jack trailing after Alan. Alan raises his head in my direction. It was as if heaven was opening up right in front of me and the wonderful angels parading in all of their glorious dazzling, spotless white ropes. Our eyes meet and instantly lock together. Suddenly, I feel everything around me moving in a slow motion… slow enough for me to digest his wonderfully symmetrical face with killer sideburns making his way towards me. If heaven looked like this, I was definitely enjoying it. The closer he gets, the closer I tell myself... Siberia, you must compose yourself! Whatever is causing this shiver down my spine must be stopped before he gets close to me. And whatever I do, I must not let him see my bald head! The musky masculine scent wafting from him fills my nostrils as I battle with my displaced scarf, adjusting myself. I hear his side-kick yell after him but it was unclear what he was saying. My eyes collide with his friend's, right when I'd finished adjusting my scarf. It seemed like Jack noticed my desperate move to cover my head. He grins in my direction and pulls back a little, leaving enough room for his friend to arrive at my side first. The man's face, after the unbridled horror of hitting me, lights up as if he'd seen an angel.

"What a paragon of beauty," he muffles under his labored breathe.

"Hello there, my name is Alan. And that is my friend Jack... And your name?" Before I could respond, the two begin an onslaught of argument between them.

"Say what?" Jack inquires.

"Nothing."

"That was not ... nothing ol' boy," he murmurs as Alan ignores his comment.

"You look like you just won the lottery," Jack adds jokingly, glancing in my direction too. He walks up to the enamored looking Alan and whispers gently into his ear.

"Easy boy... down... down boy. You are

showing your hand too early in the game."

"Oh stop it Jack! Must everything be a joke to you?"

"Just saying partner… Just saying what I see." He replies shrugging his shoulders.
Alan nods in disapproval and walks towards me while his friend backs off.

"Don't worry about me, I will just stay here and watch this" He continues in sarcasm. "Oh, by the way, don't forget your old lady at home, yes?" Jack playfully reminds Alan.

"Since when do you care about Fanta? Please spare me your sarcasm. We have a serious issue to address here!" Alan yells at him.

"From the look of things, your prey is fine" he looks in my direction again.

"You are a real buzz kill, that's what you are. Whatever suits you, stay there…suit yourself," Alan leans in, his stunning brown eyes still fixed on me. I sat in the middle of the road, totally captivated by his body next to mine. The sudden soft breeze blowing gently set the perfect ambiance. The lapels of his nicely fitted navy blue jacket flaps gently in the wind that swirls around me. With his eyes locked on to mine, I try looking away but cannot resist the power lurking behind his daunting gaze. Whatever this is, I want to explore it, ignoring the pain shooting down my spine. I jump up from underneath his fresh breath, place my palms on top of his heated truck while eyeing him. He too jumps up and comes to my side.

"Are you alright? Are you hurt young lady?" His baritone voice booms through my ear drums. If this is heaven, I don't want to come back from the bliss. Gosh, I am so enthralled … completely enchanted so that I uncontrollably and foolishly blurt out the most silly phrase anyone could have ever said to a man....

"Am I in the light?" shouting shamelessly.

"What light? Perhaps I need to get you to a hospital." His deep tone eliciting erotic feelings within me. These are certainly feelings I have not experienced before. I am afraid of it all. What does this mean for me? And why will this quivering, unnerving, tingling excitement not stop?

"Hey Jack, you know any close by hospital?" He yells out.

"You tell me, you are the one who lives here, remember?" Jack responds in sarcasm.

"No, I don't need a hospital," I interrupt.

"Miss? Lady?" His firm, bold hands warming their way towards my quivering body. "Are you alright?" He either keeps repeating or my overactive brain is tricking me. His last effort to help me finally pulls me out of my dream world! My reality is that this dude practically ran over me! Reality number two, that this blissful hunk could have killed me, that was my reality! My other reality? Well, this eye candy takes my breath away and no one has ever done that… until now! I fling my eyes open, feeling his firm hands resting on my shoulders. Mama always told me to be careful of people who try to get in your space quickly. I instantly shrug them off, carefully inspecting my body for any bruises or bumps.

"Look Miss, I am only trying to make sure you're okay! That's all." He speaks yet again.

"Yeah, sure, right! Don't you think you've done enough helping mister?"

"What do you know… the damsel in distress speaks," Jack speaks out from his position.

"And what's that supposed to mean?," Alan interrupts Jack.

"Oh please ol' boy, carry on," he begins laughing out loud.

"I don't need all of this ridicule! You and your friend can leave now. I am fine!" I blast out, startled by Jack's comments.

"Oh, take it easy young lady. I know he doesn't mean any harm by that… right Jack?" He pauses looking in Jack's direction for a bail out. "You didn't mean that insensitive statement, Jack, right?" Alan repeats in a firm tone.

"Oh, whatever you say Casanova. You know me, I am never serious." Jack grins in my direction.

"I see you are limping.. let me help you,"

he reaches out to grab my arm. "

"Never mind, I am fine…I am just peachy!" I snap at him as I gaze in Jack's direction… who stands aloof, waving at me with his sheepish looks. What if this man was behaving this way because he has figured out what was in my mind? Back in Africa, Naiya always told me that it was never a smart idea to let a man know how you felt; a theory I was about to explore in all its validity and reliability right in the middle of the road in America. Lost in my thoughts, I suddenly hear Naiya's opinionated voice chanting! In response, I retreat from my fantasy and dish out a blaze of anger at the man standing in front of me. My cover up story? Him almost running me off the road with his expensive looking truck! In my mind's eye, a perfect way of turning him off … advice given to me by my wise sister, Naiya.

"Next time, you may want to watch the intersection before you pull out!" I continue my cover up, unsure if it was helping him or me mostly. Shaken by my irrational misconduct, Alan stands perplexed as I proceed to catch up with my friends. Completely flustered, he glances at his friend, staring him down and stopping Jack from making any of his smart remarks.

"Whatever it is, I don't want to hear it. Seriously!" He speaks out to Jack.

"What? Watch me do nothing!" Jack responds with relentless cynicism. As his amusement escalates, so is Alan's lack of patience with him.

"Seriously Jack... stop!" He continues, looking as serious as ever.

"Touchy! Touchy! Aren't we? I'm just amused by you partner," Jack continues giggling. He curtsies in my direction and makes his way back to the truck. Alan's perplexed gaze rests on me. I slightly limped away from his magnificent presence and onto the road again.

"I've got to run." My African accent deliberately prominent.

"Are you sure you are alright?" Alan asks again.

"And if I'm not, I will find my way to the hospital, okay? Just watch where you are going next time please!" I reply, trying to arouse his anger.

"Same goes for you too, lady!"

"What?"

"You practically jumped into the street, remember?" He continues.

"Look mister, to each his own. You and I both know you were not paying attention either. So, let's cut the bull right here, okay?"

There was a sudden silence between the two of us; as if we were both waiting for the other to gracefully adjourn the lingering meeting. As he reaches out to grab my flexed arm, electricity surges through my body. Then and there, I know I need to stay away from him! If I know what's best for me, if I truly want to get rid of this distraction and not be sidetracked from my goal of someday becoming famous for my writing, he is one person to stay away from! Gazing his way, I keep telling myself… Siberia run… run as fast as you can!

@@@@@

The girls arrive at the place where my jalopy is parked. They are out of breath. They had been running non-stop and finally look back to see me panting and dragging my hurt leg towards them. Jessica and Josie look concerned, watching me carefully as I approach them.

"Okay mama, what is wrong with you?" Jessica yells out as I get closer to them.

"Que?" Josie echoes Jessica.

"Long story girls… long story," I turn towards the tow truck man.

"You are such a magnet for trouble Siberia," Josie exclaims. It only took us going ahead of you to get into trouble?" Josie continues.

"I said I will tell you later." I slam down hard on Josie.

"What? You gonna yell at me like that?" Josie upset.

"Serves you right," Jessica comments.

"Sorry, I didn't mean to. Just need a break," I add. Our discussion was soon interrupted by the grinding noise coming from the tow truck man yanking his chains toward my car. We all look on as he attaches the hook.

"Do something girl! Do it fast!" Josie whispers pushing me in his direction.

"Hey! Wait a minute, what's going on?" Yelling at him in my frustration.

"Repo. Just doing my job ma'am." He replies politely with a rich and thick southern accent.

"Can you just wait one minute and talk to me?" I demand of him.

"Sorry ma'am, I'm on the clock." He responds still on track with pulling my car up onto his toll truck. He walks around the car, marking on his paper all of his inspection points.

"I can't let you take this car. This is the only transportation I have." I belt out in desperation.

"Please step aside and let me do my job." He suddenly turns off his southern charm and continues unsympathetically.

"Please have compassion. I have a job interview today."

"No can do ma'am. You need to contact your finance company." Dismissing my friends and I.

"What is your name again?" I asks trying to make small talk.

"Didn't say ma'am. But Andy ma'am" he continues on with his process.

"Nice name Andy," Jessica speaks up.

"Right Josie? Nice name?" Jessica continues her distraction.

"Sure..." Josie replies.

"Nice try folks..." I add, turning my full attention in Andy's direction.

"If you leave this car here. I promise I will pay up first thing tomorrow morning."

"Sorry ma'am. I'm afraid I can't help you there. My order is to retrieve the car. I can't make up rules as I go along ma'am. That will get me fired!"

"Just till tomorrow Andy," Jessica begs.

"Can't do it ma'am." He walks away. Andy pushes his way through the ladies, gets in this truck and drives off. Jessica realizing how distraught I am, reaches out to hug me. The street is suddenly quiet as the sound of the tow truck fades into the distance. Josie joins me in my pity party, right in the middle of the street.

"Don't worry girl. You'll see. Things will work out." Jessica attempts to console me.

"Come on mama, let's walk you home," Jessica laments. She observes me limping more as we walk down the street with me guarded on both sides by the two sisters.

"I know you didn't want to talk about it earlier. But are you ok?" Jessica asks

"When it rains, it pours!" they look on, expecting a legitimate explanation for my limping.

"I took a bad fall back there." I reply,

39

not flinching or eager to continue the trend of discussion.

"Where? At the juncture?" Jessica inquires more.

"Where else Jessica? If you gals had stopped a little or perhaps looked behind you, you would have noticed." Instantly rebuking them.

"Look sorry about that. It was this slave master driving me onward!" Jessica replies.

"People, don't be blaming me for all of your problems. I ran faster, so you ran faster too. I didn't force you to." Josie replies in her own defense.

"You guys are not going to be arguing right here after my little car drama. Seriously, this is not about you, alright?"

"Oh, my bad Siberia. Sorry, okay." Jessica apologizes, looking in her sister's direction, expecting some remorse from her.

"What? What are you looking at me like that for?" Josie asks.

"Well, Jeez let's see… may be you should say you are sorry too." Jessica replies.

"Just mind your own business Jessica. Did Siberia tell you I offended her?" Josie lashes out.

"Okay gals, I think I am going to leave you both here and let you sort it out. I have bigger fish to fry!" I begin leaning away from them, when Jessica pulls her back towards them again. They walk me quietly to my porch, Jessica opens my door and they both enter into my sitting room with me.

"Come on mama, let's get you settled," Jessica nudging me towards the couch.

We all landed on the couch at once, with a sigh of relief.

"Are you okay mama?" Jessica asks again.

"I am fine now. Thanks Jessica," I reply as Josie tucks a pillow behind me.

"Here... this should help," Josie joins.

"See. It doesn't hurt to help, right Josie?"

"I don't know what you are talking about. I am always nice to Siberia." Josie responds, looking in my direction for approval. A big and profound silence fills the room as we both look at each other, waiting for who will respond to Josie's fishing for compliments.

"Sorry, you were saying something about being run down..." Jessica asks attentively.

"Are you two sure you are through bickering for now?" I sat between them, looking back and forth from Jessica to Josie.

"Look, don't mind us. Carry on with your story, okay?" Josie adds.

"That silly guy who hit me, I am telling you, he should have paid me something for running into me like that," ready to share my experience.

"Mama, what guy?" Jessica leans forward

ready for all of the juicy details.

"Just now? Out there?" Josie's inquisitive mind finally kicks in.

"I am fine. I think I practically ran into him too. I was day dreaming." I reply, hiding my true feelings about the whole incident. "That aside, what am I going to do girls? I need a job asap."

"You just keep looking mama, you'll see. Something will come up," Jessica encourages me.

"I wish I can help you more. I would like to have seen that guy who ran into you....girl, I would have faked it to get paid..." Jessica insinuates.

"You are one crazy person, you know that, right?" I sigh.

"Oh please spare me Siberia. Call me crazy, somebody would have been paying today... period!" She adds.

"What do you mean? You know what, as a matter of fact I am not listening to you right now" I continue to move off the couch.

"Then listen to this... Yes girl. I would have laid flat and made that sucker pay." Josie eagerly adds. By the way, what kind of car was it?"

"Looked like the latest edition of an Escalade, I think. Oh... I don't know these things. Besides, I was too consumed by... Oh never mind." I abruptly stop the conversation, looking away from them. Those two are too smart... they will figure out what I am thinking if I keep looking their way.

"What? A What?" echo Jessica and Josie in unison.

"You mean to tell me you let that dude go just like that? Mama mia! Qué clase de tonto es este?" She sighs in Spanish.

"I can't believe this! You let him go just like that Siberia?" Josie repeats, frantically.

"Yes, just like that Josie. I've gotta run. You are about to drive me crazy," finally rolling off the couch and away from them.

"Hold up people, there is more to that story. I can see it in your eyes. What aren't you telling us Siberia?" Jessica asks. "Inquiring minds want to know Siberia," she continues.

"Don't read too much into the whole thing Jessica. It's no big deal." I tried to change the subject.

"Well then, let me be the judge of that. Start spilling. Or else, I won't let you rest and you know me, once I get something in my head, I don't let it go! You do it now, or you do it later. Choose your poison cuz either way, I will get it out of you." Jessica continues looking on with her curious eyes.

"I am exhausted from all this drama today. Go ahead, I told you there is nothing to tell. I take my leave now." "Lock the door behind you please, okay? I will call you later."

They sit there perplexed at my reaction.

"I am telling you that girl is crazy. Algo

43

and a mal con ella… Something is wrong with her!" Josie exclaims.

"Be quiet for a second. Don't talk about my friend like that." Jessica looks pensively.

"Lord save us all from this girl's foolishness! She gets a chance to make big bucks and she won't take it! Me doy por vencido. I give up!", with her hands in a surrendering mode.

"S-s-s-h! You be quiet. You don't know what you are talking about. Jokes apart, you think it will be that easy to get money like that?" Jessica whispers.

"Now, whose side are you on?" Josie inquires. "Please don't be a two-faced friend Jessica. Just tell the girl the truth!" Josie lashes out, raising her voice.

"I said be quiet! You don't know what you are talking about. Besides, why do I have to say anything when I have your big mouth to speak for me."

"I can hear you both in here. You need to go now please. I need time to myself to figure all this out…"

"See, you made her upset again." Jessica drags Josie off the couch.

"Talk to you later mama," Jessica yells as they find their way out of my house.

"ONKA & ONYE TONKA" STORM AMERICA FROM AFRICA~ DID THEY GET SIDETRACKED FROM THEIR MISSION?

"ONYE TONKA" ON THE SET GETTING ACCLAMATED TO THE EXTRAS ON SET.

"SIBERIA TONKA" IS DISTRAUGHT ABOUT SOMETHING! CAN ANYONE GUESS?

AND THE PLOT THICKENS. WHO WILL SAVE NAIYA NOW?

4 COME RAIN OR SHINE!

AASHISH BABU, MY PRECOCIOUS, OVER-BEARING, AND TOTALLY IRRITATING LANDLORD WILL NOT TAKE NO FOR AN ANSWER THIS MORNING! Despite all of his years of living in America, he has refused to adjust his thick Indian accent … as he would tell me in one of his heated discussions with me, this is his way of holding on to his culture and a daily reminder of where he comes from. An Indian immigrant who I expect to at least understand and empathize with me regarding what I am going through… trying to keep a roof over my head, eating and everything that goes along with taking care of oneself in America, is making my life miserable. Today, he comes unwavering on his mission to collect his long over-due rent from his unfortunate tenant… me… Siberia! Aashish storms out of his car, which has been parked along our winding street, studiously watching my house and waiting for the opportune moment to make his unwelcome presence known… a game now so familiar to both of us. He stalks the house while I watch him from behind the curtains, ready to ignore his next move. He bangs on the door with his fist, at the risk of breaking down the door to the house… a door he would have to pay for if broken. His noise seems loud enough to disturb the neighborhood; as he watches one of the neighborhood kids glance at him curiously while riding off on his bicycle.

"Hey, what are you looking at? Didn't your mama teach you manners to not to butt into peoples' business? Run along now!" he yells at the boy on the bicycle.

"Why did you have to do that pops? That kid didn't do anything to you!" Sanje speaks up.

"Did I ask your opinion? As tiny as you are, who are you to say anything? You need to be quiet and mind this door for me!" Aashish replies, his voice rising.

"I am just asking you not to embarrass me. That boy goes to my school pops."

"Great, then you will both have a lot to talk about then! Now man this door for me and mind your business." Aashish warns his son again.

Banging away at the door is nothing new for Aashish Babu and myself. Only this time, he comes with more commitment to breaking down the door if need be. For all he cares, his noise will eventually get me to succumb to his nuisance behavior, if I care enough about my reputation in the neighborhood! He was right!

"I know you are there! Open this door or I will break it down myself!" Aashish's Indian accent heightens. "I don't care how much it will cost me to fix this door again! I want you out of my house period!" he continues, progressively banging away at the door.

"Wait for her response, pop, before you knock down the door." Sanje, Aashish's young son yells from across the lawn.

"I know you are not talking to me junior! What

do you mean wait? You know what, I don't have time for your rubbish today. I will deal with you later!" he carries on his tirade, his fury rising with every strike against the door.

"If you think I am joking, watch me Siberia! I am deadly serious young lady! I will break this door down if you don't pay me today! Come out now Siberia, if you love yourself… pay me my rent!" He continues relentlessly. Aashish raises his threatening voice; every explosive sound louder than the previous.

"You are leaving my house today! Period! That's it! I am done being Mr. nice guy with you. Sanje! Sanje, get me my hammer, anything… I don't care… now!" He resigns.

"Need anything pop?"

"Did I just speak French? Yes, anything dummie!"

"Here we go again. Where is your hammer?" Sanje asks, walking in Aashish's direction. At 13, Sanje is wiser than most kids his age. With a foul-mouthed bully for a father, he has learned to defend himself aptly and retreat to silence when required. This is the day he will strike a balance … a day he will defend himself, then be quiet when it gets heated.

"Are you kidding me? Of course where my tools have always been! The back of my truck fool! Is this what I have paid big tuition for? A boy who can't use his brain to troubleshoot a simple task! Unbelievable! " Aashish belts out.

"Oh come on pops, it isn't that serious." Sanje replies.

"Sometimes, when I hear your voice and I'm not looking; I almost forget it's you talking back at me. In

India boys your age cannot look me in the eye and respond back! Learn manners boy before I give you what you deserve this morning!" Aashish continues.

"There you go again pops! This is America. I was born here and raised here. I just don't think the way you do!"

"That's obvious. That is the problem right there. America or no America! You are raised in an Indian home and you will respect your father, you hear me?"

"Look pops, I'm just saying...,"

"You are saying absolutely nothing boy!" Aashish cuts him off. "The words coming out of your mouth are too big for your age... watch them before I do it for you" he concludes.

"Whatever you say pops!" Sanje resigns.

"Look boy, I have told you several times not to call me pops... like a Popsicle or a drink! I am not a drink.... I am your father. You hear me?" Aashish raining more of his anger and frustration at Sanje.

"Yes pops...oh sorry dad, " Sanje cynical.

"Oh and by the way, I will certainly remind you that you said collecting this money is not that serious. Just remember that when you need money for school and I tell you it's not that serious! Now! Just get me the freaking hammer! Hurry!" He explodes yet again.

"Got it dad!" Sanje walks away mumbling his discontentment. "This dude is really losing it for real." He murmurs. "Just call the freaking cops and let them handle it. Man! This is America. Not India!" Sanje continues his soliloquy loud enough for Aashish to hear. Aashish leans against the door, straining his ear, attempting to listen to ascertain if there is any movement inside of the house.

"I thought so! Come out this very minute! You don't want to feel my wrath today!" Aashish screams out loud, after hearing a television sound streaming out of my living room.

@@@@@

I watched all of his outbursts from afar. I have had enough so I proceed to quickly join him at the door before Sanje gets to him with the hammer. I walk up to him on the porch, carrying my purse against my chest.

"Beautiful day isn't it Mr. Babu," I speak from behind him.

"Argh! There comes our princess! What is beautiful about today Siberia? Tell me, what is beautiful?" he continues.

"See pops, Siberia was not home" Sanje interjects.

"How many times have I told you to not talk when older folks are talking?" to his son who nods, resigned.

"You just get me the hammer! That's your assignment for today. Stick to it and earn me my money's worth!"

"It is always a beautiful day Mr. Babu," I speak up, voice quivering as I attempt to walk around him and approach the door.

"Well then beautiful day for me and not so beautiful for you!" he says.

"Then good day Mr. Babu"

"Save your compliments young lady! And what is good about the day with you as a tenant? Tell me?"

I continue on, quickly pushing back my door; I ran inside to lower the volume from my laptop.

"See this is how you waste money! Money you don't have. You are not home yet you turn everything else on for the whole street to hear!" Aashish continues.

"I live alone Mr. Babu. I do that to make sure people think there is someone at home." Whispering my explanation.

"Call it whatever, that is still a total waste… reason why your electric bill goes through the roof and I am stuck with paying that too."

"Mr. Babu, regardless of what is happening, it is still a good day."

"I see, alright then Missy, since it is a good day, I am sure you agree with me, it is certainly a good day to pay me my money, right?" At the sound of what I'd dreaded throughout the day, I become dumb-founded. "Where is my money Siberia?" He repeats, his anger rising with every syllable rolling out of his mouth.

"First off, this is very unprofessional! You need to quit yelling. I don't want the whole neighborhood hearing my business." Defending my stance, while glancing out my neighborhood streets, especially in the direction of Jessica's house.

"I can't believe this! Now, you want to insult me over my money?" Aashish replies. At the car, Sanje stands there battling to open the door with the key fob handed to him by his dad. He chuckles quietly, after hearing my harsh and defensive response to his dad.

"I am not trying to insult you Mr Babu. I am just asking you to please keep your voice down." I cautiously state in a matter of fact, still paranoid about my laundry being aired on the street for everyone to hear. This is certainly another encounter Jessica and Josie need not overhear. Otherwise Josie will be on my case for not taking a chance when an opportunity to make quick money presented itself.

"Ok then missy, give me my money. Otherwise the entire neighborhood will know that you did not pay your rent. Just give me my rent money. I mean now so I can leave." He yells.

"Well, Mr Babu…," shrugging my shoulders.

"Yes, that's my name. I'm listening… my money, young lady…"

"I'm sorry Mr. Babu…"

"Can't believe you have me out here screaming like an old fool," Aashish rambling on.

"Your rent money?"

"You know, the currency you pay people you owe! This is not a charity home nor a shelter! My rent money Siberia! No kidding! I want it now or you are out of my house today!" venting his complete frustration on me.

"Mr. Babu, I know I told you I would get you your money last week but…".

"Stop right there young lady! I don't want to hear your excuses! Not anymore Siberia! I didn't come here to collect a bunch of buts!

"Hold up Mr Babu… I am truly sorry. I don't have the money right now but I am going to get it. I promise, I will get it to you shortly." I reply panicky.

"Shortly? What do you mean shortly? Do you think the mortgage of this place is paid on a shortly basis? What about the electric bill, the water bill and oh yes, all that nice furniture I have in that apartment for you…" He continues peeking over my shoulder, into my living room.

"I know you've been very patient and

understanding with me." Appealing to him gently, hoping Mr. Babu will throw a little compassion my way.

"No kidding Siberia! Now, you are beginning to take my generosity for granted!" quickly dismissing my remorseful posture.

"I promise, I will get you your money next week." Responding somberly, disregarding Aashish's sarcasm.

"Oh no! First you say shortly and now, did you just say next week? Look around you Siberia! I gave you a decent place for what you pay, wouldn't you say?"

"Yes Mr. Babu."

"Glad you approve. Look, all I want you to do is to go back in there and bring me my money. Enough with debating back and forth!"

"It seems you are not hearing me well Mr. Babu…"

"Excuse me? You are the deaf one young lady!" He replies with escalating rage.

"Oh my Mr. Babu, I didn't say you were deaf. Please don't put words in my mouth," I reply defending my stance.

"Look I hate repeating myself, if you don't get me my money… In fact, I want you out of my house right now!" Aashish continues his condescending tone.

"Please Mr. Babu, I don't have it yet. But I will get it to you next week."

"My patience has worn out with you Siberia. I gave you all this time because I understand what it means to be in a strange country by oneself."

"Then you know, if you kick me out, I have nowhere to go."

"And how is that my business? Now that is not

professional right?"

Siberia looks consciously into the streets with Aashish's escalating voice; she backs into her living room and Aashish follows continuing his ranting and raving at Siberia. Only this time it was not clear if he was speaking in his Indian native tongue or that his thick accent has gotten the best of him.

"Mr Babu. Things are just tight right now since I returned from visiting my family in Africa. My financial aid is delayed."

"Okay... still not my business," he replies looking around the living room.

"They said I didn't submit my paper work and I didn't know I had to do it every year. I thought once is good enough. It should be here before next week. Anyways, I am getting a job."

"Good for you Siberia! It's about time you go find yourself a J-O-B!" Aashish's starring eyes lands on the image of Princess of Suburbia on my laptop and the spread out writing sheets showering my study table.

"These talk shows you always listen to, whatever they are called, they can't put food on your table. Neither can that crown you have there," pointing to a pageant crown seated majestically on a mount by the table; a remembrance of what I had accomplished before coming to America.

"You girls nowadays... you want everything easy."

"The only show I watch is the Princess of Suburbia. And that crown means a lot to me Mr. Babu."

"All well and good. They still won't put food on your table! When I came to this country, I worked my behind off like there was no tomorrow. I didn't stay in my room day dreaming. I took whatever job I could find! Nobody gave me any breaks! You hear me, nobody! "

"I am trying to do the same Mr. Babu but it's just been hard finding a decent job."

"What do you mean a decent job? I said take any job to put roof over your head and food on your table! Plain and simple! And my Golly, sell that crown off if you have to. It's just sitting there collecting dust and you are collecting debt! Which is more important Siberia? Collecting dust and ~~collecting~~ debt or being debt free!

"Okay Mr. Babu. I heard you loud and clear. I will do my best."

"See, the only free gift I have to offer you right now, is free advice. Nothing else! Take it or leave it! But if I were you, I'd take it and run with it."

"So, are you going to wait till next week?" I reply, glancing at Aashish' unpleasant and unbecoming posture.

"Come on Mr. Babu, scouts honor! I will get you your money," appealing to him. I watch as he refuses to change his stand. Thank heavens, Sanje opening my front door and joins us in the living room, breaking the tension. He comes in carrying an oversized hammer. Aashish and I, in unison, look in his direction… me wondering if Aashish will still go ahead and kick me out of the house that day; Aashish in his deep thoughts, trying to decide if it is time to finally kick me out.

"I found it Pops! I mean dad," breaking the cold stare from across the room and the choking silence in the air.

"Well… Will someone tell me something?" Sanje inquires.

"Boy, leave that alone! Can't you see I no longer need it? Somebody help this boy's brain!"

"What?" Sanje asks, ignoring his dad's nutty remarks.

"Look boy, you will not be the death of me!" Aashish continues then turns sharply in my direction.

"Ok Siberia... I can't believe I am doing this, two days and that's it!" He resigns to extending the date for my eviction. Alas, the angels are smiling on me!

"Three days please Mr Babu".

"Who told you this is a democratic decision? You don't get to cherry pick the dates!"

"I am only trying to be truthful and realistic with you Mr. Babu."

"Don't push your luck young lady. If you don't have it in two days, then you won't have it in three days. Two days, take it or leave it! The next person you will see is a court server if you do not pay my money in two days!"

"I am so grateful Mr. Babu!"

"Come on son let's get out of here now." I sigh, relieved, as I watch them move towards my front door.

"Oh Mr. Babu, you are a kind man, thank you so much. I won't forget this!"

"The only thing I need you not to forget is my money in two days!"

"Quit sucking up to my pops. You are better than that," Sanje whispers in my way as he takes his final stroll out of the house. He dashes out before I could respond. I quickly lock the door after them. Relieved that I had just dodged an eviction, I lean against my closed door, my eyes panning the living room and finally resting on my laptop, still displaying a still shot of my obsession, the Princess of

Suburbia. With my fear dissipating and my nerves gradually calming down at the sight of my heroine, I gently blow a kiss towards her majestic image.

"One day... just one day, it will all come together for me too... one day!" I sigh, finally moving away from the door.

@@@@@

The half-moon is seated majestically above a community in Oyo, West Africa. The nightly curfew has begun and the streets are deathly quiet; you could hear a pin drop. Along a twisting road engulfed by a plush greenery on both sides, lies Siberia's parents' hut; a welcoming presentation Mrs. Tonka is proud to have cultivated by herself. She sits on the floor alongside her daughter; her hands lying loosely on top of Naiya's head resting on her lap. She watches as her daughter wheezes copiously. She is in agonizing pain. The fear ~~chaos~~ in the air thickens as Naiya shrieks.

"Another day, another trouble. When will all of this end? When will my daughter get well? It's been a day past our visit to the native doctor." Mama laments.

"You know the answer to that woman! Look woman, let me hear a word here. Your cry is disturbing me. You need to be quiet for a second." Lani, our papa, says emphatically.

"Our daughter is dying and you are telling me to be quiet!" she blurts out, objecting to her husband's position. Frustrated, papa thrusts the phone in her direction.

"Do you want to call her yourself? You can take the phone then." He shoves the phone yet again at her; she turns to look in another direction, ignoring the cell phone.

"Alright then, if you are not going to take the phone, S-s-s-h! Quiet, can you at least do that?"

"Please God! Answer, my daughter. Siberia where are you?" her voice whispering. Papa's face lights up as mama looks on. The ringing tone on the phone was audible as they waited, quietly in expectation.

"Don't worry Mama." Onye pacifying her.

"Mama, don't worry everything will be okay," adds Onka.

"Enhehe... my daughter Siberia...Siberia, this is your father... your papa!" he continues eagerly.

"Please leave a message," he listens to the voice at the other end of the call.

"What is it with these young children of today?" He looks puzzled.

"What happened?" Dade eagerly inquires.

"Ah ah! What happened sir? Onka desperately seeking answers to papa's puzzled intense look.

"Siberia gave her phone to one white woman! That one self, I couldn't say anything to her," he continues. Onye and Onka are baffled. They glance at each other, unsure of what Siberia's father meant. Suddenly, Onka realizes what had occurred. He begins laughing out loud.

"What is it Onka?" Papa asks.

"Oh papa, that is the answering machine." Onka explains.

"The what?" asked Siberia's father.

"The white people call it answering machine. You speak into it Papa, to leave a message" Onka continues his lesson on answering services in America.

"You mean that woman is not a real person?"

he sighs relieved.

"She is not papa." Onka enlightens papa.

"America! Big as it is, now it's hard for me to speak to my own daughter. There are very good schools here in Africa but you people just want to go to school in America. Now, there is fire on the mountain!" exerting his frustration in Onka and Onye's direction.

"Papa, America is good oh. But wait oh papa…" Onka speaks up in defense of America.

"This can't be serious, right Papa? I mean Naiya's sickness," gazing at Naiya's anguish-ridden sweaty face.

"Look Onka, don't you have eyes to see the fire burning? It was revealed by Baba doctor that Siberia took the stone to America. We need that stone back here quickly or else Naiya dies!"

"Haba papa, never! Never! Mmmba Papa? But do we really know Siberia has the stone Papa?" Onka continues his string of inquiry.

"Did you not hear what I just said? Please, don't ask me for any stupid explanation. If we don't bring the stone back, that is it oh for my daughter! Is that clear enough for you now Onka?"

"Yes papa, sorry papa."

"Now! I need you Onka to go find my daughter in America!" He laments. "And bring that stone back."
Both Onka and Onye are extremely stunned at the latest news from papa.

"You mean it papa? Are you serious?" Onka queries him yet again.

"Please go and find my daughter and bring that stone back quickly before it is too late." He continues. "I have enough money saved for the trip" He adds.

"Thank you papa. I am going to America on a mission. Just Like Mission Impossible." Onye says joyfully dancing around the room.

"Look at him, bush man! Shut up my friend. Papa is not sending you. He is sending me." Onka interrupts his dance.

"You know you can't go without me? I'm Onye the man of wisdom." Exuding much pride in himself.

"Let's see the wisdom ... the one you got from books and movies? Joker!" Onka sarcastically.

"Be as it be, street smart will take you further. That is why I am the man of the hour." Onye responds determined not to be undermined by Onka's rude comments.

"Enough of the argument. I have a dying daughter and one I don't know if she is alive or dead in America and all you can think about is arguing over who goes? Discussions closed....Both of you, go and bring back the stone!

" Papa...papa, please get Siberia here... I saw her taking pictures of ...." Naiya begins to cough profusely. Suddenly she spits out blood.

"Oh my God, I am finished Baba Naiya. We are finished!" Mother screams even louder as she wipes the blood dripping from Naiya's mouth.

"Say no more child, you are in pain already. Your mother and I will figure this out! Look, leave now!" emphatically states to Onka and Onye's direction.

"Hurry oh! Hurry kids!" The mother continues her uproar. "Who have I offended to do this? Why should this have to happen now Baba Naiya? This is my enemies at work!"

"We have a solution now that we know the stone is in America."

"But why will Siberia do such a thing? She knows our tradition! What was she thinking?" Mama continues her lament.

"Mama, she will never do such a thing," she coughs profusely with more blood. Mama helps her daughter to a clay pot sitting next to her mat.

"S-s-sh, no talking for you please!" her father warns.

EXECUTIVE PRODUCER & SCREENWRITER, Princess FUMI HANCOCK on the set: The Party Scene.

EXECUTIVE PRODUCER ACTING AS HERSELF, THE PRINCESS OF SUBURBIA

WHEN IT RAINS, IT POURS! SIBERIA IS HIT
BY A CAR!

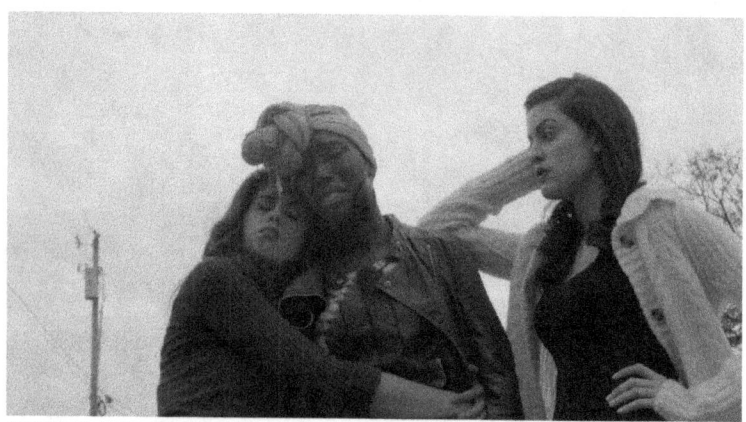

WILL THIS RAIN OF MISFORTUNE END FOR
SIBERIA? HER CAR JUST GOT TOWED AWAY
AND HER NOSY NEIGHBORS ARE
CONSOLING HER.

5 THE CLANDESTINE

TWO MONTHS AGO, THE COMMUNITY OF OYO
WAS CHOCK-FULL OF COVERT ACTIVITIES.
Countless curfews, stopping villagers from parading
themselves at the market square in the evenings; young girls
walking around the township half naked during their yearly
virginity initiation; men seeking young girls' hands in marriage
even when the girls are too young to understand the
institution of marriage. Oyo citizens, including the popular
Tonka family, are no exception to the repercussions for not
following tradition.

The clicking sound of my camera sounds very loud in the
room as I hurry to take my last picture before leaving to
board the airplane back to America. I quickly snap my final
shots with my Canon 7d, a camera I'd brought home from
United States where I now live... a place I have called home
for a little over one year. Enthralled by all the traditional
drawings hanging on the wall, I zoom in and out of each
image and let the lens do the rest. Suddenly I realize the time
to leave is close and my eyes close, remembering what I will
be leaving behind in Africa, my home... family... and a few

friends I had garnered to myself. My vacation back home with my people has been awesome thus far; the incredible show of unconditional love and the warmth of traditionally simple things overwhelmed me as I pan tearfully through my room, taking snap shots, one after the other, of the paintings gracefully adorning the wall, the African print curtain draping the window frames with my weary eyes eventually settling on the SILLERI, a captivating, multifaceted stone from which multicolor rays of light spiraled outward when caressed...The Silleri, though small in size, held great significance... a stone that had been passed on from generation to generation by my paternal ancestors since the 1800s. It was a symbol of where my family emigrated from within the African continent and the power that lies dormant within the secrets of the family. This mysterious iridescent stone... one of a kind, mama and papa once told me and one that needed to be handled with caution, rested on my overloaded dresser. I beam with joy as I stand in the middle of the room admiring it.

"Yello! What do we have here?" carefully examining the iridescent stone. "Papa and Mama with their spooky stories." smiling while snapping more pictures of it. Suddenly, I hear papa's firm voice ringing in my ears...

"Silleri is powerful! We must guard it my daughter." His voice rumbles.

"Jeez, I am still here and I can hear papa's voice in my head already. Papa and mama with all of their superstitions. I'll have to write an essay about this when I return to school." I jolt back to reality as my photo session soon comes to a screeching halt as Naiya yells out for her.

"Hey sis' Siberia! Come on out! It's time to go! Siberia!.... Siberia!..." Naiya repeats. I grab my camera bag, place my camera in it and proceed to leave the room.

"I'm here Naiya. Coming." I hasten as Naiya peeks through half open wooden door.

"You don't want to miss your flight, you dreamer." Naiya chuckles. As usual, captivated by my sister's signature giggles, I grab my camera lens abruptly and slide them into my camera bag. I hear a thumping sound.

"Did you hear that?" I asked Naiya as I begin looking in the direction of the sound.

"No, I didn't hear anything. Come on sis' it's time to go." Naiya repeats, this time helping to pull my suitcase out of the room. I lock the camera bag, do a last minute visual sweep of the room with my eyes and follow Naiya out of the room.

"You'd better take good care of my room Naiya." Tugging at her ear.

"Now, who is the oldest…what is that about? You know, no one uses your room. Besides, I have mine. Remember sis'?"

"Sure! Who are you kidding?"

@@@@@

I gaze out the window to an empty dark street… speckled streetlights yielding pools of light. The night quickly crept in on me as I have been writing all day long. For once, I have a lot to write about, particularly since my return from Africa… more stories to tell.. more voices in my head.. more characters to flesh out. Though my nights have been pre-occupied with the mystery woman constantly disrupting my rest, she has also given me a new lease on my writing. Her strange demeanor in my dreams nudges my writing to suspense… a genre quite unfamiliar to me but I'm loving every moment of it. I refuse to continue to be powerless over this enigma… If I have anything to do with it, she is going to be exposed in my story… my very first novel. Indeed, it has been a very fruitful day as the stories just keep invading my thoughts. With darkness quickly eroding, I stop, close my typed script and sit pensively staring at the laptop. This time, my eyes are resting comfortably on pictures of my family in Africa… my formidable papa, beautiful and high-pitched mama, the always optimistic Naiya and our township. I am utterly lost recalling all the places I have gone with my family and the things we have done together. Suddenly, a jingling sound from my laptop abruptly announces the arrival of a new email. This unexpected occurrence precipitates a sigh.

"One day, I will see you all soon.... I'll be back as a big, rich girl from America. One day," smiling, finally standing up and pacing around my room as I head for my comfy bed. There is nothing else to do now. I tuck myself in gently and prayed I quickly doze off … before Yemoji begins her tirade in my dreams again.

@@@@@

The mystery woman, Yemoji strikes again! Her face enlarges, eyes bulging from sockets, grinning like a mad woman. The bubbling sound emanating from her magical pot ever more disturbing. She instantly stretches out her arms marked with green and white traditional chalk; pointing her extremely long claw-like nails, beckoning me to come closer. Her wicked mirth is airborne, etching the blackness around her. I struggle to get up from this nightmare but to no avail. I am now convinced, this is my punishment for being too inquisitive in Africa. Is this my penance for not believing the tales told about the iroko tree in the village? I wonder if all who sat underneath it are going through this hell? Or is this something else? What is this manner of disturbance that won't let up? I have to fight my way through this... I have to learn to waken from these horrendous dreams. My subconscious is alert, my mind is battling, my eyes repressively fixated on hers, my head shakes, my body tossing back and forth on my ruffled bed yet my spirit is caught up in Yemoji's evil whirlwind. All of a sudden, her devilish, yet alluring, face morphs into Naiya's. I am startled and utterly confused. How can this be? This time, she approaches me differently...she says nothing but continues to beckon me to come to her, then sheepishly looks distressed. As I struggle with this demonic force, I watch an image... my aura rising, leaving my helpless body behind in bed. This is the mystery papa and mama had talked about... stories I'd watched in our African movies... stories of people's spirits flying in the middle of the night. Papa says witches fly, necromancers hover over their territories and those who wizards are after do fly to their initiation ceremonies... so which one was I? A mystery to me, until now! I am forcefully dragged towards Yemoji, her intimidating voice resounds across the dark skies. The closer I get to her, Yemoji's true facial gestures emerge, more intense and angry. She points her magical finger my way, she draws me closer, all against my wishes.

"Come... come to me Siberia! Come to me... Siberia... Come!" She screams, chaos and fear palpable. "That's right, closer...closer...closer...that's my girl...come just a little bit closer..." Yemoji continues her wicked manipulation. After much struggling, I succumb! Reaching out to grab Yemoji's powerful arms, mama's face suddenly appear off to one side.

"Don't do it Siberia! Don't go there!" I welcomed her entreating voice, just in time to save me from Yemoji. "Daughter, you must ignore her callings! Push back Siberia! Push back!" She disappears before I could respond, but not without igniting a bolt of energy in my inner being.

@@@@@

Alas! I jump out of bed, having bathed in a pool of sweat, my night dress completely drenched. Pulling vigorously at my ears, desperately attempting to block Yemoji's controlling voice. Her voice gets increasingly loud and unsettling and I fear that this diabolical mystery in her dream is penetrating further!

"What is all of this about? Why am I being haunted by this thing? What kind of dreams are these? Who can I tell that would understand?" My self-evaluation is soon stopped as rays of sunlight creep through the flowery curtains, hitting my face and jerking me out of my thoughts. I manage to snap out of my recent nightmare, though still baffled. I settle down at the edge of my bed.

"Since my return from Africa, everything is just going wrong! Frankly, I don't get it…. This has got to stop! Not knowing what to do, I revert back to what I know best… that is, watching The Princess of Suburbia.

"Well my people, I have someone quite exciting tonight. You know her already… Shaynia Colts, CEO of Let's Go Innovate. Get ready! Get ready! Get ready! It's getting hot up in here," my icon's voice echo through my room, my way of getting rid of Yemoji's toxic aura.

"That's right! Princess why don't you share with your audience that story you were just sharing with me before the show? How you got started in your business?" Her guest's voice follows suit.

"Now who is the host? Sure, I most certainly will. Anything to inspire my friends. The road to success is never easy! Many are always looking for a quick fix but we know there is no quick fix except the one straight to hell, excuse my French! Patience is the key," now fully engaged in the day's inspirational moment with The Princess of Suburbia and her guest, I was certainly due and absolutely ready for a morale boost today and I was going to get it from these two women, who sit proudly, basking in their wisdom vault, across my screen. I watch this epitome of grace, confidence, much deserved success and agility ... all virtues I desperately need and want in my life. Between juggling school, unpaid bills, the mystery woman's nightly harassment, the possibility of fulfilling my dreams daily erodes. The only lifeline I see in front of me is just holding onto the Princess of Suburbia's advice.

"That is what separates the successful stories from the not so successful!" Shaynia's voice crashes my long-winded thoughts, thrusting me back to reality.

"When I came to this country, I had no money, nobody to take me in... I mean nobody! I was so desperate that I began pawning off everything I had in my name and went for broke! All for the dream of becoming a bestselling author."

"And look at you now." Her guest responds, amazed at what the Princess of Suburbia has accomplished. Suddenly, a light bulb went on in my brain! A solution I'd been waiting for came through the tube. I instantly feel a surge of energy running down my spine. My very first breakthrough... I got from watching the mesmerizing conversation between the princess and her guest, Shaynia. In awe of what I'd just heard, I move closer to my laptop; my face lighting up like someone who had finally won a jackpot!

"Wow! That is amazing. I am not alone in this rat race!" jumping out of my chair and running around my little room in celebration of my breakthrough, then quickly settling down to watch the rest of the show.

"What price are you willing to pay to make your dream come true?" the Princess' voice echoes one more time.

"Great question Princess!" her guest continues.

"You bet it is!" She continues on the path to empowering her viewers.

After a few minutes of gulping down Princess' invigorating message, it was finally settled in my mind! At last, what I needed to do to get a temporary fix to my monetary problem suddenly preoccupies my mind. I intentionally fly off the side of my bed and begin dancing my victory dance again.

"Yes! Yes! Yes! I believe…. I can do it. I am somebody," consistently repeating after the her idol. I am relieved, ready to take on whatever life has in store to dish out today. I was parked and fully loaded with inspirational words. Whatever purports to go wrong, I was prepared, right? I laugh hysterically, finding my way to the refrigerator in my kitchenette. My face turns cold, as I am confronted by a cold, empty sight. The only thing in the refrigerator was a bottle of water and a loaf of bread. An image too familiar in Africa amongst the villagers. Only at the village, there was an excuse for it… people were living in poverty. How then would I explain this? I am in the land of milk and honey, yet even ordinary food eludes me. Realizing the heap of trouble riding my tail, my hysterics quiet at the sight. I swing open my cabinets. They were empty too! Then, as I look through the lower cabinets I find a box of cereal. Whew! What a relief! I pulled out my bowl and pour some dry cereal while finding my way back to my study table. If there was something I could count on... my emotions swinging back and forth. One minute I feel like I can conquer the world, other times my frustration and uncertainly is profound! Today, my goal is simply to do exactly what the princess shared... pawn her valuables off! Guarded by that knowledge, I scope out my place, looking for anything of sentimental value I can either pawn or sell.

@@@@@

Thirty minutes has passed, and I am still plundering my place, combing down each room assiduously. I eventually become tired of throwing things around and settle at my night table, feeling a tad-bit defeated. I take a breather from the chaos I have created in my room, raising my head up and my weary eyes unexpectedly rest on my beloved camera. I had taken this article of beauty, as I call it, since it had taken so many wonderful pictures...I had taken it on my recent trip to Africa! Behold, it had not failed me... as I'd won a local contest as the best photographer of the year in college just few months ago. This win was indeed a great morale boost for me, after all the mishaps going on in my life and because of the sentimental value it holds, I was certain that nothing would make me ever part with the camera, nothing.... Until now! My conflicting emotions about adding the camera to the mix to raise funds quickly rushes to the surface until I finally gave in... pawn the camera or get thrown out of my place... the decision was quickly made for me by my circumstances.

"Bingo! I can pawn this and pay my bills until my student loan kicks in." Unconvincingly relieved yet still gloomy.

With a sudden weariness rushing through me, I pick up the camera bag, set it on the table and begin to run through its contents. I carefully bring out the camera, pull the SD card out of it and insert it into my laptop; a last attempt at reminiscing about the recent African trip. In an instant, an image of a cinderblock wall covered in African artifacts flashes across my screen. I sigh as my eyes rest on the picture of SILLERI, the magnificent stone, as it pops up on the laptop screen! I had no time to react to its beauty when suddenly the lights in my room begin to flicker, an unusual occurrence I cannot very well ignore.

"Gosh, I wonder if Mr. Babu stopped paying my light bill. I don't know how much of this I can take." I begin looking around fearfully as my lights increase their blinking throughout the house.

"I've got to get out of here," I grab the camera bag, my pageantry crown, brush my fingers through its' imprint… the African Sunny Star winner, a title that I'd held dear ~~to me~~ and dresses I'd worn during the event. I place them all in a big shopping bag and dash out of my home, still wondering why my lights had flickered.

No sooner has I reached my mailbox, when my noisy neighbor, Jessica accosts me. Though Jessica is very intrusive and most times outright nosy, her heart is ~~often~~ in the right place. People in the neighborhood trust her to make newcomers feel welcome as she is the recently elected head of the neighborhood watch... a responsibility she values highly, and proudly takes very seriously, I might add.

"I know what you going to say but I had to

come check on you 'cause you did not call me," in her accusatory way.

"Because I have been busy and I still am. I have to run." My first attempt at leaving Jessica at the mailbox.

"Where are you off to?"

"None of your business." I unexpectedly snap at her.

"What? Hold on mama! Keep your claws in! I was just trying to help. Besides, you don't know the bus route around here yet? You can easily get lost." Jessica making a concerted effort.

"Didn't mean to insult you. I just have a lot on my mind right now. Anyways, you were saying..." quickly adjusting my posture and manners, realizing Jessica's true intentions.

"Apology accepted. That's settled then. I am coming with you, right mama?" Jessica replies pushing her skinny frame into my path.

"Well then, let's go and thanks for looking out for me."

"You are welcome. Hold up mama, someone is coming over," Jessica says gazing past me.

I turn around and we both see a cable man walking towards us, peeking out from behind my house.

"Are you Miss Tonka?" his southern accent drawled.

"Here we go again! Who wants to know?"

"Ma'am... are you Ms. Tonka?" the cable man firmly asks again.

"Yes? What is going on and why are you in my backyard?" my hasty response.

"Just so you know, your cable was turned off. I

am just here to ensure everything went well without a glitch."

"What do you mean by that?... without a glitch. Would you please speak in language I understand? "

"There were some activities detected after your cable was turned on. Look, Miss, you need to contact the cable office, if you have more questions."

"Well then, can you do something to turn it back on …hold off for a few days? I promise, I will make sure I pay my bill." I reply, heart racing.

"I wish I could help but I only follow orders ma'am. I'm afraid I can't do anything about it unless you pay your bills. Besides, I am not really responsible for this. I am just here to make sure it was completely turned off!"

"Please mister, just this once. I promise I will pay in few days."

"Yes… please pardon my friend. She will pay her bills." Jessica interjects apologetically.

"Sorry, can't lose my job over this. Have a great evening ma'am. Can you please sign here that I was here please?" He hands me the notice from the cable service.

"Are you kidding me? A great evening? Did he just say have a great evening after shutting me down?" looking in Jessica's direction.

"Take it easy mama, it's just cable service."

"I'm going to pretend I didn't hear you say that. Can you do without your cable Jessica?" signing the paper and watching the cable man take his leave.

"Okay mama, just forget I said that. Not sure what to say to you right now… that's all. I just don't want you getting worked up over this." She replies in a somber voice.

"Come on, let's hurry up before the

consignment store closes" I respond, anxiously grabbing my mails. "Besides, I've got bigger fish to fry right now... my overdue rent!"

"Don't get all worked up girl. I'm just tying my laces" Jessica bends down tying her sneaker laces as I shuffle through my most anticipated mail... chock full of over-due bills! The red stamps splashed across each bill haunting me. I needed a ray of hope, there and then. Then I see a colorful flyer sticking out of my mailbox. I quickly haul it out from the rest of my over-stuffed mailbox. It was the announcement I had been waiting to hear... one I'd heard for so long on the television and ached that someday I would be a part of. It was an announcement about my idol. Alas! The Princess of Suburbia is in little town, visiting a book club! If anything was set to brighten my day since my return from Africa, this was it! My dream to meet my icon is suddenly within reach and nothing is going to get in my way of meeting her. I am ready and certainly due for some one-on-one wisdom nuggets she could share that would help me fulfill my writing dream in America too.

"Yes! At least some good news..." I shriek and begin jumping up and down invigorated with happiness. I pull Jessica up from tying her shoe lace, and she instantly joins me in my hysterics.

"What? Did you win the lottery? Your father sent you some money right? I told you mama that all you had to do was ask your father. I am so happy for you girl!" Jessica rambles on.

"Good news is not always about money girl." She stops jumping and starts looking dead serious.

"Oh really? Not in my dictionary mama. You of all people know now, you need money to pay your bills!" She disagrees.

"Yes, really Jessica. This is way bigger than getting money in the mail Jessica!" I continue my hysterics.

"Okay then humor me. Why are we both jumping up and down?"

"Simple! Four scrumptious words Jessica, The Princess of Suburbia!"

"Is that the lady you are always watching in there?"

"Yes, my idol. I came to this country because of her! All of her interviews… her books… everything inspires me Jessica!"

"I don't get it but I'm listening. What does it have to do with us acting crazy and jumping up and down the street Siberia?"

"Look, she is coming to town!... Our town… Right here! Can you believe it, the Princess of Suburbia is coming out here!" I continued my raving. "Anyway, who cares about cable being switched off? Who needs cable after all?" I respond, now dancing off the curb and into the street.

"So how is that going to pay your bills girl? How is that better than money? But you know what, if you are happy… then I am happy for you" Jessica concludes, baffled by Siberia's seemingly erratic behavior over the announcement about the Princess.

"Let's go Jessica!"

Jessica follows her into the streets.

6 WHEN IT RAINS....

ALAN AND FANTA, ALAN'S LIVE- IN GIRLFRIEND,
ARE RIDING TOWARD THE NOW INFAMOUS
INTERSECTION IN HIS LAND CRUISER. They are on
their way to their various business appointments, looking
away from each other, tension rising in the truck. His anger
reflects on his face as he approaches the infamous
intersection where he'd met me.

"I'm not happy about being late today Alan!
Not happy at all!" the famous model flips out, exuding
colossal arrogance. Alan focuses on the road, ignoring her
comment.

"Did you hear what I just said Alan? Alan?"

"I heard you quite well the very first time Fanta!
I am just choosing to be silent for now! Can I be quiet
Fanta?" his African accent heavy.

"I know you don't care about my fans
hounding you but could we not take this route ever again...
particularly when I have special events to attend to?" She
continues her nagging.

"Look woman, Alan this... Alan that. When

will you stop all of this nagging?"

"I don't know what you are talking about? What do you mean nagging? Who is nagging you?"

"You are never satisfied woman! I can buy you the whole world and you still won't be satisfied!"

"Now, you are going off on your own tangent here! Don't forget I make my own money!"

"Yeah right! How can I forget that when you are constantly throwing it on my face? Eih Fanta! Who wears the pants in this relationship? You need to quit the theatrics Fanta. It's getting old, even for you!"

"I am going to ignore your foul mood today. Just get me to my appointment please."

"If all I am going to continue to get from you are your flippant responses, then I am glad we didn't go through with the marriage yet! I feel like I am married already... drama queen!"

"Are you kidding me? Did you just say that Alan?" They both pause, with a quick glance in each other's direction then back on the road. The tension in the truck thickens again and then Alan quickly breaks the ice.

"Look, you'll be fine. George will understand. You've never been late before now have you?" Alan speaks up softly, watching Fanta repeatedly checking her expensive Rolex watch.

"You are not getting it Alan. That is beside the point!" She becomes combative. Alan pulls over at the same spot where he'd stopped a while ago.

"Alright then Miss big-shot, enlighten me! What are we talking about right now? Your fans or the meeting you think you are about to miss? Which is it woman?" he continues prodding.

"Both and you know it! And why are we stopping when I already told you I am running late?" Fanta replies.

"I am not going to have an accident on your account woman. So say all you have to say now and when I do get back on the road, you will not say anything until I drop you off. Do you understand me?"

"This is pure foolishness Alan!"

"For months now, you've been on the road and you finally get to spend few hours at home with me but no, you had to find something else to occupy you again. Your fans! Your events! Your plans! That is all I hear every day."

"That is my life Alan! Get over yourself. You are barely home either, so what are you talking about?"

"We haven't even spent a little time together; you are already screaming bloody murder about the hours spent!" Alan completely outraged.

" Oh please spare me the tantrums!" She continues.

"What? Did you just say I am throwing freaking tantrums?"

"You heard me!. Look, you knew what I was all about when you chose to get engaged to me, right?" She continues. "And I most certainly won't apologize for what I do!. It's that simple!" She persists.

"Perhaps, that's my mistake then! " Alan concludes.

"Well then, perhaps it is... suit yourself! Just go!" She resolves, moving her face towards the street. With his face still partially turned in Fanta's direction; Alan pulls right into the intersection.

@@@@@

I approach the ill-famed junction a few miles away from her home. Since the last incident, I'd promised myself to always be extra careful at this intersection. The last time I'd crossed over I barely escaped with minor bruises and an aching body. This time, I was going to be very attentive... I was going to keep all of my faculties in check. This time, as I contemplate crossing the road yet again, I would make sure ... only I didn't! The thoughts at war inside me were overwhelming enough to make anyone absentminded. I dashed into the street, and came to myself, just as my body almost slams into Alan's truck again, coming to a screeching halt!

"Siberia!" Jessica yells!

Thank heavens Jessica is with me this time. She pulls me out of the way and I stumble over her.

"Ouch mama! Are you okay mama?" Jessica's voice penetrating my confusion. From the raucous screeching, if I'd been hit this time it would have been fatal! Alan looks ahead in horror, immediately recognizing me.

"You see what you made me do Fanta?" He tenses, attempting to jump out of the car. Fanta pulls him back into the car.

"Like hell! You are not going out there! As you can see no one got hurt. Let's go... now!" screaming at Alan.

"Let go of me Fanta! Life is not just about you."

"Look... does anyone look hurt out there?"

"Be a compassionate lady for once in your life and help out too!" He pushes Fanta's well-manicured hands off his own and jumps out of his truck.

"You can stay in here and continue to act like a prima donna you are or you can do something nice for someone else! It's your choice!," he leaves Fanta dumb struck.

Fanta hesitates for a while then finally steps out of the truck, still furious.

"Are you deaf or what? Can't you watch where you going?" she spat out to me.

"Hey! Hey! Hey! Whoever you are, you don't talk to my friend like that. Do you know how to drive?" Jessica perks up defending me, as I attempt to get up off the ground where I'd be thrown.

Alan interrupts what was quickly becoming a hostile bout between Jessica and Fanta, with his heartfelt apology.

"You might want to learn one or two things from this man... it is called manners!" Jessica continues in Fanta's direction.

"You will not talk to me in that tone, young lady!" Fanta responds.

"Please accept my apologies. Especially to you." Alan interrupts their arguments, while staring in my direction.

"Are you ok? Seems like we keep running into each other." His silky baritone vibrates the air in Siberia's direction. He instantly turns back in Fanta's direction.

"Take it easy on her please. It's bad enough that I ran into her before. I almost hurt her."

"Oh yeah? I see!" Fanta suspicious.

"My Golly! I am glad to see that you are okay" he whispers softly in my direction yet again.

"You have got to be kidding me. You are having a family reunion while I am late. Hand me the keys Alan!" she screams, attempting to pull the keys off Alan's hands.

"What has come over you?"

"I said hand me the car keys now. You stay here and have your little chat with your friends. I am leaving for my appointment. You have wasted enough of my time today" Fanta yells, set in her ways.

"You will do no such a thing. We need to give them a ride, so let's find out where they are going."

"Have you lost your mind Alan? I think you have lost your marbles! Give who and who a ride?" She lashes out uncontrollably. Alan ignores her comments, as he walks over to me.

"Sure! Go ahead. Knock yourself out!" Fanta snatches the key from Alan's hands, gets in the truck and drives off; leaving a perplexed Alan who turns and runs after Fanta. Jessica grunts at Fanta's unruly behavior.

"I tell you, I know her type! That man should let me handle her." Jessica speaks out as we both watch Alan run after the truck.

"Mama, that is one fine dude," Jessica exclaims as she helps me off the ground. "What do you think mama?" she inquires and looks on, eyes dazed like she'd seen an angel.

"Hey Siberia, what do you think? A hunk of a man, right Siberia?" she adds, disrupting my deep thoughts.

"You look like you have seen an angel or something. What is it?" Jessica looks on. "I tell you what, that man can hit me over and over again." She flirts.

"Okay mama, this is weird. You are not saying anything ... Siberia." She continues.

"Yes, a hunk," I responding.

"Oh my, wait just one minute, he said he's met you before right?" Jessica investigating as she is assessing my body for any injury.

"Stop prodding at me… it hurts."

"Oh so sorry. Is that the dude who ran you over before?" Jessica suddenly lights up. "Well, I am waiting for your response. Is he the one who got away before?" she inquires.

"Keep your voice down Jessica." Replying cautiously.

"Well then, answer me. Is this the man?"

"Will you please just leave that alone? You are embarrassing me," whispering and leaning on Jessica for support.

"And mama, you look really funny right now… all doe eyed."

"I don't know what you mean by that," desperately hiding my emotions.

"Unh, you are not stupid Siberia. I bet you do. You feel something for that dude." She giggles away.

"What? You don't know what you are talking about. And quit playing like that!"

"And who is playing? Your face has given you away mama. Just quit denying it." She continues tormenting me with her barrage of inquiry. How could I feel something for a total stranger? And what was in the cosmos that was bringing all of these unruly emotions my way. I'd been fine with my plans all along… to come to America, make a name for myself, go back home to help my people, then perhaps only then can I think about settling down with any man. That was my plan… still is my plan, if I can get this man out of my head.

"You are impossible… you know that, right?"

"You know me mama, I will dig until I find out

the truth."

"What is it to you Jessica? Who cares if he was the one or not. Just help me out of this place. I am really running late now."

"That voice is music to my ears girl! Lord have mercy…" she continues her praise of Alan.

"I don't know what you are talking about Jessica. Please just get me out of here. Will you?" I respond, hiding my stomach's butterflies… this heart thumping experience coursing through my body.

"Just saying…" replies Jessica.

"Just saying nothing Jessica. Please, let's go." I end the awkward conversation, attempting to leave the scene before he shows up. Only, I was too late! Alan suddenly appears on the scene, running towards Jessica and I.

"I am sorry for the incident. My name is Alan. Alan Hamilton." His voice streaming beautifully in my direction. A powerful name, spoken with firmness and exuding much confidence.

"Siberia Tonka" I reply in a quivering voice, with eyes locked on to his sizzling deep brown ones.

"Jessica Hernandez. Did anyone ever tell you… you are one gorgeous dude?" Jessica joins, softly breaking the serious stare between Alan and I.

"Girl stop" I whisper in Jessica's ear yet again. "Besides, he looks like forbidden fruit," I add.

"Mama, I don't know what you mean. What fruit is forbidden?" Jessica ignorantly inquires.

"You can't be serious about not knowing what I am talking about. That woman who stormed out of here…"

"Yes, what about that fool!" Jessica asks blatantly.

"It's obvious there is something between them, right?" Asking, hoping secretly I would hear something encouraging.

"But we don't know who she is yet. She could very well be a business partner!" Jessica answers.

"I don't know about that. Business partners don't talk like that to each other."

"What? Look, if you don't want him, I don't mind taking him off your hands" Jessica continues smiling sheepishly in his direction.

Alan spots their tete-a-tete and becomes curious.

"Is everything okay ladies?" he inquires moving closer to them.

"Everything is just great... totally cool.... With you in it," Jessica whispers undressing him with her eyes.

"We are fine!" I exclaim using Jessica as a crutch.

"You have a beautiful smile. You should smile more often," declares Alan. In all my twenty-something years, no-one or nothing has ever made me shy. His deep baritone caresses my ears and his presence dazzles me. His scent, a strong musk fills the very short distance between us. This man is one of a kind... rugged and soave. Anyone who would catch my attention in this manner is worth knowing more about. Perhaps suddenly developing these instant unshakable feelings for him is still a result of the misfortunes in my life lately. Or perhaps, it was fate compensating me for all of my recent hardships.

"Thank you." I respond sheepishly.

"Where are you ladies going to?"

"I'm ordering a couple of taxis right now." He continues.

"By the way, I have to apologize on behalf of Fanta." Alan interjects.

"You have absolutely nothing to apologize for," Jessica interrupts, gently caressing his body with her looks. "Is she your wife or something?" Jessica asks.

"Come on Jessica. Don't be so upfront. Please, you don't have to answer that. It's none of our business! Right Jessica?" Grinding my teeth in Jessica's direction.

"I know I don't have to say anything.".

"Well then, you see Siberia. Let the man talk. Nothing wrong in asking." Jessica inquires further.

"No… Please!" I shout.

"Mama, you'll thank me later." Jessica edges on.

"No please I insist! It is none of our business!" Though my heart was burning and wanted to know the truth.. the whole truth and nothing but the truth, I interrupt the flow of discourse with a raised voice.

"Alright then, where do you want to go?" Alan asks after a few seconds pause to gauge our reaction.

"Just few miles from here. The Consignment Shop on Harris Street. You don't have to help us. We can find our way out there. Besides, it's not that far." I interrupt.

"I insist. I am paying for the ride."

"No, really … please. I insist too," I continue.

"What kind of crazy is this mama? Let the man be a man, will you?" fervently whispering into my ear.

"Stop embarrassing me Jessica," I whisper back in her ear, teeth clenched.

"What?" Jessica screams out loud. "I don't mind the ride, thank you" She quickly moves closer to Alan.

"No! Jessica. I mean it!," I yell at startled Jessica.

"Has anyone ever told you, you are stubborn? Look lady, I am only trying to make up for my horrible faux pas," Alan continues.

"We are not a charity case, that's all."

"Charity case, who says anything about charity case?" Jessica butts in.

"Be quiet" grinning my teeth, muttering in Jessica's direction.

"I know the owner... He's a great buddy of mine. I've done business with him lots of times." He adds, attempting to soften the mounting tension.

"Look at that. What a small world. You know what, since my friend is very indecisive, how about I make the decision for us both." Jessica continues in a stern way.

"I thought I made my decision already" I interject.

"Well then, I will make a reasonable decision for both of us." Jessica continues, facing Alan exclusively and avoiding my perturbed gaze. "We accept the offer."

"Terrific! Alright then," Alan responds, me looking overwhelmed by it all.

"My feet sure can use some rest right about now and I am sure yours too, with your banged up self," Jessica adds jestingly. "Don't worry mama, you'll thank me later. Did I say that before?" She whispers confidently. Entrenched in our heated debate, Alan's truck suddenly pulls up with Fanta hopping out of the truck, still incredibly furious.

"You are lucky that my fans adore you. If not for the sake of protecting my public image, I should have left you here." She whispers in Alan's ear away from Jessica and I. She looks curious and extremely suspicious of what may have transpired in her absence. Jessica and I strain our ears to catch the quiet but seemingly heated one-sided conversation between Fanta and Alan. She jams the keys in Alan's hands.

"Let's hurry now... please." Fanta adds, making her way back to the truck.

"They are coming with us. Yes?" Alan asks.

"Suit yourself. I'm late anyways...." Fanta replies.

"Well ladies, the offer still stands." Alan explains.

Jessica smiles, rushes towards the truck before I could respond. I follow, leaping towards the truck.

"Tonto ignorante! Stupid fool! I will dump a bucket of water on her crazy behind if I were you." Jessica mumbles in Fanta's direction.

"What?" I inquire.

"Oh nothing. Hope you enjoy the ride..." Jessica avoids her remarks as they all hop into the truck. Ignoring her present company, Fanta lights a cigarette and blows out smoke while Alan shakes his head disapprovingly and drives off.

SIBERIA FALLS AND HELL IS UNLEASHED!

SIBERIA IS DISTRAUGHT; HER NOSY
NEIGHBORS COMFORT HER.

SIBERIA VISITS THE PAWN SHOP WITH
FRIEND JESSICA

SIBERIA WELCOMES HER COUSINS FROM
AFRICA. Oh, IF SHE ONLY KNEW?

7 SIBERIA'S D-DAY.

THE HEAT IS ON AT CLASS N SASS CONSIGNMENT SHOP ON HARRIS STREET! Jake O'Conner, the co-owner is arguing with his younger brother, Simon over what their deceased father wanted them to do with the store. He is frustrated with Simon's nonchalant attitude toward everything... in particular the store! Simon, on the other hand, is bent on avoiding the long overdue confrontation when Jake finally pins him down. While some brothers play and enjoy life together; it's different for these two brothers, especially since the death of their parents. Their noise often escalates enough to create a resounding echo outside of their store, an occurrence their aunt Jennie tries to avoid at all cost.

"Look brother, I need you to take this business seriously. I can't do this alone." Jake laments, still upset at Simon's blasé attitude.

"I don't know what you are talking about Jake. I'm here, aren't I?" Simon manages an incredulous snort through his congested nose.

"No doubt, your body is here and so is your ability to remove things out of this shop and not return them!

We can't keep losing money because of you Simon" Jake's frustration on the rise.

"And we can't keep giving things away either! Wait a second, are you accusing me of stealing bro?" Simon inquires in a serious and defensive tone.

"We need to come to a mutual agreement for this business to succeed. I am not accusing you but I want us to take steps towards a positive change that will benefit us and make dad proud." Jake adds.

"Who says I am not?" Simon yells.

"Alright then. Get this bro, these goods do not have legs Simon! For starters, you and I know, we are the only two who have access to the inventory." Jake continues.

"Really? Are you kidding me? We are? How about Jennie?" Simon throws conversation into a heightened gear.

"Of course, Jennie too but she won't be taking her own stuff, will she?" Jake states emphatically. "Jennie is like a mother to us now! Don't even try insinuating anything!"

"Look, you are the one throwing accusations around, not me. I am just telling you the facts, period!" he walks aimlessly around the store.

"This is exactly what I mean. You have absolutely no discernment. Accusing Jennie is like accusing mom of stealing her own stuff! For crying out loud, she calls you son. What is wrong with you?" Simon walks around sheepishly ignoring Jake's last comments.

"Like I said Simon, you have access to the inventories."

"I see. And you think I would steal my own goods, eih bro'?

"Let the facts speak for themselves Simon." He continues watching Simon goofing around with an antique guitar displayed at the front desk.

"Hey, be careful with that, will you?"

"Aren't I always? You are killing me here with all of your crappy talk."

"See, you won't even sit still to discuss this and neither will you take the time to look me in the eye on this issue" Jake adds.

"You don't know what you are talking about bro'," Simon replies.

"Simon, don't forget dad wanted us to be successful. That is why he willed this shop to us, along with Jennie, right?" Jake in a somber mood.

"Don't you think I know that brother? One thing I also know is that dad and mom accepted you and Jennie more than they did me! So excuse me if I am probably taking after my biological father!" Simon lashes out ignoring Jake's recent remorse.

"There you go! Spare me please with your biological blame and guilt trip again," throwing his hands up in total despair over Simon's denial.

"My what? What did you say?"

"You heard me, your biological bull crap! You need to man up to your own responsibilities. We were both raised and treated equally. Mom made sure of that." Jake continues.

"Is that right?" Simon replies.

"Darn straight! You know that's the truth. That's why I can't have a decent conversation with you. Every time I mention something is missing, you bring our biological bloodline into it. Stop Simon. It's getting too old…really, quit now! I'm getting fed up with your nonsense" Jake explodes.

"Oh! Yeah! The funny sassy name Jennie calls this place and all the fruity stuff we carry; heck, they once named the store after you." Simon responds.

"See what I mean, you never stick to the facts…always jumping from one topic to the other. Seriously, bro' whatever you are on, has really gotten you screwed up!" Jake fuming.

"As always, you have no clue what the heck you are talking about," Simon continues moving around the shop without purpose.

"And quit roaming around the shop. You are making my head spin!"

"Yes sir! Your royal highness! Tell me, what else do I do to rattle your feathers, your highness?" Simon cynically replies.

"You are now taking this to the extreme."

"Which part of my conversation is too hot for my dear perfect bro'?"

"You are loony Simon, seriously someone needs to check your brains. Something is missing in there…"

"Always trust you to resort to insults when the truth comes out."

"And you are the truth bearer Simon? Do you really believe the nonsense you speak? If you do, then you are in more serious trouble than I thought."

"Was the store not originally called Jake's? Was that the truth or something I conjured up?"

"Dad's name is Jake! Have you forgotten that too?" Jake lashes out. "Here is an idea you need to wrap around your mind, dear little bro'… perhaps he named the store after himself! How about that… yes bro'?"

"Okay, I'll give you that. How then do you explain them sending you to a private school in London while they left me in a riff-raff school ~~out~~ here in the states? What's fair about that bro?"

"Look. I am not going to stand here and debate dad and moms' decisions with you. Neither am I going to add Jennie to the mix of your baggage. I am done with this rubbish Simon, seriously… I am so done."

"Now, who is avoiding," Simon slurs.

"One more thing, adopted or not, you are my brother! Are you saying dad and mom treated you differently? Is that it?" Jake bellows.

"Bingo! Well, you just hit the jack pot! You got it!" Simon replies, now playing around with the guitar, slurring some words, attempting to sing.

"Oh stop it! You are driving me insane with that guitar and that song. Better keep your day job! Oh wait a minute, you don't have one… Oh, let me rephrase that, you don't want one."

"Ah…ah…ah funny bro'," making fun of Jake.

"You know what I think bro, this is your excuse for making the same mistakes over and over again! Get over this inferiority complex before it destroys you, dude." Jake replies.

"Is that what you call it now? Inferiority complex?" Simon asks.

"All I am asking you is just a little cooperation and consideration for others." Jake answers.

"And all I'm asking you is to quit dismissing my feelings." Simon adds.

"Look, I need you to be serious about this

business. Is that too much to ask?" Jake belts out.

"I am! You either believe it or you don't... period! Besides, perhaps if you take this sassy girlie stuff out of the shop, maybe, just maybe, I'd be pumped!" Simon insinuates, glancing through the racks of women's clothes, purses and shoes displayed across the store.

"Let's have a manly store, not a fruity fruity store."

"Right, this fruity fruity stuff puts food on the table and sent you to college. Is your manhood threatened Simon? Is that it?"

"Woo…woo…woo chill brother. My manhood is intact, thank you!"

"I see. Just thinking maybe we need to add that to the mix now." Simon walks away putting a healthy distance between him and Jake. "That's right, another flimsy excuse. Class & Sass is what the shop is. It was when dad was alive... it was when mom was too and it still is with Jennie! Get over it! Get over yourself!"

"Then you quit hounding me!" Simon concludes as their aunt Jennie walks into the store front from behind the curtains leading to the backroom.

'What are you two bickering about now? You know if your dad were alive, he'd be sorry right about now?"

"You know Simon… the usual garbage! He's blaming everyone else for his screw ups! Grow up buddy!"

"I don't know who is at fault and don't care! I have given you guys room to bring in your own toys; against my better judgment. Jake, you are the oldest, fix it!"

"But…" Jake exclaims in frustration at Simon.

"No buts… just fix it!" Jennie responds.

"And you Simon, I have my eye on you! Being your aunt doesn't mean I can't correct you if I need to. Get yourself together son! I mean it!" She walks into the back room, leaving them in the front store with thinly repressed anger hovering over the two men.

"See what I mean? Argh! Proves my point! I'm done!" Simon walks away with Jake shaking his head disapprovingly.

@@@@@

Alan halts his car in front of the consignment shop. Jessica and Siberia get out of the truck.

"Thanks for the ride. You too Miss." Mustering all the effort I need to speak to the barracuda sitting next to Alan, I finally opened my mouth to wish her well. Her response to my kindness? Well, I watch Fanta puff on her cigarette, looking ahead without a word from her sassy little mouth.

"Tell Jake I said hello. I will be seeing him tomorrow or whenever I get the chance." Alan quickly adds; obvious he is attempting to make up for Fanta's rude silence.

"Okay. Will do." I finally make my way out of the truck, look ahead as Alan zooms off, till out of sight. Alan drives off carefully spying on me through his rear view mirror. I could sense his eyes all over me even as the distance between us grew.

@@@@@

Fanta gets a wind of Alan's intent looks in my direction.

"You may park the car on the side road, so I can take over!" Fanta finally speaks to Alan since the ride to the store.

"And why will I do such a thing Fanta?"

"Oh…oh, perhaps it's because you are busy gawking at your rear view mirror for a certain… oh, I don't even know how to describe the thing!" Fanta blows up.

"Woman, I don't know what you are talking about," He glances yet again into the rearview mirror.

"You just did it again. You son of a gun… you just did it again!" she continues her rampage.

"You need to hush woman. You are killing me here with your drama!" Alan lashes out, his foot pressing on the accelerator.

"Just pull over. I won't let you kill me!" Fanta replies.

"You can do that all by yourself woman! You don't need me to kill you. Your mouth is enough to give any one a coronary!"

"Yeah, right! Pull over Alan, I mean it!"

"We won't start this again Fanta, Okay? I am exhausted from your bickering and lambasting everyone in your path! Enough Fanta! Enough!" He pushes hard on the pedal yet again.

"That is a message you might want to take up yourself. I will quit bickering, as you call it, when you quit flirting with every skirt that come your freaking way. Honestly, I am sick of it."

She watches Alan's eyes fixate on the road, the blood vessels on his neck pulsing like they are about to burst. The stern anger in his eyes suddenly max's out, exploding… with absolute disgust written all over his face.

"You used to get turned on by my charm Fanta!" he speaks solemnly and exhausted.

"That's when it was directed only at me Alan. Well, just so you know, it's no longer cute."

"I see." He cranks the engine, driving like someone in a high speed chase ignoring all of the traffic signs and just zooming through. He was on a mission to get rid of Fanta as quickly as possible!

@@@@@

Jessica and I stand in front of the store, watching as Alan zooms into obscurity. She cunningly clears her throat, an attempt to disrupt my blissful stance.

"Okay mama, are you ready to go in now?" Jessica attempts to get my attention. After no response, she tugs at my shoulder.

"Mama, are you going in or what?"

"Ouch! That was rough. What?" returning back to planet earth.

"Well mama, just trying to get you back from wherever you were. You were the one shouting how late you've been, right?"

"I heard you Jessica."

"Yeah, right. Who are you kidding? Mama, you are in so much trouble... I see it all over your face," Jessica laughs.

"Oh hush your mouth Jessica. Did you see that barracuda by his side?"

"Yes and we don't know who she is, right?" Jessica edges me on.

"Are you serious? Now, what woman will make

such a fool of herself and not have something going on with the dude?"

"This is America mama. You never know until you really find out."

"At any rate, let's not talk about that now please. I have other important things to handle, like my rent?"

"Oh mama, I'm fine with that. You are the one lost in your own head."

"Whatever Jessica. You are impossible."

I pull Jessica by the hand and we both walk into the consignment shop, the door bells chiming our grand entrance.

My eyes instantly landed on the owner, Jake… an extremely good looking fella, with muscles bulging out of his tightly fitted t-shirt; his powerfully featured side-burns, caressed by his well-defined jaw and dazzling eyes, was looking my way. This epitome of gentile and endowing magnificence slowly finds his way from behind the register and walks up to us smiling.

"Hello there, Siberia, right?," squinting his set of stunning blue eyes as if trying to place my face. This very minute, I realize I am once again mesmerized by the beauty of yet another man. The thoughts flowing in my mind of what could happen if anyone knew what was going in my warped brain… between the hunk and deliciously rugged looking chocolate of a man who had just dropped me and the subtle yet fiery set of eyes penetrating my soul at this very minute. I am certainly not prepared for this unexpected mental battle in my mind! It feels like my head is about to explode through my conspicuously colorful African head wrap. This emotional turmoil is an absolute taboo in Africa! One I dare not share with anyone!

"Hello" I managed to whisper in a soft and shaky voice, avoiding any eye contact but using my bag of clothes and my other valuables as a point of focus. Hopefully by not looking into his eyes, he won't figure out the sudden mayhem in my pounding heart.

"Yes, I remember now … from Tao's grocery store. We bumped into each other a few weeks back, remember?" His interest displayed on his striking face. I quickly glance in Jessica's direction; who seems very fascinated by his reaction to me and the obvious and sudden connection between us. Here and now, Jessica does what she does best… she whispers into my unwelcoming ear.

"Oh mama, just look at your sparkling eyes." I jumped away from her, trying to compose myself in front of this man while attempting to stop Jessica from saying any stupid thing out loud or worse yet, tell my secret.

"Be quiet Jessica, I mean it," through clenched teeth.

"Just one thing," She continues again into my other ear, with Jake amused by the awkwardness in the room.

"Whatever it is, I don't want to hear it," I whisper back in Jessica's ear.

"You will hear this man magnet! Here goes another one of your potential prey," she moves away smiling sheepishly before I could respond.

"S-s-s-h, be quiet please."

"I don't know what is going on with you girl… first, that man we just left and now you are all glassy eyed over this one. Whatever you got when you went to Africa, you need to give me some of that mama. Seriously!"

"Pl-e-a-s-e!"

"Mama, I wish I were this lucky!" Jessica stands

at my side, scoping out Jake from his head, to his perfectly framed face, down his well-shaped torso and bulging muscles… all the way to his tightly fitted jeans.

"Wow, you remember! Jake yes? Meet my friend Jessica" I blurt, with emphasis on the word "friend", quickly summoning Jessica's presence with my hand twirled in her direction. Not surprisingly, Jessica looks our way, pointing her finger at her chest, pretending not to understand what I'm trying to accomplish by pulling her into our conversation. If I truly needed a more arduous time today, I know just where to get it… from my obnoxious foul mouthed landlord Mr. Aashish Babu, who has threatened to kick me out if I didn't get him his rent and certainly not from Jessica's blabbing mouth! Jessica's embarrassing ways are undoubtedly uncalled for at this time… her prank is absolutely not welcome when everything suddenly seems to be spinning around me. After what seems like eternity, she finally gets it. Jessica figures out that I am in no mood for her embarrassing mannerisms. She walks up to Jake with a giddy gaze.

"Nice to meet you Jake. I'm going to go over there and let you two handle your business" I quietly pinch her on the side, dragging her close to me for a swift tete-a-tete.

"You will not be the death of me. What are you cooking up in that head of yours now Jessica?"

"Are you serious about that question? Are you kidding me?"

"Do I look like I am kidding?" Continued whispering.

"All in one day, your African man magic is working. You are the one who's got some explaining to do."

"I don't know what you two are talking about."
Jake suddenly interrupts our tete-a-tete excusing himself and
walking to the register.

"See, what you made happen now? That man
will think we are a bunch of gossips Jessica!"

"Like you always say, I don't know what you
are talking about either. He left because it's just common
courtesy. A man with great manners... I like that!"

"For crying out loud, will you quit clowning
around and answer my question... what are you cooking up
in that head of yours?"

"If anyone's head needs to be checked...
girlfriend it is yours." Starts laughing sheepishly, looking in
Jake's direction. "Quick suggestion, you may want to go back
to your new hunk. You don't want to keep him waiting, yes?"
Jessica adds with us both gawking at Jake.

"Gosh, I have no idea what I am doing
here...."

"You owe Mr. Babu money... you are here
to..."

"I know that! I am not talking about that
Jessica. I am in serious trouble here!" I interrupted her.

"I tell you what, while you are busy deliberately
over your whorish behavior!" her pique increases.

"What did you just call me?" startled by her
words.

"Well my dear, that's the name they use here in
America!... Love you girl..."

"I am going to ignore what you just called me
and as a slip of the tongue."

"Look, its' obvious you can't have them both.
When you are done messing around in your own head, you

may want to help this sister out in that department… yes mama?" She walks away, her attention fully directed to the colorful summery dresses on the rack.

"We are not done yet. We will finish this discussion later Missy!" I unleash my pent up emotions as Jessica walks away smiling, her eyeballs glinting with mischief. Right at this very moment, the awful truth dawned on me, that this delicious hunk, standing across from my embarrassed fickle self, had been watching all of the drama play out between my nosy and impressionistic neighbor and myself… whatever the consequences now, I turn around and face the music … and Jake's reaction.

"Sorry about that! You know friends, how impossible they can get…" raising my disapproving voice, loud enough for Jessica to hear me from across the store floor. "Glad you remembered me," stumbling through my words.

"I never forget a face like yours. And you… it seems you remember my name too." Jake responded in a warm and seductive manner.

"Thank you… I think," I reply now, battling my insipid babbling and stuttering while preoccupied with what I'd brought into the shop to exchange for money.

"I wanted to take your number that day but by the time I turned around from my discussions with the store owner, you'd left." Jake added.

"Oh?" kept stumbling and blushing, only black people don't blush… or do they?

"It seems someone up there must be looking out for me for bringing you into my store today…" he continues.

"Flatterer," I joined in, quickly adjusting myself

to the beat of his voice.

"You are quite welcome. So, how can I help you?" Jake asks, totally fixated on me. "How can I be of service Siberia?" His sudden firm voice kicks me back to my senses and the problem at hand. Suddenly, I begin to hear Mr. Babu's mean heavily accented Indian voice, lashing me with his wicked tongue and threatening to throw me out of his house, if my rent was not paid! I instantly checked out at the thought of the disastrous event that might occur, if I didn't get him his overdue rent.

"Siberia?" His soft and gentle voice echoed throughout the store, enough to jerk me back to real time… the store.

"So sorry, I heard you the first time. I just needed to pull my thoughts together for what I am about to ask of you."

"I see" he replies, watching my every move.

"I was out of the country visiting my family in Africa" increasingly stuttering my way through my muddled words.

"That's awesome Siberia. One of these days, I hope I can visit Africa. Perhaps with you." Jake replies attempting to soften the discussion.

"I bet you will!" Jessica yells out from across the display floor, her face peeking out of the overstocked clothing rack in front of her.

"My gosh, is it hot in here or is it just me? huhhhh?" Catching my infuriated stare, she quickly moves further in-between the racks of clothes.

"Gosh, you guys have nice stuff here, seriously. I will just stay right here and do my thing, yeah mama?" Jessica shouts across the store floor digging further into the stacks of clothes, parading herself as she holds up dresses to her bodice.

"I need some serious cash. What can I get for this?" Eagerly awaiting Jake's response.

"Let's see all you have right now. May I?" He asks sorting all of my valuables… my pageant clothes, the zirconia-crystal fully loaded pageant crown, the bedazzled shimmering shoes I'd used for my pageant while I was in Africa. I gaze at him in anticipation of his offer and closely watch his mannerisms, hoping it would give him away. Jennie O'Conner, Jake and Simon's aunt, stands by the door to the inventory room, closely monitoring all of the discussions and the flirting between Jake and I. She makes her move towards us as Jake is right at the cusp of delivering his decision. Dressed in a white elegant top and her shimmering tight short skirt, she dashes towards the counter top where Jake is. Jennie begins to nit-pick at all of my sentimental valuables. She throws a condescending stare in my direction then goes back to Jake, frowning at him. First, I'd looked behind me, hoping there was someone else there that she was looking at with disapproval. I turned back in their direction confirming that it was truly me she was against. My thoughts suddenly began to race. Had we met before and I had done something really bad to rob her spirit? Why was she acting so arrogant towards me? Watching her, hoping I would understand her behavior towards a total stranger like me. Her abrasive opinion broke into my consciousness and speedily brought me back to the conversation.

"Hey Jake, I'm going to help you close shortly." She intentionally interrupts our transaction; staring bluntly at my prized possessions.

"Meet my aunt… She is like a mother to me.

The brains behind this joint" Jake states pulling the somewhat reluctant Jennie to his side and imprinting a kiss on her forehead.

"Oh son... flatterer!," she smiles pulling him forward and planting a kiss on his cheek.

"Good day ma'am," I said, as Jennie sizes her up; from head to feet wrapped in her multi-colored, bright-eyed and gargantuan scarf know called the Afro-centric do.

"We can't take those clothes!" She finally detonates like a bomb.

"I haven't finished looking at them, Jennie." Jake replies, his face desperately covering up his embarrassment.

"I see" she pauses still sizing me up.

"I've got this, let me do it" Jake whispers into his aunt's ear.

"I know you can. At any rate, you don't have to spend time on those things" She adds.

"Did you mean my valuables ma'am?" I interjected, offended by her condescending behavior.

"Yes, those things. Whatever you call them," she replies, her nose up in the air.

"I think all you have seen now... those on the countertop are all you need see" facing Jake squarely.

"You mean I can't get anything for them?" Speaking out in desperation.

"Look young lady, you do know we are a consignment shop and not a pawn shop. Perhaps you are mistaken what we do here and I'd be glad to point you in the right direction" Jennie continues in a stern voice.

"I'm sorry, I don't understand. I am not following you" I genuinely inquire, frustrated by her rude remarks and shenanigans.

"Jake, you might want to explain this better, right Jake?" she continues arrogantly. I gaze into her face, pretending not to be moved by her arrogance. If she only knew the truth that I, at this very instant, my only thought is to do her bodily harm... the urge to pound her down on the heavy duty wooden counter top... anything to stop her mouth from moving as they were spitting callous words. I look in Jake's direction; who looks equally embarrassed and perhaps as frustrated as I am with his aunt or mother whatever he wants to call her!

"I told you I was handling this," He gently yet firmly whispers in his aunt's direction. The sudden urge to bail him out of the humiliating incident overcomes me; an unexpected feeling, one I dared not explore. One thing I could count on was my African accent which never fails me. Being in America, I have always tried to mask it as best as I can. However, in the heat of the moment such as this, I could rely on it to save me! Today is no exception! Jennie starts ranting her insults, showing her ignorance and boy, tumbling out of my mouth, and without any caution, came my African flare. I could always count on it to relieve me without anyone knowing what I was saying, even if it was raining insults on them. Few minutes of ranting in my mother tongue certainly brought me a level of balance. With a cold stare stretching across the counter top, I quickly jump into the strained conversation between Jake and his aunt.

"But I heard your store just changed your policy... you are now giving money right away for the goods and some I could come back for if I am able to get the money... right?

"Oh that?" Jennie comments flippantly.

"Isn't that what your advertisement said? Or did I misunderstand … was just that a gimmick to bring people in here?" my voice rising uncontrollably.

"Sorry we don't play pranks here!" Jennie continues her tirade of snide remarks.

"Ma'am, I'm not trying to cause trouble. I need help and I am in trouble. I just want to get some of these things offloaded and I'll be out of your hair," I add, desperately wishing that she would remove herself out of the equation. Jennie looks at me directly with a blank stare, then turns in Jake's direction.

"You heard what I said Jake, no deal!" She adds walking away from the counter and into the back room. I stand there completely flabbergasted! How could she treat me like that? What had I done to deserve such a crappy attitude? Before I could compose myself, Jessica zooms to my side, infuriated and ready to take action!

"Oh no, she didn't! Did she just talk to you like that? Are you going to take that rubbish?" Jessica continues her tirade.

"S-s-s-sh! Enough Jessica. Need to focus on what I came here for, remember?" I plead.

"Oh quit it mama, don't shush me on this one! I mean it!" She faces Jake who is now looking pale.

"Is this how you guys treat customers? Are you going to let her get away with that?" She yells at Jake.

"I am so sorry about that. She usually is not like that. She's been under a lot of stress lately…" Jake defends his aunt.

"That is no excuse! Is she a bigot or how do you call that?" Jessica continues.

"Oh no. It's nothing like that."

111

"You could have fooled me!" Jessica continues. "Whatever she may or may not be going through, she need to keep it in that room back there. You hear me?" Jessica concludes.

"You are right. I truly apologize." Jake laments.

"Are you sure you want to do business here mama?" facing me, her angry mood now subsiding.

"I have no choice Jessica… I am fine. Need to do this so we can quickly get out of here," I respond.

"Sorry!" Jake shrugs his shoulders in defeat.

"Have I met your aunt somewhere or something? Why the animosity?" I ask Jake, who stands there with his arms crossed across his chest.

"What can I say… so sorry Siberia. Truly sorry for the embarrassment. I will take care of it," Jake speaks out in his soothing voice.

"Got it. So what do you have for me?" After an awkward few seconds of silence, we went right back into business. Jake takes my bag away from me and begins to shuffle through what I'd brought to the shop.

"Well, I am anxious. What is your verdict?" I was eager to hear his response.

"Truthfully, all of this is worth nothing." Jake responds in a sober mood.

"Are you going to be like your aunt now? Please take a look again. It has to be worth something… I got this at my last pageant in Africa" Pulling out my crown.

"What are we going to do with that Siberia? It's a pageant crown from Africa." Jake adds.

"But it can be a souvenir for someone, right?" I reply. "Alright then, look at other stuff in there… come on Jake, and those clothes? Your shop is filled with clothes. You can certainly do something with that…" my frustration rising like a rolling thunder with lightning roaring across an African prairie.

"Well, with the clothes, you heard her, right? I don't know what to say… it is not worth anything."

"With all the aggravation I got here today, you've got to help me out."

"All the glitz on it is fake!" grabbing the crown again and perusing it with care.

"Jake… Jake, I need help desperately… please" my voice cracking in anticipation.

"By the way, aren't you supposed to keep this for the next pageant queen?" Jake inquires.

"I am desperate right now. If I don't get my rent to my landlord, he will kick me out!" grabbing one of his arms, pulling him across the countertop, enough for our eyes to meet in the most intense and awkward way. For a second, our eyes lock on each other's; accompanied by total silence in the room.

"I see. Do you have something else for me?" He quickly grab my red glitzy shoes.

"I think I can do something with this" he continues.

"Arhhh! Great we are getting somewhere. But I need more… Keep looking please." Finally, I reluctantly pull out my treasured camera. I had won it at a writing competition held at my post graduate college. I had taken it with me on my trip to Africa, taking memorable pictures with my family as I was not certain when next I would see them. Besides the pageant crown, this camera is the most valuable to me. After watching Jake desperately trying to find a way to assist with what I brought in, I reluctantly hand over the camera bag with its content.

"Let's take a look. This looks interesting." Jake lightens up.

"I was hoping it wouldn't get to this. How much can I get for it?" quickly putting the crown and clothes back in my black grocery bag. Jake had a glare in his eyes. He looked like he was overthinking the whole situation.

"Can I ask you a question first?" He asks.

"Sure. What is it?" I glanced at my wrist watch. "Gosh, I've got to hurry up now. I've spent way more time in this shop."

"This is a great camera. You want it sold right away?"

"Oh no, I am not here to sell... not yet" interrupting his trend of thought.

"Oh?" Jake inquires.

"Can you just keep it and loan me the money? I promise you I will give you back the money when my student grant comes in." cautiously glancing behind him, ensuring that what I'd shared would not be heard by Jake's aunt.

"I see" Jake looks on.

"You said it. It is very valuable, right?"

"Yes, I said so" Jake adds almost reluctantly.

"Alright then, how much can I get for it now?"

"Come on Jake, you hold on to it while I sort myself out and then I'll come back for it." I continue.

"The rest of the stuff, you can sell right away." One can literally hear a pin drop amidst the silence and if there truly was a pin in the room. I watch carefully, anxious to see what Jake would decide. He was still, studying the camera yet again; glancing from the camera to my face. He leans forward gently, looks behind him, making sure no one is there, then gently whisper in my ear what I had been hoping for.

"I want to do this for you" he says with me looking on, panicking.

"How about $2,000. Just for you," pushing across the overloaded and congested counter, with all of the rest of my stuff. His whisper was dreamlike, echoing in my mind. Did I just hear him say $2,000?

"OMG! Really?" screaming in sheer ecstasy.

"S...s...sh! Don't let my aunt hear you or the deal is off" He chuckles my way.

"You are a life saver. Thank you so much." I shout in sheer ecstasy. He is a hunk of a man with a heart of gold too, a combination no woman could resist; perhaps I will be an exception or maybe not.

"You are quite welcome, pretty lady," He replies looking quite content with his decision.

"You have just saved my head from being chopped off and displayed on my landlord's mantle!" replying with a grin plastered all over my face.

"I totally get what you are going through" he answers, still being cautious about raising his voice for anyone else to hear. Unfortunately, Simon stands in the shadows, at the entrance of the back room shaking his head in total disbelief of what he'd seen his distrustful brother do. His anger is rising to the surface.

"Don't thank me too much, my dear Siberia. Hopefully, if the situation were reversed, you would do the same, right?" He adds to the elating conversation, as I stand there in shock that I'd finally gotten money for Mr. Babu and a few of my overdue bills.

"You can return the money with interest in 90

days. Hopefully, we would have sold the shoes and bags by then too. What do you say?" He continues putting away some of Siberia's valuables while settling her. Simon continues to sigh, shaking his head profusely, a sign showing his disapproval for Jake.

"Little Mr. goodie two shoes! There he goes again giving away what belongs to both us!" forcing with himself as he watches the transaction conclude.

"Jennie must see this rubbish!" he continues his groaning behind the curtain.

"Thank you... thank you... Thank you. Yes?

"It's a deal! Thank you so much" my voice seems to echo through the store.

"You are quite welcome. Let's do the paperwork and get you out of here quickly, okay?"

"Alright yes! Thanks!" replying while glancing at my wrist watch. Afar, Jessica is alerted by my initial scream. She quickly walks towards me as Jake and I walk through the paperwork.

"Jeez mama, someone is excited" she says, her bulging eyes jumping from Jake to me and then back to Jake.

"Well, is someone going to share?"

"I'll tell you all about it. Let's just be done here, okay Jessica?" I reply quickly going over the papers Jake had tossed my way.

"You go girl! Those black African eyes are good for something after all! I told you... magic happens when you use what your mama gave you" Jessica whispers in my direction, her look more curious than ever.

"Oh stop. You are impossible! For real!" I look in her direction for a minute.

"Alright mama, I won't rock the boat... for

now," Jessica replies still looking as inquisitive as ever.

"Just so you know, if we don't catch the next bus on Harris in the next 10 minutes, we won't make the bank, that is if you are still going to the bank" Jessica quickly warns spying at her colorful wrist watch.

"I know Jessica. We are rushing through now. Yes Jake?" I respond, battling through the heap of paperwork handed over by Jake as he nods in agreement with my statement.

"We will be late for school too mama. I need to show you the route for next time. I don't want you getting lost around here." Jessica adds.

"That's neat. You are in school too?" Jake inquires.

"Yes. I came to this country to finish my master's program. It is killing me right about now" I reply, quickly rushing through the paperwork, signing all of the dotted lines displayed on each of the fifteen pages.

"What are you in school for, if you don't mind me asking" Jake asks, pointing to those parts of the documents that still need signing.

"One day, I will be a bestselling author... my novels will be made into movies... and my family will be very proud of me... and of what I have accomplished here in America" replying with my head suddenly enraptured by my dream.

"Great dreams for a great gal like you" Jake states, his face lightens up.

"Yeah, but it's so hard achieving it" I respond, bringing my mind back to mother earth.

"Well, you know what they say about America... a land of opportunity and where dreams come true," Jake continues his show of support.

"Look mama, that dream is jeopardized if we don't get our tails out of here now" Jessica interrupts, her eagerness is displayed visibly for all to see.

"Yes mother!" looking in the direction on her fidgeting body.

"I am studying to be a writer" I blasted in Jake's direction, ignoring Jessica's warnings.

"That is great! I am excited for you" Jake replies still pointing me through the document.

"Thank you. Hopefully, the dream will come true someday. Gosh, if I don't get my rent money to Mr. Babu today, I'll be in serious trouble! Is this all of the paperwork I need to do?" sighing. I quickly scribbled my way through the last of the papers.

8 WHEN DARKNESS BECKONS

AASHISH BABU DRESSED IN HIS FLOWING INDIAN
REGALIA, AND HIS COLORFUL TURBAN,
complimented by the bluish sky, charges onto my porch
alongside his son, Sanje. Aashish Babu viciously slams a duct
taped eviction notice on to the front door.

"Pops, I still think you should have waited for
her…" Sanje interjects.

"Who asked you for your opinion?" Aashish
charges on, his thick Indian accent suddenly accentuated, his
hands smoothing the tape around the door edges, ensuring
no room was left for me to get back into the house.

"I am just saying, you gave her today to come
up with her rent. At least you can wait till tomorrow, then
you do something," Sanje continues disapprovingly.

"Did you just say something again? I can't
believe this boy is still talking."Aashish raising his voice to yet
to another height, anger spewing from his nostrils. "I need
you to shut your mouth right now, before I do something I
will regret! Is this what I am wasting my hard earned money
on… one with a flippant mouth?"

"Here we go again pops… the old school joke."

"You call it a joke Sanje? You call your parents wasting money on your training a joke?"

"Okay pops, I apologize. Let's not start another round of your stuff!" he begins to work his way away from the porch.

"You are such a daft boy, you know that. I don't blame you. I blame your mother who insists on leaving you in this country to be trained!"

"Alright pops, enough…please! I don't want anyone hearing all of this, please"

"Then quit acting like a Jack-ass! Perhaps, then I won't say anything. I most certainly can rectify the mistake your mother made. It's not too late to ship you out of this country… send you where you can learn proper manners." Aashish raves.

"You are kidding me, right pops?"

"Do I look like I'm kidding?"

"Look, for once, I agree with you… mom keeps pushing us together… father son bonding she keeps saying. It is time for her to just let things be. You need your space and I need mine," Sanje walks even further away from the door.

"How old are you again? I can't believe what's coming out of that mouth. Anyway, I will deal with you later. I know your medicine!" Aashish concentrates on the last taping of the door.

"Now, let's see what she'll do," he sighs in contentment as his cell phone blasts out on an Indian ring tone. He instantly pulls out the phone from his pocket and sees my name pop up. Aashish ignore the call, walking towards the parking lot to catch up with Sanje. The cell phone continues to ring, repeating the Indian music ring tone, tirelessly.

"Pop, you may want to pick that up. That ring tone is driving me crazy." Sanje says.

"Good! I finally have something to rattle you. Deal with it." Aashish responds, ignoring the phone call.

@@@@@

Simon continues on his ranting war with Jake, after seeing his deal with me. He walks out of hiding and throws a disapproving stare in Jake's direction.

"Dude, you are one big hypocrite!" he slams Jake.

"What are you griping about now Simon?" Jake responds with his back to Simon, a visible sign he was not interested in whatever he had to say.

"Are you kidding me? Did you just say that nonsense?"

"Look bro', it's been a long day for me and I am pretty exhausted... too darn exhausted for what you are about to start here. Some of us do work hard for a living, you know," Jake tries to stop Simon from escalating the discussion.

"Oh there he goes again. Mr., goodie two shoes!"

"Just knock it off bro'... I am dead serious. Stop this foolishness! I am certainly not interested; so quit while you're ahead."

"Easy for you to say. Let me see, since when does this consignment store cough up that much money for anything? Tell me Casanova!" Simon blasts out. Jake is quiet, looking on with his chest raising against his tightly fitted t-shirt.

"Yeah right! I thought so! I'm so freaking out of here right now that I may blow a gasket! Simon continues pulling his guitar across his chest.

Mr. Wise guy, Wait just one minute! Where do you think you are going?"

"Argh! And he speaks again. Taking a break from stupidity!" He replies pushing through the inventory on the store front.

"Well then, are you coming back to close the shop? Remember I have an appointment later tonight." Jake adds.

"That depends!" Simon replies.

"You are one crazy dude, you know that! Oh! Never mind Jennie will. You get outta here before you make me lose my mind" Jake replies.

"Yeah bro' I'm crazy. It takes one to know one."

Jake shakes his head and walks out from behind the counter; pacing around the shop as Jennie walks out and into the store front.

"What's eating you up son?" She inquires of Simon, blocking his path.

"Nothing. I just need to go. Jake told me you are closing for him so I am making sure." Simon replies, gazing in Jake's direction.

"Yes I am, so go ahead. I'm just doing some inventory right now. I will come back to the front when I am done." Jennie replies looking on suspiciously, from Jake to Simon.

"Well, I'm going to have to do mine from home. Please don't tell Jake I said that. I really can't take any more of his snotty and smart remarks!" Simon whispers in her ear, with a raised eyebrow in Jake's direction.

"Um... I see. My lips are sealed then. Just make sure you have it together when you get in tomorrow. Okay sweetie?" Jennie adds planting a warm kiss on his forehead.

"What do you mean, have it together?" quickly pulling back from Jennie.

"Now who is being snotty and smart? You know what I mean Simon! I was speaking English!" Jennie blasts back, with a slight attitude.

"I don't need you jumping on Jake's band wagon," getting agitated by the impending argument about to erupt between him and Jennie..

"You my dear...are impossible. Hard headed like your father.

Jennie walks away while Simon grabs the camera bag and a few other items not yet priced. He rushes out of the shop.

"I am out! Later." Simon says sneakily watching Jennie attend to some customers.

"Bye honey... Good luck. Not that you need it, right?" Simon walks out and into the backyard where his car is parked.

@@@@@

Fanta and Alan finally walk into their mansion. They hug each other whilst Alan ruminates over who he'd seen that day... namely Siberia. he quickly brings himself back to the conversation.

"You were amazing with your fans tonight."

"Thanks. I wish you did the same with me. Why can't things get back to what they use to be?"

Alan is quiet, taking it all in.

"You were so amazing when I met you. I miss us." Fanta continues.

"I am freaking exhausted from fighting you every day Fanta. This is not good for my health."

"But the way you were staring at that girl today. Are you sleeping with her ?"

"What! Are you accusing me now?"

"I need a cigarette, excuse me…" ignoring the comment.

@@@@@

Simon is sitting in his car. He begins to remove the contents of ~~in~~ the camera bag onto his passenger seat. Suddenly, there is a bluish glow coming from the bag, but Simon is not paying attention. He makes a desperate call to one of his dealers.

Hey dude, I need to see you right away. I have some goods I need to offload. Are you game? Tomorrow is too late! Need the funds now!"
Simon hangs up in frustration, banging his fists on the steering wheel.

@@@@@

Tiger, one of Tee's henchmen receives a phone call. He pulls himself aside from his boss who is busy puffing at his cigar and the other henchmen.

"Hello?... Yes! Are you sure? Ok then. Thanks."
He quickly makes his way over to Tee.

"Sir?" disrupting the conversation at hand.
Tee looks up, along with the others in the office.

"We found him… Simon. He's trying to
offload some goods."

"Good! Alright guys, we are going to take
our time with this one. I want to show him what really
happens to a punk who refuses to pay what he owes!"
Tee puffs his cigar hard, blowing smoke into the air!

@@@@@

The night has slowly crept in on us. We walk from the
bus station back to Jessica's house. We are so tired
because of the long day we've had. Jessica wobbles
towards her house, not paying any much attention to me
walking away.

"Mama, this has been a very long day," she
drawls.

"I agree. Thank you for coming with me."

"Sure mama, what are friends for?" I quickly
cross over and walk up to my house. I looked up and see
an eviction notice glued to her front door with a duct tape
across the doors. My worst nightmare has come upon me
and I have no one to help. The shame that this will bring
to me and my pride will not let me reach out to Jessica. I
turned around to see Jessica about to enter her own house.
This is yet another frustration! Another day of
disappointment! Another opportunity to feed into my self-
pity party. I sit down at the edge of my porch, completely
exhausted and unsure what my next move would be. I
have no choice but to reach out to Mr. Babu. I summon
courage and dial his number.

"Mr. Babu… This is Siberia." Words stuck to the back of my throat. Mr. Babu's voice was quite audible as he blasts his hysterics through the cell phone.

"Who?"

"Siberia… You know who Mr. Babu?"

"I have nothing to say to you! " his screams getting even louder through the phone.

"I have your money… Please!"

"And I have a big fat notice for you. Do you see it right in front of your door?"

"Yes Mr. Babu… I missed the bus home, Mr. Babu."

"Great! I am not in the mood for any of your excuses. We had a deal, you will pay me my rent today or else I kick you out!"

"Yes but the day is not over yet Mr. Babu!"

"For me, it is over! I am not going to be crawling around in the middle of the night to collect rent from you."

"Mr. Babu, I just couldn't make it on time but I do have it now. Please, it's been a long day for me."

"So what are you suggesting… that I come out of my comfortable bed to open the door for you now? Is that what you are suggesting young lady?"

"Yes please. I need to get in the house to take care of myself."

"You are a joke! I will do no such thing. You may as well take the money and go find you another place. My charity shop is now closed to you."

"Mr. Babu? Mr. Babu" the phone finally goes dead. He hangs up abruptly. I look aimlessly around the porch, uncertain what my next move would be. Mama always tells me to look for a silver lining in the midst of any tragedy that may come my way, at all times. In this case, the only silver lining I can see is not sleeping and the mystery woman will be unable to disturb me as she is constantly interrupting my dreams. I looked down and my cell phone is blinking. These are messages I'd been unable to retrieve since my running around today. If there was a better time to retrieve them, it is now. My very first message pushed me to jump off the porch floor immediately.

"Siberia, this is your mother. Please call us… it is urgent o." her voice echoes.

"Oh no! What else can go wrong now?" I gaze into the sparsely lighted skies. "Why can't I just get a little rest?" I push the next message and this time papa's urgent tone blasts through the phone.

"Siberia my daughter… your father here. … your papa. There is fire on the mountain. We need to put it out before it becomes a calamity. Call us back please. It's about your sister… Fire, o my daughter! Fire!" The message ends brusquely. My phone goes dead at that very instant. I realize the battery had died and it needed to be recharged. Exasperated, I slump to the hard, cold floor in an attempt to sleep, desperately wishing that when I wake up, this will all be a bad dream.

9 COLOSSAL RESPITE

INSPITE OF THE HARDSHIP I'D GONE THROUGH THE NIGHT BEFORE, I dozed off, my back against the hard floor waiting for another day to chart my course.

"Siberia! Wake up Siberia!" a voice I'd heard before and wonder if someone from beyond was calling me. I lay down, unsure if I was dreaming yet again.

"Siberia!" the Indian accent erupts. Suddenly I feel two hands pushing hard against my shoulders and shaking me immensely.

"Young lady, get up from this place... Now!" This was my clue to push through the sleep and wake up.

"Mr. Babu?"

"No. It's a genie! What do you think you are doing on this floor?"

"I told you I had nowhere to go. I was trying to explain to you last night," gradually pulling myself together.

"I have your money Mr. Babu," I state.

"I heard you the first time you said it last night. I am not deaf!"

"Okay then, let me give it to you so you can open the door."

"I told you I was done with you. If I take this money now, what will happen next month? Another drama?"

"Mr. Babu, please just take this and let's call a truce. I am really tired right now and need a shower and a hot meal." The silence stretches as they both look at each other, each one waiting to hear what the other would say.

"Where is the money?" He finally speaks.
I bring out the money from my wallet, count out what I owe and hand it over to Mr. Babu. He walks over to the door, pulls down the eviction notice and the duct tape. He removes the lock on the door and surprisingly lets me back into my place. Perhaps things are beginning to look up for me. Last night, Mr. Babu was adamant about not wanting me to be his tenant anymore. Today, he looks happier; glowing with generosity and kindness, attributes which had eluded him previously. So I conclude, whatever causes him to be this way, affording me the opportunity to have a roof over my head… whatever changed his actions, I am grateful. I walk into my home breathing a sigh of relief. I rush to play one of my inspirational CDs yet again, a daily ritual I'd gotten used to.

"Hello girlfriend. I bet you've missed me."
Speaking loud at the laptop. I take my seat in my favorite spot by the laptop and begin my every day routine. The Princess of Suburbia's voice comes blasting through the speakers.

"How does it really feel to be doing all you believe you were born to do and yet, you've achieved no head way? How do you move past your disappointments?"

"Tell me about it Princess. I sure can use some help right now."

"Do you know that your yesterday and today's disappointment is an undercover cop for your future success? This is your gal, the Princess of Suburbia. Let's go people. It's going to be a great day..." She continues in her cheerful mood. The show's theme song comes on as I settle further in my sofa, pull my blanket over myself and attempt to doze off yet again. I slowly drift off to sleep.

@@@@@

A sudden banging on my door barged into my sleep. Whoever is at the other side is bent on opening my door. The banging continues increasingly disturbing until I finally get up from my sofa.

"Hold on. Coming. Who is it?" There is no response except for the continuous door banging.

"Gosh, it better not be another bill collector."

I make my way to the door, reluctantly open it and there they are... my two rascal African cousins, Onye and Onka, all dressed in mis-matched colors... long pants but not long enough to cover their ankles... colorful bow-ties that looked like that of a clown... sun glasses adorning their heads rather than their eyes. If there was ever a contest for the worst dressed, they would win it hands down! They jump at me, grab me and throw me up in the air. I landed in both their arms as they begin ranting and raving about being in America. I quickly invite them inside the house before any of my neighbors could see them. They drag in their big goofy looking bag; another clown asset.

"What in the world... Onye... Onka, what are you doing here? Is this all you brought?"

"Sis' what else are we to bring? It's not like we have all of these clothes that you celebrities wear here in America."

"Celebrity? Who's a celebrity?" I reply.

"You now. Isn't that what you are here for?" Onye asked while looking around the house.

"Not sure where you got that news from. Look around you, does this place look like where celebrities live?"

"You talk true... my sister. But you are on your way, right?" Onka inquires.

"Well, that's the plan. But thank you for the flattery."

"I am so tired. Long trip to this obodo... America" Onye states.

"Look at him, illiterate man. You are in America now. You can't be saying obodo... America anymore." Onka lambasts Onye.

"I beg you, mind your own business," Onye re-iterates.

"Brother, you have been liberated from the village. Recognize that now before you go out there and start to embarrass yourself and me too." Onka insists.

"I can and will call America whichever way I like." Onye replies, his heart beating profusely and anger at the brink of erupting.

"Then get ready to be disowned by me!"

"By you? Who are you? Don't start any trouble here Onka Tonka! Leave me and my English alone. You hear me? Leave me alone!" Onye emphasizes.

"I can't leave you alone. Do you want to shame me?" Onka continues.

"Wow! You two are still at each other's throats!" I interrupt. "Unbelievable! Okay guys, how are mama and papa?"

"They are fine... we thank God." Onka ignoring Onye.

"I tried to reach mama and papa last night but my phone died. The truth is something must be going on cause why are you two here? What is really going on?" I inquired trying to compose myself.

"It's Naiya." Onye answers.

"What's going on with my sister? Please cut to the chase."

"Yes, your sister... she is sick." Onka finally replies after much silence.

"Sick? Has she seen a doctor?" ignorantly asks.

"Not that kind of sickness cous'," Onye replies.

"What then?" intensely staring at her cousins.

"Spiritual sickness." Onka responds as I looked on confused and puzzled as to the meaning of his riddle.

"I am not following you Onka. What do you mean spiritual sickness?

"Quick question, did you bring that stone?" Onka asks

"What stone?" then I turned to Onye who shrugs his shoulders. "What stone is he talking about?"

"The one mama left on your table at home... did you take it?" Onka continues his interrogation.

"Onye, can you please help your brother out? What stone is he talking about?"

"The gods have revealed that you took the stone. It is here in America." Onka states.

"When will you all stop this fetish behavior… which gods again? Are mama and papa still dabbling into all of that nonsense?"

"S-s-s-h! The gods have ears. Don't you dare challenge them with your insults! They will retaliate!"

"You guys need to start coming out of the village more often. For crying out loud, you are more educated than the average person in the village yet you believe all of these things." I add.

"Perhaps if and when you remember this stone, you will understand it all. So did you bring the stone here?" Onka continues.

"You are testing my patience. Why are you all over the map like this? Just tell her what we came to do." Clenching his teeth.

"Shhhhh Onye. Help me understand what he is saying. Why are you all looking for this stone?" Suddenly, I remember the Silleri stone.

"Ah…ah! The one your parents told you about. We must return it home right away. No time for questions please. We have to find the stone quick." Onka interrupts my thoughts.

"Wait a second! Silleri? Is that what you guys are talking about?" I ask.

"Yes. That is it, Silleri. Do you have it?" Onka asks again.

"I wouldn't take such a thing without letting mama and papa know."

"This is trouble…" Onye sighs aloud.

"What do you mean trouble? I did take pictures

of it while I was home. I have always been fascinated by that stone cause it has a sentimental value to our family. I remember Papa always warning us to guard it and never let it leave the family."

"Where is it cousin?" Onka asks.

"I told you I don't have it. Why would I take it?" I continue. Onka suddenly starts another bout of argument with Onye and quickly gets sidetracked from what Siberia is telling them.

"I told you before bro', she couldn't have taken it!" Onka speaks out loud.

"My friend shut up. I don't know what you mean by that. Did I tell you she stole it?" Onye defending himself.

"My friend you are not serious. Have you suddenly developed a case of amnesia?" Onka says.

"Be quiet my friend. Real people are talking and you too join in. What rubbish." Onye attacks back.

"Stop! Get to the point. What is wrong with Naiya? And what does the stone have to do with it?"

"Look cous', your sister is really sick and if we don't find that stone she can die!" Onye blurts out.

"What? Naiya die?"

"You just dropped a bomb shell. There is a certain kind of way you do it bro'... Not like that!" Onka complains.

"I'm getting a nasty headache. Will you both please quit arguing and let's reason together? Seriously, I need for you now to be quiet." I state emphatically.

"Did you hear her Onye?" Onka adds.

"First of all, the last time I saw it, was when I was leaving Africa and quickly taking pictures of it to bring here. I remember pulling my camera off the table where Silleri was placed. I put myself back in time and traced my steps from the last time I saw the Silleri till I returned to America.

@@@@@

Naiya's voice is echoing in the hut. As she approaches my room, she peeks in, asking me to hurry up.

"Siberia your car is here." I remember pulling my camera off the table, right where Silleri was placed. I did hear a thumping sound but didn't make anything of it. Could it have dropped into the camera bag when I was hurriedly putting things away in Africa? Could it be the thump I heard and didn't pay attention to? While I would like to believe these are just fetish beliefs from my people, could I really risk the life of my sister, Naiya, to find out if the tradition still holds or not. I have a decision to make and fast. I know I cannot stay on both sides of the beliefs. On one side my African tradition, culture and beliefs and on the other is the American way of doing things, into which I have since been indoctrinated. Be it as it may, my goal today is to do whatever it takes to help Naiya get better, including finding the stones the family believes it has mystical powers, if mishandled, as we have done. I come back from my memory lane, and back into my living room.

"Oh my God, I just took the camera to a pawn shop."

"What do you mean you pawn the camera? That stone must return home in 7 days oh, so your sister don't die. Is the stone with the camera?" Onka wonders.

"Will you quit mentioning death as if it is mere

cho-co-late you are eating? Onka interjects.

"Didn't papa tell you that it must not exchange hands?" Onka inquires.

"Yes but what does that have to do with me?" I ask.

"Think cous'... think! If you don't have it then someone else has it. Change of hands... get it?" I find myself immediately flustered by the latest occurrence.

"Think cous'... Think real hard. We must find this quickly." Onka piles on the misery I am already feeling about the whole ordeal. Suddenly, I am overwhelmed by panic. What if what they say is really true? What if Naiya dies because I had mistakenly taken this stone and transported it to America? This is no longer about my own belief but the belief of my people. I cannot take the chance! I have to find the stone quickly.

"Well, that's what I am doing, if you let me be... I am thinking Onka!" the panic increases.

"Onka, can't you see she is racking her brain? Give her room to breathe for a second." Onye spits out. Onka hisses in his direction ignoring his latest remarks.

"What am I going to do now? I will never forgive myself if anything evil happens to Naiya." Screaming in despair.

"Nothing will happen, if we find the stone quickly," Onka consoling me.

"What a minute...,"

"You remember something?" Onye pushes forward.

"That explains the bad dreams I have been having since I got back from Africa?" They look ahead waiting in anticipation for me to tell them what the dream is

137

about.

"What is it cous'?" Onye pushes his question ahead of Onka's.

"You know that goddess people are always talking about at the village? The one they say comes out during the festival from under our famous tree?" I continue.

"Argh… you are talking about Yemoji." Onye queries.

"Yes! She has been disturbing me in my dream. Is this why?"

"Haba! This is another palaver… another trouble. How can you be seeing Yemoji just like that cous'?" Onka blurts out.

"Did you ever go under that tree when you were home in Africa?" Total silence befalls the room as I looked on, attempting to avoid answering the question. This was a secret that I only know as I would always sneak out of the house to do just that.

"Well cous'. Did you or did you not?" Onye joins Onka in this inquiry.

"Never mind. My problem is just not sleeping and my dream. Naiya on the other hand has a bigger problem. Let's focus on that." Avoiding their stare down.

"If you say so cous'. But I certainly hope you did not go under the tree when you were not supposed to! Otherwise, you are heaping another trouble on yourself. But we will focus as you have said." Onka concludes, still glancing my way suspiciously. My heart sinks hearing the fright imprinted in Onka's voice. What have I done? Have I unleashed terror on my family due to my ignorance? What have I done to myself and to my family? My heart begins to race rapidly, my body shaking in fright that I may have chewed more than I can handle.

"What have I done? What have I gotten everyone into? The stone has got to be in the camera bag. Please let the stone be there." I conclude, getting up from the seat.

"This is not the time for blame but time to take action!" Onka's attempt in consoling me.

"Look my people, let's wrap this up and find the stone... Please, enough talk now." Onye warns.

"I believe I know where to start the search! I have to run. You guys have had a very long flight from Africa. Stay and get some rest. I did groceries last night. Eat what you like, sleep where you like, I got to go get my car then, we will meet up later."

"Oh no cous', we will go with you." Onka says.

"Yes cous'. This is why we are here." Onye adds.

"Not now. Just rest up okay. Let me figure the first step out and I will come get you two later. Okay?" I insist.

I rush out of the sitting room and into my bedroom before either could respond. In my bedroom, I quickly called Jake.

"Hello Jake?" exchanging quick pleasantries with him. I go straight into my reason for calling and point blank ask him for the camera bag. As I delve into the discussion with him, a sudden static overcame our conversation. I try my best to hear what he had to say but the static was overpowering.

"This is America. What is this static all about?" I drop my cell phone, change my clothes, secure my head tie and head straight for the door.

"See you guys later." Leaving them in the sitting

room.

"Bye cous'," Onye answers, getting up from the couch. They watch me leave the house I silence.

"I'm going to shower my brother..." Onye announces to Onka.

"Great! Who is stopping you?" Onka replies. "Just hurry up." He adds.

"My friend shut up. You arrogant thing!" Onye responds walking away as Onka notices my laptop. He walks up to the laptop and opens the internet.

"There you go," Onka sighs at the sight of the internet.

10 THE HUNT FOR SILLERI

I ARRIVE AT THE CONSIGNMENT STORE, THE CHIMING OF THE DOOR BELL ATTRACTS THE NOTICE OF OTHER CUSTOMERS IN MY DIRECTION; a disconcerting feeling at the pit of my stomach magnifies as I swiftly approach the front desk. This is day one of my quest for the Silleri stone. If there was ever anything I would focus on, this was it!

"Hello there Siberia... How are you?" Jake trying to make conversation.

"Peachy!"

"Sorry we got cut off over the phone. I just couldn't hear what you were saying." He pauses. "So how can I help you?"

"Listen, I need that camera bag back?" in a very serious and no nonsense tone.

"Oh? You've got the money now? Good for you Siberia." Jake ecstatic.

"I wish man. I need to check something in that camera bag back please. I think I left something very valuable in there." Uncontrollable panic written all over my face.

"Is everything okay Siberia?" Jake inquires.

"It will be when I find what I am looking for."

"Sure! Let me grab it then." He walks away from me.

"Thank you so much Jake."

"The pleasure is all mine." He walks to the back of the shop to retrieve the camera while I peruse the store awaiting his return. Jake returns into the store empty handed but looking frazzled.

"Where is the camera bag Jake?"

"Give me a second, let me make a quick call."

"Oh Gosh! . Where is it Jake?" So very weary.

"Please keep your voice down. Don't want the rest of the customers thinking there is something wrong." We both glance in the direction of the customers, ensuring no one heard me.

"Look! This is a life and death situation and I need that camera bag right now… Where is my camera Jake?

"Please just give me a second. I think I know where it is... Probably my brother has it. He is in charge of inventory. No worries." Jake blurts out unconvincingly.

"Well, he'd better! You promised me you'd wait for me to pick it back up! You promised Jake!" hysterical, completely ignoring Jake's effort to keep me quiet and undisruptive.

"Please Siberia, keep your voice down. Seriously, I'll find it. Just give me a second, alright?" Jake hurries off to the back room in search of Simon.

@@@@@

Jake is in the back room talking to Simon over a phone. He

intentionally lowers his voice, making sure that his firm voice is not heard in the front store.

"Where are you now Simon?" he pauses for a response. "The camera dropped off by that young lady, Siberia, has suddenly disappeared from this shop. I know you have something to do with it. Where is it?"

"What now Jake? What camera? Ask Jennie not me." Simon's speech slurred over the phone.

"I see you are having your own party there again! Are you high Simon? Are you?"

"Okay bro' which is it… are you calling about the camera bag or are you calling to harass me about what I do or I'm not doing in my own crib?"

"You know what? You are right? It is your life and if your decision is to sniff it all away on drugs, you go ahead! Go right ahead pal! I am through trying to help you."

"Thank you! Now, you were saying?"

"Seriously, I am not playing with you right now. I need that camera and the bag back! The customer is here to take it back."

"Is that right? Okay, well I don't have it so you better ask Jennie." Simon hangs up before Jake could respond.

"What a dork? I know you took it…. Jennie doesn't handle that department. It better be still intact!" Jake dials back and he picks up yet again.

"Yes what do you want? I ~~too~~ am busy Jake… I already told you, ask Jennie!"

"Don't you dare hung up on me again. We've got to finish this. The customer is right here waiting"

"You mean your lovely Siberia." Cynical.

"You are the last person I want to be joking

with right now. Look Simon, I need you to bring the stuff back now! All she wants to do is check the camera bag for something she thought she left in it."

"Alright bro'. It is on the inventory list I brought home with me. Will bring it in later. Now leave me the heck alone!"

"And when is later Simon?"

"You heard me, later! Perhaps tomorrow. I am busy right now."

"Sure, busy frying your brains."

"Whatever! Look you are wasting my time right now. I don't want to be rude, but you need to get off my line before I drop it again on you."

"I thought you and I had an agreement not to take any inventory home again? Why did you do this Simon?" Simon snorts in response.

"I am so done with you! Tomorrow you better bring that camera back." Jake retorts.

"Alright boss, tomorrow Jake." Simon hangs up before Jake could say another word. Jake reluctantly heads back to the store front.

"Well, did you find it or did you not?" screaming at him, anxiety on the rise.

"I'm afraid it is currently being inventoried outside of the store. Come back this time tomorrow, I promise you; you will have it then."

"I do not like the sound of this. Don't like it at all. I truly appreciate you Jake, but, if you don't deliver my camera bag tomorrow, I will have to sue you and your store." Ignoring my recent interest for him. Saving Naiya at this point trumps whatever feelings I may or may not have had for him.

"Come on Siberia, it hasn't gotten to that yet. I promise, come back tomorrow; and I will have it for you."

"Like I said earlier, this is a life and death situation."

"What do you mean by that?" I looked his way, deliberating in my head whether I should tell him the whole truth or not. I opt to storm out of the store leaving Jake perplexed and few of the shoppers staring at him.

@@@@@

Onye and Onka have settled down in my house. Looking refreshed after a warm bath and change of clothes, they settle in front of my laptop, surfing the internet.

"Bro' this is life oh." Onka exclaims.

"I agree. Siberia must be having great fun living in America. Look at the sitting room, I tell you what I will give to live here." Onye agrees.

"But eyes on the ball bro'. We need to focus." Onka concludes as he continues surfing the internet.

"So what are you looking for?" Onye asks.

"Just looking at the internet. Who knows, we may find something leading us to the stone." Onka replies.

"Bro' how did you know how to use this?"

"Are you joking Onye? Well, it's simple, when we were being taught in school, you were busy chasing the girls in your class." He bursts out laughing.

"Don't start your insults! You know I can dish it out too." Responding to Onka's sarcasm.

They continue to surf the internet until an image of a similar stone surfaces on the screen. Onye wipes his face in amusement and disbelief at what he is seeing on the screen.

"Am I seeing right? $500,000... for that stone? Is that true?" Onye screams with Onka quickly launching at him and covering his mouth with his hands.

"S-s-s-h! be quiet my friend!" Onka cautions him slowly releasing his hands from his mouth.

"My brother you are too much. How did you find this?" Onye whispers.

"That's why I tell you reading is very important. Our forefathers, may you be praised! That kind of stone is worth all that much ? Onka continues.

"Yes oh bro' isn't that what we are seeing with our eyes?" Onye replies as he jumps up and begins dancing.

"Wait oh Onka Tonka, before we kill ourselves with dancing; why people go buy this kind stone for that amount?" Onye suddenly stops dancing.

"Look my friend, who knows why people do anything? This is America where anything can happen." Onka responds.

"Are you sure this is not a joke?" Onye queries.

"I beg you, who knows you here to joke with you? This is what they call rare stone. That stone is a rare stone Onye." Onka further explains.

"Enhe ... he... hen. Rare stone. This America Obodo people. Na real wa o." Onye sighs.

They jump up in unison, beat their chests against each other's like Tarzan, the ape man, and then quickly regroup, settling at the table again. Onye pulls the picture of Silleri I had printed earlier and they compare with picture on internet. They jump up and clap each other's' hands in excitement.

"This is jack pot bro'" Onye says watching Onka still dancing around the room.

"All of our lives, people have treated us like second-class citizen, even in the village where we all wear poverty like a Sunday church clothes."

"Maybe now, the villagers will respect us more. And maybe we can go back home to our parents now." Onye continues eliciting response form Onye who suddenly calms down and sits by the laptop, just gazing at the stone.

"If we get this money, do you know how much our lives will change? In fact, we wouldn't even have to go back to our village again. Perhaps, stay here and live the life... yes!" Onye continues.

"I don't know... This is tough. What do we tell cous' and her parents?" feeling a little remorseful. "How about Naiya?" He adds.

"I don't know what to tell you bro'. I am tired of suffering. With this money, we can take care of everyone. I love my cousins but I don't want to suffer for the rest of my life." Onye concludes.

"We have to think this through Onye. Too many things riding on this. Besides, we have to find the stone first. No use counting our eggs before they hatch Onye."

"I have counted this one. We will find it. We must find it. Anywhere cous' goes now, we follow her. Deal?" Onye reacts.

"I'm not comfortable with letting anything happen to Naiya. I have to think about this. What if we end up cursed for the rest of our lives?" Onka suddenly panicking.

"Which curse my friend? There is no curse... Please, no curse here."

"Are you willing to risk the curse Onye?"

"Yes oh. To get that kind of money, I will risk

anything." Onye replies.

"Nawa oh!" sighed Onka.

"Look, our mother and father are at home dying of poverty! And if we don't find a solution, we too will die. We all have to die someday, don't we?" Onye hoping to dissuade Onka from changing his mind. "For once in our lives, our parents will respect us too and quit seeing as village louts." He continues.

@@@@@

In the alley behind their store, Simon is getting punched in the face by guards who work for Tee. He wants his money back.

"Where is my money punk?"

"I told you, I don't have the money yet. I swear, I will find it!" Lifting up his bruised face, spitting out blood.

"Oh, you don't need to swear. By the time I am done with you, you're going to wish you were dead! I want my money pronto!" Tee shouts.

"If you kill me, how do you get your money back?" Simon lashes back at Tee, flippantly.

"Shut your trap or I'll just finish you off here and not even bother about the money!" Tee ordering his henchmen to pull Simon up close. His henchman throws a hard punch in Simon's stomach, Simon explodes in pain.

"Now, this should keep your mouth shut when the boss man is talking!" henchman roars in Simon's face. Tee walks around Simon. He signals his guards to search his pockets and all he was carrying with him.

"Let me go please, I will have the money."
Exhausted, he pleads for his life.
" I said, shut your mouth punk!"
He slaps Simon real hard across his already bruised face.
SIMON screams in anguish yet again. Tee pauses on hitting
Simon again, he signals to his henchmen to look around,
ransack Simon's pockets.

"You either give me my money or return the
merchandise. Either way, I will get back what's mine. And I
don't want to hear you sniffed it all through your nose. You
sniff, you pay! Period!" Tee yells.

As Tee paces back and forth, he notices a light flashing from
the camera bag. Tee is drawn by it. The henchmen points
their gun at Simon's legs, ready to shoot at Tee's command.
Tee grabs the camera bag and raises his hand in the air
instructing the Henchmen not to shoot. He opens the bag,
pulls out the camera then throws the bag in one of the
henchmen's direction. Out came tumbling the sparkling
stone. Tee not making anything of the stone, picks it up and
places it in his pocket.

"The next time I see you, you better have my
money man." Tee concludes his discussion with Simon.

"I promise Tee, I will. Just let me go and take
care of this." Simon stutters.

"Your promise's worth jack to me. You've got
this weekend to bring me my money or else!" replies Tee,
nodding at his guards who immediately drops Simon to his
knees giving him a lasting punch before sending him on his
way.
TEE and his henchmen leaves hysterical Simon at the alley.
In desperation, he quickly grabs his phone and makes a call to

one of his dealers. He is left alone,
squirming in pain and wiping blood off his battered face.

@@@@@

Onye continues to speak endearing words to Onka, ensuring
he does not change his mind about finding the stone and
selling it to the highest bidder.

"See bro' if we know what's good for us, we
keep our mouth shut." Onye carries on.

"You don't have to worry about that. Who are
we telling here in America? I am just worried about what
could happen to us or even Naiya if we go through with
this?" Onka responds.

"Good thinking bro' but it won't get us closer
to our freedom" He says. "Let's just keep it quiet for now?
You see all these American movies we watch in Africa. Don't
want my face rearranged by American mafia." Onye says
shrieking at the thought of being brutalized.

"Onye, the whimp! Can't you tell the difference
between a movie and real life anymore?" Onka replies.

"Just saying... obodo America has a lot of mafia
people o." Onye answers.

@@@@@

Siberia drives into her drive way and parks her car. Thank
God for getting the money to retrieve it from the car dealer
who'd towed it away just recently. Just as soon as I lift my
head up, there is Jessica, my nosy neighbor and friend,
banging away at my window. There are times, I wonder how
Jessica knows when I am around and no matter how much I

try to avoid her when I am not feeling up to her talks, she always seem to know when I am at the house. Today is no exception. I come out of the car, holding grocery bags.

"God deliver me from this woman!" I sigh.

"What girl? I'm excited. I see you have your car back. That's good mama." I nod in response.

"Are you alright girl. You don't seem okay. Let me help you."

"Thanks but I have my cousins visiting from Africa. I might be busy for a while but I will call you." Dismissing her.

"Ok mama! No worries. I'm leaving but call me or else I will be back again" She insists.

"Thank you, I will call when I need you." With strong emphasis on when I need her. I promptly walk towards my house, leaving Jessica on the front lawn.

"Cuál es el problema de esta chica? What is her problem?" She mumbles in Spanish, walking away from my house.

The cousins hear my exchange of words with my neighbor. They are instantly alerted of my presence.

"Quick! Turn that internet off now!" Onye screams at Onka.

"Hold on, I want to print this page." Onka replies watching Onye peek through the curtains.

"If you don't get up that place now, she will see what we are up to. You can print later!" Onye whispers hearing my footsteps closer to the porch.

"S-s-s-s-h! You are the one who needs to be quiet before she hears you by that window." Onka warns, printing the page and tucking it right into his pocket. They take their seats by the small television and begin laughing sheepishly, pretending to be enjoying the show. I enter the living with the grocery bags and watch them immersed in the show.

"Hello…hello…hello," I finally scream ensuring they hear me; all to no avail.

"I tell you bro' this obodo America is really full of comedy."

"I agree with you. Just look at that…".
I finally walk closer to them, there a quick glance at what they are watching. Truthfully, I didn't get what they were immersed in… I didn't understand what was funny about the news show they were watching. Lately, I decided to take the news channel off my radar as all they flung out were peoples' misery…other peoples' misery. I have enough of my own to last me a life time. My eyes moved from Onka to Onye with their animated bodies being thrown across their seats really into the news channel and laughing like one who'd lost his mind.

"I don't get it cous'…what is funny?" I ask.

"Hey Cous' welcome back." Onka manages to speak through his laughter.

"You missed the fun. This America is full of so many funny stories." Onye's attempt to cover their intentions, as he begins fidgeting . He jumps up in the seat.

"Here, let me help you with that." He pulls one of the grocery bags away from me. Onye joins them, pulling the second grocery bag from me.

"So, how did you make out there? Did you find the stone?" Onye begins with his small talk.
Siberia shakes her head.

"I see. So what do we do now?" Onka

inquires as we all enter my little kitchen together.

"I am going back there tomorrow." My weary response.

"You think they have it? Whoever they are?" Onye inquires of me.

"Time will tell! Tomorrow they'd better have the camera bag ready."

"You didn't tell them what you were looking for, or did you?" Onye probes.

"No, at least not yet." My response as we all place the grocery bags on the kitchen countertop.

"You can't tell them!" Onka exclaims.

"Why? It is of no value to them here in America though it means a lot to us."

"Oh no, you cannot tell them what it is cous' You never know what they could do with it!" Onye adds. "Besides, we don't have time."

"I know... I know." I exhale, exhausted from the day's running around.

"I am so tired, cous'. I just need to rest my eyes a little for now." Yawning through my speech.

"You both can take my bedroom." I tagged on to my discussion with them.

"You sure? We can manage this living room, you know" Onka answers with Onye poking him on the side, disapproving his suggestion.

"My friend stop it," Onye warns Onka, hoping I would not see what he was doing.

"Please, spear me your dramas you two.. I sleep in the living room most of the time anyway. It's no big deal." I reply.

"Okay then if it is no burden to you." Onka

says.

"It is no burden, okay?"

"Okay then cous', we will do as you as you have said." Onye interrupts the discussion, making his way into the bedroom.

"There is food in the refrigerator now, you guys can eat anything you want. I need some rest." Walking away from the kitchen, heading straight for the living room which stands adjacent to my kitchen.

"Good night, glad you are both here."

"Us too cous' . More than you know… us too. " Onye adds looking in Onka's direction.

"I pray tomorrow is a good day." Yawning through my statement and getting myself ready in the living room.

11 THE CHEATING BAIT

I RUSH INTO THE CONSIGNMENT SHOP, ONKA AND ONYE TRAILING ME. Today, I cannot bring myself to be distracted by the handsome Jake, his physique and beautiful face… his sparkling eyes… his muscles filling out his t-shirt. I am determined to stay focused on the goal, to retrieve the camera bag and get back the family artifact, Silleri. I glance up and see his smiling face, his glittering blue eyes beckoning me to come on over. I will not be moved, I tell myself over and over again. My messed up feelings for him is not what matters at this moment. Jake looks in Onka and Onye's direction. He seems like he is expecting a formal introduction. I painstakingly ignore his captivating baby blue eyes, walking straight to him.

"Where is it?" Clearing my throat, avoiding my usual stutter which often comes out whenever I am in his presence.

"How are you Siberia? Good seeing you too." Insisting on carrying on a conversation.

"What do you think Jake? I'll be fine when I get back what I came here for."

"Simon, please bring the camera bag here." He yells across the countertop towards the back of the shop.

"Are they with you?" Attempting to calm me down. Suddenly deciding to gaze into his eyes for just a brief moment, I knew I had to make up my mind, to fall captive to his overpowering allure, or remain dismissive. Another thought that cross my mind is to flat out pretend and to guard my heart.

"Yep! My cousins are here from Africa. Now can we see the camera bag please?" Onka and Onye are dumbfounded by the amount of goods displayed on the floor. They ignore me and begin to play around with clothes and anything they can lay their hands on.

"Stop you this bush man. This embarrassment is too much." Onka announces.

"My friend get out. Please, let me enjoy myself without you harassing me. It is you that is an embarrassment. Look at what you are wearing." Onye replies, sneering at Onka.

"Isn't this better than what you are wearing my friend... Ah! You are not serious. You know what they call me back home the king of fashion." Onka responds.

"The king of fashion my foot. Whoever calls you that is a blind bat, I swear." Onye laughs. I quickly grab their attention by calling out their names and grinning sheepishly their way. Mama and Papa have always said that in our African culture, you can carry on a whole conversation with a child with your eyes. I remember growing up in Africa, when we would visit a friend's house. Whenever they offered food, it was customary never to eat outside of the home. While the host is attempting to persuade us girls into trying their food; mama with a smile on her face, turn to us girls and begin to make silent conversations with the contour of her face and the movement of her lips. We quickly understood what she meant and obeyed. I decided to do the same where Onka and Onye were concerned. They refuse to follow my leading. Rather, they are looking at each other pretending not to understand my body language and my facial expressions.

"Stop you two. We are not here for that." My frustration flaring out uncontrollably.

"Sorry cous', don't mind that illiterate, Onye. He is the one causing trouble back there." Onka responds. Jake walks up to Onye and Onka, overlooking my disapproving gaze. He stretches out his hand towards Onka.

"And how are you sir?" Onka asks. Before Jake could reply, Onye jumps in the way of the conversation, grabs Jake's hand and shaking it profusely..

"Oyibo, we are fine... very fine. My name is Onye....Onye Tonka." He continues to shake Jake copiously, pushing Onka aside. Amused by his reaction, Jake looks in my direction. Baffled, I shrugged my shoulders. Onka clears his throat, a sudden air of arrogance emanating from him. Jake whispers in my direction, attempting to pull his hand away from Onye, though amused at their reactions.

"Speak English my friend! You are in America now!" Onka interjects, eluding to his own superiority of over his brother.

"Waitin? Isn't he oyibo? Are you going to teach me how to speak English now? Who died and made you my teacher?" Onye gearing up for another match.

"Just don't confuse the man. Say what he understands... that is all I am saying Onye! When in Rome, you do as the Romans do... simple logic!" Onka continues.

"Look mister! Just keep your mouth out of my

business. I no get time for you! Simple... period!" Onye sarcastic. "I don't understand it... you read a little book past me and that makes you an expert on English speaking?"

"Well, you said it... not me!" Onye mockingly.

"What is O-yi-bo?" Attempting to spell out the word Onye had just used.

"White man." whispering back in his direction. He seems amused by that and turns back in Onye's direction.

"Are you done introducing yourself now Onye?" Onka, his attempt to disrupt Onye's stance and cause him to let go of Jake's hand.

"I will let you know when I am done." Onye replies, his eyes fixated on Jake.

"Amazing, I finally touch a white man today. Kai. I have died and gone to heaven o" Onye exclaims.

"I told you bro' you are bush man!" Onka responds. "Look mister, my name is Onka Tonka, we are Siberia's cousins." Onka attempting to speak more eloquently than his brother. After watching their stupidity for few minutes, I pull towards them, yanked Jake's hand away from Onye.

"I say you are done now.!" My anger rising. Instantly, my felt like apologizing for my cousin's ignorance and the fact they Onye hijacked Jake's hand.

"Sorry." I whisper, a little embarrassed by my cousin's' behavior.

"That's alright." His smiling suddenly breaking through my initial wall and melting my deliberately fortified demeanor.

"You do have some interesting cousins' here" Jake speaks.

"Thank you my brother. Great compliment."

Onka interjects adjusting his oversized black pair of trousers.

"Well, not sure about that. But thanks for the compliment. They just flew in from Africa a few days ago.

"Wow guys, long way from home. Right?" Jake continues his conversation, only this time with some distance between them.

"Yes, indeed. Nice meeting you Mr...." Onye answers back.

"Jake O'Conner. But my friends call me Jake." He throws one of his deadly charming smiles their way.

"Well, any friend of Siberia is a friend of ours, right?" Onye jumps in.

"Absolutely," Jake replies. The pleasantries flying across the room are beginning to get on my nerves and it was time to break up the chitchats and focus on my mission to the shop today.

"Right! Please go get the camera bag 'cause your brother is still not out here." Interrupting the moment and pointing everyone concerned to what's important… the retrieval of the stone.

"Simon!" Jake calls out again.
Simon walks out of the back room sluggishly and with a non-caring attitude. He brings with him my camera bag. He places it on the countertop and proceeds to leave the room; trying hard to hide his bruised face. Regardless of his attempts, we all see red blood shot left eye and the black and blue marks surrounding the eye. I am baffled bur focus on my own business.

"Stay here Simon, don't go in yet. Attend to the customer first." Jake says sternly.

"I thought you were. You wanted the camera bag. Here you go. Now, if you will excuse me, I have some inventory to conclude back there." He answers flippantly. I rush over to the countertop, grab the camera back and quickly ransacking it with my shaky hands. To my horror, the camera is nowhere to be found! Simon had brought in just an empty camera bag.

"Am I missing something? Or am I delusional right now?" I blurt out.

"Do you want to tell me what you are looking for, perhaps I may be able to help." Jake inquires.

"Alright then, let's start with a simple task....Where is the camera inside?" Looking in Simon's nonchalant direction.

"Miss, are you here to collect the camera back or just to look at the bag?" Simon asks offhandedly.

"But where is it? Where is the camera inside of this bag?" Looking in Jake's direction.

"You will have that when you are ready to pick it up. There is the camera bag you requested." Dismissing my question and heading to the back room.

"Get the camera please!" Jake intervenes.

"I am sure you heard me, she will get it when she has the money to get it back!" Simon insists.
Jake looks mortified by Simon's response. A horrendous panic at the thought of not seeing the stone overtakes me, I take another look at the bag, this time scrutinizing it inside out. The only things which come tumbling out of the bag were the SD cards I had hidden in one of the compartments. My frustration gets the best out of me and I find myself banging the camera bag against the counter top. I am disappointed yet again at not finding the stone. Perhaps I am tired or angry or overwhelmed by guilt, whatever the reasons, tears come rolling down my cheeks... an unexpected

occurrence.

"What do we do now?" Onka asks, appearing to be genuine.

"What kind of trouble is this? Bring it, let me take a look properly." Onye reaches for the bag. He grabs it away from me and begins pulling the inside compartments apart. Onka grabs it away from him and begins tugging at it too. Simon is amused at the way they are playing with the camera bag, he seems unmoved by my concerns but fixated on Onka and Onye's stupidity. Jake on the other hand, looks frazzled and appear not to understand the urgency being displayed by me, regarding the camera bag and the camera. He walks up to me, pulls me aside a little, as best as he could, looks me straight in the eyes and poses his question one more time.

"If you tell me what you are looking for, perhaps Simon and I can help you." He repeats.

"Mister, are you sure you didn't see anything in this bag?" Onka walking up to Simon.

"I didn't see anything valuable in there but the sd cards and the camera." He responds unapologetically.

"Think hard please? Did you by chance see a stone in it? It's got to be there." I interrupted their discussion. In the heat of the moment, I blurt out what the misery was... the stone, Silleri. My cousins froze! You would have thought I announced the death of a loved one. It was never my intention to talk about the stone.

"Haba cous' What are you doing?" Onye screams after me.

"What? Well, the cat is out of the bag now... All I know is that we must find it period! Enough of the secrecy!" Defending my stance. Jake glances in Simon's direction as if soliciting a response… a trigger for an answer. Simon slowly retreats from everyone, avoiding direct eye contact with Jake who is staring at him from across the room.

"Did you say a stone? What kind of stone?" His gaze still resting on Simon for clues.

"What? Why are you staring me down like that?" Simon begrudgingly asks.

"Oh, I don't know, you tell me Simon." Jake continues until everyone begins to look in Simon's direction too. Onka steps forward in an attempt to add more to the discussion when Onye quickly pulls him back, a deliberate attempt to stop him from telling all their recent discoveries about the actual worth of the missing stone.

"Let me be, my friend. We need that stone or Naiya could die. Right?" winking his eye at Onye mischievously, a move only understood by them. "Stop my friend, I know what I am doing" he whispers at Onye. Onka suddenly becomes dramatic! He drops to his knees and begins begging Simon.

"What is he doing? Can someone tell me what this dude is doing on the floor?" Simon looking around the room.

"My brother, this is how we beg people in Africa." Onka replies, all eyes on him.

"Dude, you better get off that floor."

"Then you too answer him now and he will get up." Onye continues the foully.

"I beg you, my brother, please help us. We need the stone please. Maybe it fell on the ground somewhere…" Onka continues.

"In fact we need to turn this entire place upside down 'cause you see hen…hen… No stone No going back.

We are sleeping here." Onye adds, joining Onka is a display of hysterics. Suddenly, Simon begins to laugh out loud, being entertained by Onka and Onye.

"Oh... I am finished! Is this one making fun of me?" Onka stands up.

"Bro', you have suffered oh... in obodo America... this rascal oyibo making fun of my brother. In fact..." Onye continues.

"You guys! This is not about you. You need to stop this foolishness!" I yell out, frustrated.

"I feel like I'm in a twilight zone or something...This is a joke, right?" Looking in Jake's direction with a smirked face.

"This is no joke Jake! Tell your brother please! How dare he take this callously? He stands there aloof and laughing!"

"Calm down Siberia," Jake whispers.

"Yes... chill broad!" Simon even more sarcastic.

"Are you truly for real? My sister is dying as we speak! I don't have much time to find the stone and return it back to Africa."

"I am not understanding all of these Siberia. I really want to help but you've got to calm down and let me in please." Jake pulling me to his side.

"I may not understand and you may not understand it all but that's beside the point right now! I am asking you both to please trace back your steps perhaps you will remember something!" Refusing to be consoled by Jake.

"What does this stone have to do with your sister?" Jake presses on with his questions.

"What you really need to be doing is prying your brother for answers!" Instantly snapping at Jake. I glanced in Simon's direction and he seems to be lost in space for few seconds. His eyes tell it all... he knows something about the stone that he is not telling.

"Did you remember something?" I ask, Simon shrugging his shoulder and moving farther away from them.

"Well Simon, you heard her... do you know something?" Jake, supporting my position.

"I may be able to help. I took the camera home yesterday so I will check and get back to you tomorrow." Suddenly somber looking.

"Oh no! We don't have that much time. It has to be done today ok? Today Simon!"

"Calm down lady." Simon replies, quickly back to his nonchalant way. Suddenly, grief came over me, bursting into tears! My heart racing uncontrollably, I find myself gasping for air, completely hysterical at the overwhelming thought that I may cause Naiya's death! Without warning, my legs gave in to running, as I race out of the store hoping to catch some air.

"Hold up Siberia!" Jake screams, taking off after me.

"I need fresh air. I just want you and your brother to get me my stuff period!" Bellowing at them as I find my way out of the shop.

"Oh...oh, the love birds!" Simon announces.

"Are you ever serious?" What is wrong with you man? What is wrong with you?" Jake shouts, still sprinting after me.

"Did you hear that Onka?" Onye whispers wide-eyed.

"What are you talking about now?" Onye asks.

"S-s-s-h! Did oyibo call them love birds?"

"Why don't you just mind your business. Right now, we need to stay focused!" Onka replies, uninterested in Onye's latest dialogue.

"If what this man says is true, that could mean trouble oh…" Onye continues, ignoring Onka's lack of interest. "where will she take white man to? To our village?"

"That is another trouble for another day Onye!" Onka snaps. "Palaver the family will handle by themselves. Besides, what do you care, once we get this money we won't show up there, right? Isn't that the plan Onye?"

"True talk… you are right bro'… you are right. But what I will give to see the faces in the village if Siberia goes there with this man o." Onye nearing the end of his discussion.

"Shu-sh! Enough of that!" Onka warns again. They all listen to the bickering going on behind the glass doors.

"Hey hey, please calm down. We are going to do our very best. Remember, you brought the camera to us and I was only trying to help" Jake reminds me.

"You right. I'm sorry. It's just that so much is happening to me since I returned from Africa. It seems like I am living one huge nightmare, one after the other. Jake! I just want something to go right for a change." Bursting into uncontrollable tears as Jake thrusts out, throwing all caution to the wind; he grabs me tight, gently planting my head on his warm, welcoming yet strong chest. I need not lie, it was soothing… my feelings for him take over, with a tug of war going on in my head. Should I give in to my feelings or should I stay focused on what needs to be done right now. And what is this unruly feeling going on in my heart? Why is my heart pounding away, responding so eloquently to his racy heart. Regardless of this moment's heat, there is something tangible in the air. If I am right, what will I tell Papa and Mama about this white man I may be in love with? How will I break it to them without sending them to their early grave? Granted they have always called me the rebel in the family and granted Mama had always joked that I, Siberia could one day be the death of them because of my rebel ways…I certainly do not want that premonition to come to be and not on my account. But the heart wants what the heart wants! How would I reconcile all of these… my thoughts trailed off until I heard Jake's soothing voice, as he gently caresses my back with his firm hands.

"Are you feeling better now Siberia?" His voice resounded, bringing me back from my temporary bliss. "Are you okay dear?" he repeated ever so gently, his silvery voice caressing my ears and tugging away at my gelatin heart. Suddenly, my eagerness to find the stone though still in the fore-front is now subtle compared to what I am feeling with this man's hands all over me. Is this what it means to feel something different for someone? Is this love? Is this lust? Is this just my wishful thinking and this man is only trying to appease me? What is this feeling? What is this uncomfortable sensation running through my spine, pumping heated blood straight into my heart yet it is soothing? My head begins to spin at all the questions enslaving me. So I decided there and then, if I could only look into his eyes, perhaps I will sense what his motives are. I pulled myself slightly away from him, raise my head up and gazed into his bright blue eyes! A surge of incredible surge of excitement overwhelms me as his eyes reach straight into my heart like a shooting star. For once, if I am not sure of anything, this I am certain of… Jake is feeling exactly what I am feeling.

@@@@@

Inside the consignment store, Onka, Onye and Simon continue to look on, awaiting my arrival back into the store.
"Well guys, it's been fun. I've got work to do. Peace guys!" Simon proceeds to walk into the back room; as he watches Onye high five Onka.
They seem content with all that is taking place.
"Brossssss! You are too good my brother…In fact, that was an oscar winning performance." Onye complimenting Onka.
"Please brother, we do what we need to do. Rule # 1, deflect away from you… That is what I have done." Onka agrees.
"You and your big grammar, Deflect, which one is that again." Onye continues.
"I don't have time to explain that. We've got work to do." Onka adds, watching Simon's moving closely.
"Anyway, the way you de beg ah! And the way you de threaten to scatter this place ah! I don die oh! I almost believed you." Onye increasingly praising Onka for his performance, an unusual temperament where their relationship is concerned. Perchance their latest potential heist will finally reunite them.
"Nawa oh! The things we de do for money…. $500,000. Money don kill me oh. You are smart my brother. We fit scatter this place and buy them another one." Onye

concludes.

"My friend, tone down this pidgin English. You know it crawls up in my skin." Onka warns."

"Shuuuuh, I guess I spoke too soon." Onye yaps back.

"I have an idea." Onka, ignoring Onye's last comment.

"What now Mr. Smart pants?" Onye inquires, as Onka walks closer whispering into his ears, ensuring that flighty Simon does not hear his plans.

"Let's talk to the brother and offer him some money; that way he will take us directly to the stone." Onka suggests.

"My brother, I beg, high five me again. You are too much. In fact they should just call you a genius ah! My God, money is coming our way…I don die…I want money… That beautiful girl that came to talk to cous the other day." Onye rambles uncontrollably, watching Simon ransacking the counter top before his final exit from the store floor.

"Which girl? You and your roaming eyes!" Onka replies.

"That girl now…. Our very own people. You don't remember her again?" Onye persistent with his discussion until he finally jugs Onka's memory.

"Okay o, I remember. Haba, Onye, you have long throat! That psychedelic one? Do you think she will want your illiterate self? I beg, please cut your coat according to your size!" Onka comments. Simon hears their bickering, turns around and stands amused.

"And I thought my life was interesting," amusing himself as he watches Onka and Onye.

"AHEINH! I want that girl." Onye insists, Onka laughing hard.

"Joker! Forget it my friend. No money in this world will make that girl want you." Onka continuously laughing at his brother.

"Waitin you de talk now? What kind of talk be this now?" Onye sensing his anger boiling towards Onka.

"Look at you … just look at yourself. Ordinary clean and straightforward English, you refuse to exhibit." Onka, telling him off.

"Nawa for you. Wait and see. That girl go marry me!" Onye boasting.

"Let me quickly speak the language you understand….You de craze!" Onka lashes out.

"Well, this is where I go in guys. Please don't let me stop you both from whatever it is you are saying." They instantly stop arguing, stare at Simon and run towards him.

12 WHO'S ON FIRST?

ALAN IS PARKED A LITTLE DOWN THE STREET WHERE HE IS ABLE TO SEE JAKE AND I IN EACH OTHER'S ARMS. He quietly observes us through his rearview mirror. His jealousy rises to the surface. Ever since he'd met me he has been following me around town. And now, he thinks his eyes has finally deceived him! He watches as Jake consoles me and reads more into it. His jealousy soon turns into a confident smirk as he sits in his truck… just watching. Alan has never lost a battle when attracting any girl in town is concerned…. The crux of his troubles with Fanta. Though he had recently been reunited with Fanta and has simply focused on his thriving art business, I was different! I was awakening something in him that reminded him of his old self. One who is bent on conquering what he wants…. And Siberia he wants!

"Ten of you can't hold that girl," convincing himself that he has the upper hand where I am concerned. He is African! He is a very wealthy African at that! He is well respected, loved… and I mean loved by the ladies!…. Certainly a paragon of dark chocolaty loveliness. The only problem.... His shadow Fanta, whose relationship is not quite clear to the world.... Is he truly married? Are they dating and just living together? Though Fanta is a popular model who is constantly in the news, they have managed to keep their relationship a big secret! Whatever the situation is, Alan is now drawn to me...a rare African mahogany gem... he called me at the last accident scene. He keeps watching....

"Are you ready to go back in now? We will figure it all out together okay?" Jake pulling me back, so our eyes meet. I shake my head in silence, as Jake pulls me again into his comforting arms.

@@@@@

Onka and Onye quickly approach Simon with sheepish smiles on their faces

"Hello bro'" Onye deliberately blocking Simon's path to the back room.

"Whoa. Yes, how can I help you? And why are you tiptoeing around this place?" Simon says right back at Onye.

"I was watching you from afar. And it dawned on me that you will be a very nice partner to have." Onye whispers in his ears.

"Excuse me? For the record, I am not gay!" offended.

"What? Not that kind of partner. You these people self. Na sex... sex.... Sex de for him brain!" Onye complaining.

"Interpretation please or get out of my way and let me go!" Simon yelling.

"Look Mr. Man, please keep your voice down

before this woman hear from outside." Onye cautions.

"About the stone my cousin is looking for?" Onka expounds on their plan.

"I'm listening... right now, I don't know what you are talking about." Simon eagerly awaiting their further explanation and their reason for stopping him from going inside.

"Haba, fast and smooth operator recognizes one when he sees one...." "Onye says.

"Look guys, I have no idea what you are talking about. You need to hurry up otherwise, I will shout and get Jake's attention right now! So out with it!" Simon's voice increasingly loud.

"Okay! Okay, just keep your voice down. Onye replies.

"Will $5,000 jog your memory? And maybe your brother's too?" Onye blasts out confidently.

"5 grand? What do you mean jog my memory with that?" Simon digs in further.

"S-s-sh! Seriously Mr. man, keep your voice down, please. You can't say don't understand my language. You feel me?" Onye pulls closer into Simon's personal space and equally peeking at the storefront.

"Whoa ...whoa ...whoa ... man, sit a second, I don't swing like that, thank you!" Simon replies pulling back.

"It's nothing like that bro. If you can produce that stone now, $5, 000 will be yours!" Onka supporting Onye.

"Wait a second. Am I being pranked here? You are joking right?" Simon looking around for a camera.

"We are from a land where people kill lions with their bare hands. Haba! We don't joke about money."

Onye replies gloriously adjusting his loose belt.

"What? Someone must be playing practical jokes on me. Just like that? $5000 worth of it." Simon continues his suspicions.

"Look Mr. we don't have time for all these. Are you in or are you out? Hurry before Siberia and your brother come back in. Well…" Onye impatient. Silence permeates the room as they size each other up, Simon looking intensely into their eyes for possible clues of deceit. He can smell a deceitful person a mile off. After all, it takes one to know one.

"Come on bro, what do you have to lose but everything to gain. As it seems, I am sure there is a lot you can do with that money, right?" Onye continues his persuasive dialogue.

"If you do this…they call you Simon, can I call you Simon friend?" Onka steps up.

"Whatever, you can call me whatever" Simon replies nonchalantly.

"Okay then Simon. If you choose to do this, there is only one condition." Onka carries on.

"I'm all ears. Let's have the conditions" Simon still guarded and apprehensive.

"You are not to tell anyone once we get back the stone. This deal is between us three." Emphatically speaking. Simon finally gets it… the African boys were deadly serious. They indeed needed a partner to lift the stone from Tee's house.

"Alright then. Let's just say I'm interested in this deal, when do I get paid?" Simon asks.

"Enhehe. Now, we are talking real business." Onka laughs out loud.

"You have two choices… you either bring the

stone to us or take us to where the stone is. We will take it from there. Once the stone has been brought, we will pay you." Onka explains, as Simon's gaze sweeps them from their funny looking summer slippers, to their skimpy khaki pants and the dark glasses adorning their foreheads.

"Unless I am missing something, you two don't look like you have a penny to your names. I don't want my time wasted here!" Simon demands.

"Oh but my American brother from another mother..." Onka interjects.

"Say what? Your American what? Or whatever..." Simon squinting his eyes in attempts to understand what he has just been referred to by Onka.

"Don't let looks deceive you. We are going to be loaded!" Onye jumps in in excitement while Onka looks on, attempting Onye from spilling their whole plan.

"Make it 10 grand and you have yourselves a deal" Simon finally agrees.

"That is stiff! Bring it down a little now." Onye asks. But Simon declines. They both hear Jake and myself finding our way back into the store. Our voices echo our arrival into the store as they shake hands quickly and plan on meeting another time for further deliberation.

"Okay Onye, let's do what we do best.... Grab him quick!" Onka tugging away at Simon, pretending to be muscling him to a hasty confession.

"Hey stop guys!" Simon playing along.

"Shut up my friend! We are holding you hostage until you produce the stone" Onye embellishes.

"Oh my God, what are they doing?" Jake and I rush to quickly separate them.

"Stop it guys. Leave him alone" Jake shocks

Simon, who stands steering blackly at Jake.

"What a minute, did you just defend me?" Simon stunned.

"What? I know you don't think I care… well, I do!" Jake yells.

"I need to hold on to this moment for as long as I can." Simon says.

"Yeah right, do that!"

"Since you really want to know, I am fine. They took me by surprise I was just about to handle them." Simon boasts, an attempt to avoid the embarrassment.

"Are you two crazy? This is not Africa. You can go to jail right now for doing that." I yell at them, all of my pent up emotions rising to the surface.

"If you didn't stop us, we would have gotten the information from him. We have to shake him down." Onye interrupts.

"Look, I don't care whatever. You do not touch anyone here… You hear me? I have enough trouble of my own. I don't have money to bail you out if you are arrested. So I beg of you, behave yourselves." In the heat of the moment, Simon shrieks.

"I know where the stone is!" He bellows out. In an instant, all eyes are on him… awaiting further explanation to what seemed like a big confession to only Jake and I.

"Are you serious? Did you just say you know where it is? Seriously, I don't have time for jokes." I rant, still anxious that the bottom may drop and he may change his mind.

"It took you guys a long time to come back in. what were you two doing out there?" Simon asks.

"Stay the course Simon, no digression with your cynicism. There really is no room for it right now," Jake insists.

"Of course not!" Simon even more cynical than ever. "I traced back my steps."

"Okay, don't keep us waiting. Let's have it!" Joining Jake in his persistence.

"I remember Tee's boys coming to my place last night and few of our inventory was laying on my work table. I saw something fall out of the camera bag and he took it. This is all I can remember." Simon concludes.

"What?" Jake and I in unison.

"Bro, I thought we wrote the book on swagger and lies. Boy we found our match right here in America" Onye whispering, quietly carrying on a side conversation with Onka.

"Okay bro let's see where this will end. S-s-s-sh!" Onka warns, carefully guarding against Jake and I figuring their plans out.

"When I think you can't stoop any lower, you surprise me Simon?. What do you mean Tee and his men came over? I don't buy that...not for a second Simon!" Jake exerting his frustration to the max.

"Well then, since you seem to know me well and perhaps you wrote the book on me, suit yourself. Believe what you'd like. I have told you the truth!" Simon backing out of Jake's personal space.

"Hold up Jake, your brother might be telling the truth, right Simon?" I jump into his defense, focusing on finding the stone, attempting to keep my anger towards Simon in check for the greater good.

"You don't know him as well as I do Siberia!

Every time I turn around, this family's name is being dragged through the mud…all because of him!" Jake's conversation lingers.

"Well Tee has it. That is all I have to say about that. You wanted the truth, there you have it!" Simon adds, insouciantly. "Look, the stone seem so ordinary. I didn't think it was worth anything."

"So you let them have it instead? Is that it Simon?" Jake interrupts Simon's explanation.

"Who says it's worth anything?" Onye quickly jumping into the discussion, cunningly pushing discussion away from his monetary value.

"What do you mean Onye? It's worth saving my sister's life, isn't it?" Soliciting support from my cousins, as they fidget through the conversation.

"That's it cous', yes of course, it is worth a life." Further diversion away from its monetary value.

"So Mr. man, you mean to tell me that all this while, you have known where this stone is. You kept us here all these while…" Onka pretending to be upset at Simon.

"You heard me or am I speaking to thin air." Simon replies.

"Wait a minute, did you just insult me?" Onka moving close to Simon. "Onye, did this stupid Oyibo man insult me just now?" he continues, his pretense heightened.

"Cool down bro, eye on the ball" Onye jumps in.

"Okay guys, we will not go there now. Let's stay focused." I interrupting another blow of arguments, this time it would have been caused by my cousins.

"Look, thank your lucky stars. Cous' just saved you from a whipping!" Onka manages to speak up as Onye drags him from the scene.

"Sorry cous', didn't mean to cause you pain. Oyibo or no oyibo, no one insults Onka !'" Onka belts out.

"Understood. But you can't be fighting everyone here in America. You will get yourself in trouble."

"Who is Tee?" Onye asks, breaking the tension.

"Bad news, that's who he is. If you were from around here, you would know him. Simon, what business do you have with that kind of man?"

"Who says I had business with him?"

"I just did. From what I know of him, he does not go around town beating people up. Unless, your paths have crossed recently!" Jake expounds. "Do you owe the man money Simon?"

"Shall we table that for another day please? I just want the stone." Quickly cutting in.

"You are probably right." Jake exclaims, looking disgustingly in Simon's direction.

"Wow bro, if looks can kill... this man is a goner!" Onye hints Onka.

"How do we get the stone back then?" Eagerly querying Simon, hoping for the truth. We all look in his direction with great expectation, of a great solution.

"What do you suggest?" Jake suddenly dismal.

"Wow! Isn't it funny? The big Jake himself needs my help, right Jake?" Simon's on a roll, his full blown cynicism exerted.

"Come on Simon. Out with it. You know Tee... I don't!"

"Well, lucky for you.... Tee has his annual party tomorrow night. Didn't you hear about it bro'?"

"I wouldn't know Simon. We obviously don't

FUMI HANCOCK

run with the same circle" Jake's response, flippant. "Okay, maybe I heard something but I wouldn't be caught dead at that party, you know that?"   "Translation....You mean you were never invited?" Simon teases.

"I will let that go for a second." Jake speaks up.

"Well then, get this, it looks like we're all going to be partying tomorrow. That is if you want to retrieve that stone." Simon replies.

"What? ...Party?" my emotions kick in.

"You want your stone back, don't you?" Simon shouts, unapologetically.

"Hey! Hey bro', watch your tone with her, will you?" Jake butts in like a lion protecting her cub.

"Jeweez! You sound like she is your girl or something." Simon comments, Jake embarrassed by his comment. His eyes meet mine, and then quickly looks away.

"Can we just get back to the real subject here Simon?" Jake stuttering through his speech.

" You know what? Count me in! For my sister's sake...I'll do anything for my sister's sake!"

"Are you sure you want to do this? You don't know Tee. He and his guys can be brutal if anything goes wrong." Jake protecting me.

"Well then, I guess we have to make sure nothing goes wrong! But not going is no option for me." The sudden tirade of silence consumes everyone as they gaze in each other's' eyes. Simon breaks the silence, deliberating annoying Jake.

"Hey you... you may want to quit acting like a papa bear!"

"Get over yourself, will you?" Jake responds blowing off steam.

180

"We need invitations to the party and I am not one to get them for you. Not on good talking terms with that man right now." Simon answers.

"Well count me out! Not interested in his party." Jakes protests.

"I will go. I have to go… so what do you suggest.. how do we get the invitation cards?"

"I need to think a little about that." Simon responds.

"You don't have all day for your fuzzy thoughts." Jake answers.

"You know what? I've got a great idea, you leave your cousins here with me while I figure this out. You can leave for now. It's certainly been a long day for everyone, right?" looking in Onka and Onye's direction.

"Oh yes cous', we will be fine here. Let's figure this out with Mr. man. You need to rest," Onka stutters.

"We all can meet at my crib later tonight, when I have figured it out." Simon adds. "Unless our guy here has other suggestions" glancing at Jake.

"I don't. My role in all of these is simply waiting in the car for you guys, that is, if you do get the invitation cards for others." Jake surmises.

"It's just that my cousins, they don't know this town and…" my concern worsens.

"You want the stone or don't you?"

"What kind of question is that? Of course I do!"

"Then we do it my way." Simon replies, the two African boys edging him on. "I will figure out how to get the invitations. Tee does not give out his invitations to any and every one! It's an exclusive party."

"As long as it's nothing illegal…I mean, as long as you get the invitation cards the legal way."

"Who is talking illegal? I said get the invitation cards, not steal the them! Come on my African brothers, let's go do this." Simon points at Onye and Onka, who are more than happy to oblige; walking away from Jake and I and heading straight for Simon.

"Your brother…"

"What about him?"

"He has a dry sense of humor. Trying to be the tough guy but I bet deep inside that hard exterior is a good heart."

"Ummmm ! I guess! He's alright. I love him and I am so worried about him. I'm afraid he is going to get himself killed one day with him running around the streets, doing all sorts of things."

"Oh?"

"Truth is, he doesn't believe I care about him."

"Did you tell him all of this? I inquire.

"I have tried several times but the knuckle head doesn't get it that I want the very best for him."

"Well, keep trying. Perhaps you can change how you tell him that too."

"What do you mean?

"If you are constantly haranguing him with all he is doing wrong, he might continue to take offence."

"But someone has to tell him when he is going the wrong way. Our parents are dead and Jennie is all we have left."

"Sorry to hear that. You still have to reach out to him in a more subtle way. Anyway, I have given enough advice for the day."

"The advice is appreciated." The light in his eyes glows yet again.

"Thinking back now, there are things I could have done better with my sister Naiya, if I thought I may never see her again. I can't change that now but I can do my very best to make sure she doesn't die."

"A sign of a brave lady."

"Oh dear Jake, you flatter me much."

"It's not flattery. It is how I feel about you." A sudden surge of heat running through my vein and pouring right into my face. Thank goodness, my black skin was dark enough to hide the rush of heat flooding my face. I quickly refocus the discussion right back to my sister. She was what was important now, not my crush or whatever the feelings are flying between Jake and I.

"Jake, I have to find that stone." In a more somber mood. "I know you may not understand it. Half the time I don't myself. But it is tradition. My people have what is of sentimental value to them. I know you guys have yours here."

"Yeah right. But you don't have to explain yourself. If it is that important to you, then that is what's important right now." Few minutes of intense stare between us, Jake pulls himself closer, thrusting his muscle ridden arms towards him, he pulls me closer and holds me gently.

FUMI HANCOCK

13 THE HUNTER & HIS PREY

ALAN HAS HAD ENOUGH OF WATCHING JAKE AND I IN EACH OTHER ARMS, OUTSIDE OF THE CONSIGNMENT STORE. He sits in his truck, in uncontrollable jealousy. Since we met, he has been following me around town! Of course, I was not aware of it. He obviously wants something from me but since he has not approached me personally, I can't guess. If my emotions serve me right, he is into me as I am secretly into him as well. While Jake is gently spirited, smooth yet firm in his grip, Alan... well, Alan is rugged looking and charming, his dark chocolaty face severe yet alluring. If there was any other way to describe this man... ah, he was charismatic. Indeed, a lady's man he is. One who women would fight over, just to be in his presence. What then would this demi-god male want from a village girl like myself. Granted we are both Africans, the only thing we may have in common! After sitting in his truck for a long time, deliberating how to handle what he'd just seen; he decides to head into the store.

"Oh heck! I can't let this one go." He secures his truck on the side street and walks up to the consignment store. He musters his courage, walks into the store. His presence is instantly announced by the door bell … A welcome announcement, quickly saving me from Jake's enchanting gaze. The saying, when it rains it pours, is beginning to hold true for me. This is a precarious situation for my heart. Beating hard for two different men…: And now, I get to face them both in the same room. Whatever I do, I must never let them sense my inner turmoil.

"Oh my word, what a surprise?" Jake says, seeing Alan walk in; his musky scent gently wafting through the air.

"Hello friend Jake, I was in the area so I thought to stop by… see what you have. You know… a few antique gems. You are always good for that." Working his way to my side.

"Well Alan, I am glad you feel you can depend on me for great stuff."

"You are quite welcome. It is the truth."

"I should have something for you on Thursday." Jake responds.

"Oh, that's okay. Let me see what else you have here today." Alan's eyes roaming about until he lands on me!

"Oh, excuse my manners. Alan, meet Siberia." Alan's face lights up as I turn slowly towards him.

"Siberia meet my number one customer, Alan." Jake introducing us, with Alan giving a short bow.

"And a friend too, if I might add. Right Jake?" Sweeping the room with his magnetic voice. "Well my lady, fancy meeting you here. It's a small world, isn't it?" His voice directed toward me.

"I hope you aren't planning to run me over again." The words come tumbling out of my mouth.

"I see you two have met?" Jake inquires, observing the fireworks.

"You have to know I didn't mean to hit you." Alan looking serious.

"Well, I don't know what to make of that." Jake continues watching the mannerisms.

"Are you alright now?"

"Absolutely. I am fine, thanks for asking." I respond.

"Oh so sorry Jake… yes we have met in a somewhat sticky circumstance," he continues looking my way, his provocative eyes piercing my soul like a dagger.

"Well, hopefully history will not repeat itself again, yes?"

"Absolutely…" he smiles, turning to flustered Jake. "My friend, it's a long story. So tell me Jake, what can I get here today?"

"It all depends on what you are looking for, man." Jake replies. I needed something to happen right away, breaking the fiery tension rising in the room. Where are my cousins when you need them? They have chosen this moment to go to the back room with Simon! Where are they when help is needed to whisk me from this magnetic man's presence? Where are Onka and Onye to help me figure out these pent up emotions… being torn between the two men. Funny, none of them had really told me their true intentions. Just flirting here and there, yet it all looked so real. In my moment of confused chaos, Simon and the boys walk back onto the floor. Simon looks up and instantly recognizes Alan. He smiles at him; his own way of acknowledging his presence.

"Can I talk with you for a sec Jake?"

"I'm busy right now… need to tend to our customer," with teeth clenched.

"No, seriously, I need to speak with you… now." Simon insists, Alan's roaming eyes resting once again on mine.

"Excuse me please" Jake saying to both of us.

"Oh sure, I am not in a hurry. Go ahead. I will keep her company till you return." Jake, looking suspicious, ~~but~~ leaves our presence.

"So…" his captivating smile radiating.

"Well… so…." I reply.

"I see you shop here."

"Not really… Just needed to… well, not really."

"I see you are a woman of very few words." Alan continues.

"On the contrary, my family would say otherwise. Just don't have much to say to you right now."

"I see. Meaning we will talk some other time right?" Alan flirting.

"Meaning nothing." Smiling sheepishly.

"A hard nut to crack too." He sighs.

@@@@@

"What do you want from me Simon?" Jake exhibiting his complete lack of patience with Simon.

"Chill for a second dude and listen…"

"Alright then, I'm all ears but please do not waste my time Simon!"

"That man who just rolled into the store could not have come at a better time."

"What do you mean?"

"He could very well be the answer to getting into Tee's party tomorrow."

"Please explain yourself and quit beating around the bush! I'm getting very impatient here."

"Jeez! I didn't think I needed to explain further. He is Tee's friend."

"Alan? Tee's friend?" I think you may be mistaking him for someone else. There is no way they can be in the same circle. No way Simon!" Jake attempting to walk away from Simon but he grabs him hard in his shoulder.

"I meant what I said! You want in, then approach him. It's that simple!" Simon whispering.

"How do you know all this?

"I have seen him several times at Tee's house."

"If you are right, I am surprised that someone like Alan would be hanging out with Tee."

"No one is perfect dude except, of course, you. At some point, you will need to get rid of your grandiose expectations for people. The rest of us struggle through life everyday dude!"

"I haven't asked you for anything beyond the basic life necessities, have I? You either learn to fly yourself or you'll be run over. Plain and simple!"

"Anyway, he is our ticket to the party. At this point, I can't face Tee myself."

"Why? What have you done?" You know what, I don't even want to know." Jake leaves Simon and heads for Alan and I.

"You are welcome dude!" Simon yells after him while Jake ignores his comment, shrugging his shoulders.

"Sorry to keep you waiting Alan," Jake says,

standing right next to me.

"Nothing to be sorry about. Besides, I had a beautiful lady here to keep me company. So you see, nothing lost." Winking at me.

"Say, there is a party going on in town tomorrow night… 'Make the Night Beautiful' Annual party." Jake continues.

"Ahhh yes. It's going to be a great one." Alan adds.

"I need invitations man. Can you swing that for a brother?"

"Well… well… well, this is the first. I had no idea you like partying." Alan replies, his eyes still on me.

"These are for some friends of mine." Jake replies.

"I'll say. Matter of fact, I have two extra invitations in my car. A couple of my business partners missed their flights… they are all yours."

"Awesome, thanks man. I owe you one." Jake shaking his hands profusely.

"That's right. You owe me more than one. So remember that the next time you are billing me." He laughs jokingly. "You know what? Better yet, I have a great idea…" Alan walks up to me. "Perhaps my lady would like to accompany me to this party."

"Quite a turn of events" Simon whispers in Onka and Onye's direction. While I was busy battling between my two hunks, Onye and Onka had taken their place beside Simon, just watching us, Alan, Jake and I.

"What does that mean? Turn of events?" Onye whispers in Onka's ears.

"I'll explain later." They watch as Alan make his

way over to me.

"Bro' do you see what I see?" Onye inquires.

"What now Onye, what do you see? You might as well say what's on your mind now, so you can let me rest."

"Do you see what those two men?"

"Yes?"

"They have a thing for cous'? Look at them, circling around her."

"Huh Onye, you and your suspicions. You better keep that to yourself my friend!"

"Seriously bro', I know when a man is circling around his prey and those two are definitely circling."

"I bet you do! Now, will you let me rest?" They move closer to the three, watching Jake's unpleasant look at the latest news from Alan. Suddenly, everyone's eyes are on me, seemingly awaiting a response or reaction to the recent turn of events. On the other hand, Jake is not pleased by Alan's proposal. The tension in the room sent me straight back to Naiya! Her face is suddenly haunting my mind, her painful cries stabbing at my heart and the evil laughter of the wicked mystery woman... all were enough to help me reach a decision about the party... painful as it may be.

"I'll be delighted." I say, staggering away from my flash back and into reality. I look straight at Jake.

"Jake? Is that alright with you?" I ask.

"Oh yeah, sure..." he stammers through his response. It is all clear that he is desperately hiding his hurt as Alan leaps forward with great excitement.

"Well then... awesome. Where do I meet you tomorrow? Your home? Or here?" Alan rushes to seal the date.

"This place will be just fine. Right Jake? That is,

if you don't mind" I ask.

"Oh, yeah... sure..." Jake answers unconvincingly. "I guess it is okay." He adds. Still stuttering.

"I guess I will see you tomorrow then, ok?" Alan reaching out for my hand. "Say 7-ish?" Siberia smiles as Alan leaves.

"Bingo! And the bigger lion beats the small!" Simon whispers to Onka and Onye.

"You too have lions in this country?" Onye asks.

"Dude, that was a figure of speech." Simon walks away from them.

"What is he talking about Onka?" Onye asks.

"As usual, your ignorance is rearing its ugly head. I am not your dictionary. Go figure that out for yourself. I have a bigger headache to handle." Onka turns to follow after Simon. Looking in his brother's direction, he notices a cloud of disapproval once again on Jake's face; he halts for a second, redirecting his steps towards Jake.

" Say brother, before I leave, remember that adage you just threw at me a while ago... You either learn to fly yourself or you'll be run over; you may want to think about it a little. Well my dear brother, a man who does not hasten to grab what he wants, gets squashed to the ground like a roach. Think about that."

"Look you, let's go! Too much talk spoils the soup in the pot!" Onka states, Simon looking on not understanding the adage.

"Hold on a sec. I need to speak to Jake!" Simon replies. Onka moves back in position, alongside Onye.

"I thought you were in a hurry, pursuing that one like a rabbit in a hole?" Onye cynical.

"I'm not even going to dignify that with an answer!" Onka looks ahead awaiting Simon's next move out of the store.

"Let's talk after Alan leaves okay?" Jake replies embarrassed by Simon's rude interruptions.

"You bet we are going to talk some more about it... Now who is getting snowed?" Simon continues.

"These oyibo... white people, they are different... all talk in riddles." Onye sighs in frustration.

"My friend, if you stayed in school you will know they are not talking in riddles. It is common English you are supposed to know." Onka responds unsympathetically.

"Come on partner, let me get you the rest of the invites." Ignoring Simon's recent outbursts as he walks out of the store with Jake.

14 LET THE GAMES BEGIN

ROXIE, A FLAMBOYANTLY DRESSED JAMAICAN, THE WIFE OF THE INFAMOUS TEE is enjoying the sun beating down on her body, through the heavily decorated window blinds in one of the rooms of her mansion. She drinks her pina-colada, watching the flowery displays gracing her well-manicured backyard. She is running against a tight schedule to get everything ready for the big bash. As she settles down on a sofa seat by the window, she hears the doorbell ring.

"Somebody get that!" she yells across the room. "Hello! Will one of you gals get that?" It was total silence as none of her maids hear her.

"Sometimes I wonder why I pay these deaf girls!" She stands up as the doorbell continues to ring impatiently. She makes her way to the door only to meet Annie, her maid. Roxie reaches out to open the door.

"Please let me do that madam." Annie proceeds to open the door.

"No please! It's too late for that. I am here now. Where were you anyways?" She inquires of Annie.

"Ma'am, I was upstairs catering to Hailey. She was looking for her doll, Candice, Ma'am." She replies timidly.

"I see. Well, next time you call someone else to come down quickly. Do I make myself clear?" Roxie lashing out, the doorbell rings again.

"Yes ma'am," She curtsies as she leaves Roxie's presence.

"Did you find the doll for her?"

"Yes ma'am, it was under her bed." Annie replies and walks away.

"Good help is hard to find these days." Roxie sighs, gulps down the wine in her glass and opens the door. To her surprise, Fanta sweeps in like a queen… all dressed in a flowery, and extremely short sun dress. She places her hand over the top of her flimsy looking hat set ever so delicately on her head. She storms past Roxie and into Roxie's living room.

"Girl, it is getting hot out there," whipping her fan out, fanning herself as she makes her way into Roxie's house.

"Oh! Wow! Fanta" Roxie surprised.

"Da! Girl! Don't act all surprised to see me."

"Well sister girl, I was expecting you yesterday not today." She replies following Fanta into the house.

"Okay then, what are you saying? You want me to leave?" turning to Roxie.

"Oh no sister girl… just surprised, that's all. By the way, what happened yesterday? You stood your sister girl up?"

"Hish, long story. It's more like who happened?" It's a long story. Anyway, I am here now." She reaches out and hugs Roxie.

"Enough for you not to pick up your phone either?" Roxie asks.

"Sorry about that. You know me? When something gets to me, I shut down totally."

"I am so glad you came today anyways."

"Me too sister girl... me too." Fanta replies, taking off her sun hat, freeing her hair, combing through it with her fingers.

"Always as beautiful as ever." Roxie comments.

"Thank you sister girl... Thank you. With age riding up on us, we sisters' got to keep it together, right?" Fanta remarks.

"Tell me about it." Roxie agrees.

"Let's sit over this side of the house. The event planner is in the other room... still doing last minute touches for the party..." Roxie adds.

"Okay, did you just say you are allowing someone to touch your stuff? Wonders will never cease!" Fanta exclaims.

"I know where you are going with this. I do allow people to do their jobs for me, once in a while. This is one of those times," Roxie smiles as they both make their way further into the house. Roxie suddenly catches Fanta's somber look.

"What's up sister girl? Are you okay?" Roxie gets closer, tucking her arm into hers.

"Oh yes... I'm fine I guess. I just wanted to see you, that's all" She stutters uncontrollably.

"I know you well enough now Fanta. Spill it out now please!" Roxie pushes a service bell by the lounge, as they sit Annie rushes out instantly.

"Get me another glass of wine. And oh... what

would you like to drink?" Roxie asks.

"Just my usual… Perrier water. Thank you." Fanta replies, still subdued.

"You heard her. What are you waiting for? Run along."

"Yes ma'am." Annie makes her way out of the lounge. In an effort to avoid the discussion, Fanta quickly snaps out of her funky mood, changing the subject entirely.

"You know how loud you are … I don't want you going berserk on me if I am late to your party. That's all" hiding her true emotions and not telling Roxie that, this was actually the first time she'd heard of the party. As usual, Alan had not informed her of the party… a usual occurrence these days that Fanta is covering up, so her friend dos not realize how hurt she is. She starts to imitate Roxie.

"Girl you did not come see me before! Now you showing up at my party?" Pointing her finger in Roxie's face.

"You know you are a clown, right? You are so funny… I see why your fans can't get enough of you." Roxie bursts out laughing.

"How is your hubby Tee doing?"

"You know? Same ol'… Same ol'!" Roxie adds.

"Men… what are we going to do with them?" Fanta responds. "One minute they are hot, the next you feel like killing them!" Fanta raging.

"I hear you sister girl. I hear you! But they are all we've got, right?" Roxie follow suit.

"Not sure about that, right now."

"Take Tee for instance. Always out and about. You never know what he's doing out there."

"Regardless, he loves you, respects you and

doesn't flash a trashy prostitute in your face!" Fanta proclaims.

"That's right! He knows this Jamaican woman takes no junk from nobody! All them hootie mamas stay outta' ma house. You know me and my hot self, I be slashing someone's throat... him and his crazy prostitute!" Roxie chimes in.

"I know, that's right! Roxie mama, I need to take some lessons from you." Fanta loosens up.

"Just being real sister girl... just being real." The maid comes I with their drinks, sets them down next to them and excuses herself.

"You are hilarious girlfriend. I really learn from the best... You inspire me so much.... I wish I was more like you."

"Well now, watch it girl, there can only be one of me... for Tee," their laughter echoing through the room.

"Seriously... all the crap I take sometimes out there, I could deal better with it, if I had a little of Roxie" Fanta continues.

"Sister girl, you may want to rethink that dream wish. Seriously!" Roxie continues.

"Come one, quit saying that. Why wouldn't anyone want a little of your spunkiness?"

"Oh sister girl, I got mad blood in me, girlfriend... I go to war if someone steps on my Jamaican toe."

"Girl you are impossible...I have my share of that too."

"You are talking in riddles sister girl. What is going on?"

"What isn't? Especially nowadays with Alan, it

just seems like I am always in a war zone."

"Oh? What's the brother done now?"

"Where do I begin! Him and his roaming eyes are at it again. I don't know how much of this I can take any longer!" Fanta exerts.

"You guys just need to do the marriage thing for real this time. That fake one you did don't count sister girl… calling your friend to officiate a marriage and show your love to each other without the real officiating pastor! Real copout, if you ask me!" Roxie continues.

"But you know the whole story, Alan don't believe in the real thing… marriage." Fanta complains. "He doesn't want to be tied down but he still made us do that silly thing. Now, I don't know if I am really married or just playing house!" Fanta speaks out regretfully.

"You went along with the silly ceremony sister girl! Why you do it anyways? Why you follow him to that stupid thing?

"Truthfully, I really don't know. Trying to please him, I guess?" Fanta admits.

"Boyfriend just wants to play house with you. Nevertheless, he is still your man, right?" Roxie asks carefully punctuating her syllables. "Right Fanta?" She asks again. "Girl, drink up… we got lots to talk about… drink up!" They pick up their glasses in honor of their men.

"To our men who make us crazy yet we love them" Roxie says.

"To the ones we often feel like whacking, yet we love them!" They click their glasses, smile and gobbles down the drink.

"Okay, with this gin hitting the right spot, my creative juices are in full creative mode."

"Oh oh, should I be worried?"

"You know me girlfriend, I always got your back." Roxie smiling unashamedly, her glittering black eyes light up.

"Alright girl, spill. Lord knows, I need the help right about now." Fanta ready for Roxie's wisdom nugget.

"I know exactly what you need. Take a vacation okay. Rekindle your love before it's too late."

"A vacation? Girl, you know how busy this time of the year is for me, right?" Fanta cries out.

"Sister girl, you better love that man, love him real good... romance him until you start having babies."

"Babies? What are you talking about Roxie? Bring babies into this mess? I don't even know if I am really married or not, and you are talking about babies."

"You love him yes?" Roxie puts down her glass and looks in Fanta's direction, wearing a very serious look. "Do you love him?" She asks again in an even more serious tone.

"You know that is not in question, although most times, lately, I feel like strangling him!" Fanta replies.

"You work on giving that man babies... you settle him down with you. That's what my Jamaican mama taught me girl. It's worked for me."

"I don't know Roxie. I don't know if Alan will like that at all."

"You guys are not getting any younger, you in particular. You gonna let Alan waste your youth?"

"That is the bone of contention Roxie! One minute, he calls me his wife another I am his girlfriend. I don't know if I am coming or going with him. And lately, he has been even more distant." Fanta even more frustrated.

"Look sister girl, I am telling you the secret here… settle that man down please! Then you can war after you have really gone to the registry and you do the right marriage…" Roxie impresses.

"Something to think about Roxie!"

"Darn right! You don't need much drama now, so tone it down. Save it for later… after the real marriage, then babies come and the career gets old."

"There are times I am so angry at Alan I want out, other times I love his sorry butt".

"I know what you talking about sister girl. I was once there with Tee."

"You guys are the perfect couple. He is always loving on you in public. You will never catch Alan do that." Fanta speaks out. "His excuse is always that he is trying to stay away for my fans."

"I have been with Tee for 10 years, with one child, who is the angel of his eye. That child keeps him grounded."

"I believe that."

"Then believe it will work for you too." Fanta shrugs her shoulders in resignation.

"Don't get me wrong, I know my Tee is out there. He don't know I know… But he don't bring it in here. Here, I am the queen of this castle."

"And that is okay with you?"

"Did I say it is okay? I just say I keep my castle to myself here. Whatever he does or not do out there, I don't wanna know." Roxie explains.

"Perhaps therein lies my problem. But then again, Tee doesn't flaunt it in your face, right?" Roxie responds with a gesture.

"Okay here we go, another nugget to for, sister girl. Just ease up on Alan."

"I am trying. Gosh, I am but he makes it so difficult when he is constantly arguing with me."

"Then don't bite! Let the man be, Fanta."

"It is not that easy Roxie."

"Who says it is? Relax superstar. Let me get us something to eat, a sandwich maybe? Or what would you like to eat?"

"I love your cranberry salad. You have some of that?"

"Everyday girl… every day. Trying to keep this body in tip top shape for my man." They laugh as she reaches for the call bell.

"You hang onto that man real tight, you hear me? Otherwise he will start looking elsewhere."

"That advice may have come a little too late. I think he is already looking elsewhere."

"He is still in the house right?"

"Right. Then all hope is not lost. Handle your business sister girl. Handle your business real good. That man is not going anywhere."

"Can you believe he didn't tell me about the party?"

"What? Tee gave him the invitation for both of you."

"I just heard it from you … just now."

"No wonder you had some funny look when I was telling you about preparing for the party. That is silly."

"Beyond being silly. I don't know what his plan is for not telling me about the party." Fanta utters. "So, I don't know if I'm coming tomorrow." She continues.

"What you mean, you don't know if you will come? Now, you know about the party, right?" Roxie inquires.

"You know, I am famished. I think I have my appetite back just talking with you. Please tell your maid to hurry up with it" Fanta avoiding Roxie's last question.

"Anyways, I don't want to hear about you not coming tomorrow, okay?"

"We'll see Roxie… we'll see. Now get me some food please…"

"Well, let's drink another Apple Martini before the food gets here.

"Here… here… sister girl, here… here." Fanta pouring more of the drink into her glass, handing the half empty bottle to Roxie.

"May the party be as beautiful as it's name… Make the Year beautiful".

"I'll drink to that. Whew! So much still to do, you know." Roxie comments.

"I know your party will be great. You have hired the best to put this thing together… The best money can buy! So no worries there."

"I hope so. Come on girl, let's go catch up on our reality shows."

"You have time for those shows?" Fanta walking along side Roxie.

"I must confess, some of them are just plain stupid but there are few that I really like."

"They put me to sleep, if you ask me." Fanta explains. They walk towards the theatre located in the courtyard, right in the middle of the mansion.

African OSCAR PEOPLES' CHOICE WINNER~FAVORITE SCREENWRITER BEING PREPARED BY CJ SAVOY, OWNER BAC TO BASIC HAIR GALLERY IN BRENTWOOD, TN.

AND THE TRANFORMATION INTO THE
PRINCESS OF SUBURBIA® CONTINUES….

TRANSFORMATION IS COMPLETE….

15 CHITTY...CHITTY...BAM...BAM!

I WAS RUSHING TOWARDS MY CAR WHEN ANOTHER CAR PARKED RIGHT IN FRONT OF MY HOUSE. The relentless honking of the horn from the man behind the wheel became irritating! In frustration, I throw my school books on the passenger's seat.

"Who in the world?" turning around to see who was behind the wheel. Though his face us hidden; I could recognize those biceps anywhere. Relieved that it was Jake, I walk up to the car.

"What are you doing here?"

"I was sitting in my store and I got to thinking..." Jake starts off, cautiously.

"Oh? That is a good thing right? I mean thinking..."

"Well, it depends on if you like my idea."

"I am listening."

"You know what.... Better yet, I need to take you somewhere. I promise I will bring you right back once we are done."

"Where?" I ask.

"Don't be inquisitive. Just hop in."

"Not until you tell me where you are taking me." Hesitant.

"Has anyone ever told you how stubborn you are? You need to start trusting people okay?"

"I have had enough bad things happen to me lately. Just being cautious."

"Do you think I am going to hurt you Siberia? I am crushed by your words right now." Jake is troubled by my response. Quickly realizing that I had hurt his feelings, I reached out to the passenger door and jump into his car.

"I am sorry. I didn't mean to hurt your feelings. I am just very jumpy these days."

"I will never hurt you Siberia. Don't you get that by now?" Jake stresses.

"I know. I am so sorry, alright?" Apologizing for my rude behavior.

"Regardless, you have to get this… not everyone is out to get you."

"I am slowly getting that."

"Great Siberia. Now, I need you to relax and allow me do what I want to do. Yes?" Jake demands.

"I was on my way to my school library. You will need to bring me back on time, so I can grab my car and go to the library. Deal?"

"I have an even better offer. I will drop you off at the library and pick you back up when you are done. How does that sound?"

"Nice gesture. Thank you for offering but don't you have anything else to do in your store?"

"I'm the boss. I set my own hours. Besides, let me worry about that." Jake speaks up firmly.

"Alright then, I'll go get my books and off we go, okay?"

"Cool! Awesome. Now, that's more like it." He smiles as I get out of his car, run to mine, drag out my books and off we I go to some an unknown place. For the first time, I get a chance to take in the Tennessee scenery... the beautiful tall buildings downtown...country music blasting across the streets... the cow boy hat displayed on a giant mannequin...

"Wow, this place is beautiful."

"So, how long have you been here?" Jake asks, lighting up.

"Almost a year now and things are still a little fuzzy for me. This is the very first time I am actually taking in all the scenery around me."

"I'm glad you are doing just that." Jake replies smiling. He reaches out for my hand and gently covers it with his warm hand. He throws a quick glance at me, then goes back to the road ahead of us. His touch was warm, gentle, exhilarating, heart pumping but I was not going to let him see how his touch is affecting my thought process. In that moment, if anyone had asked me what one plus one equals, I would have screamed out loud! His touch was sending some sensations throughout my body... one I desperately did not want stopped yet I have to focus on the task ahead... finding the stone and getting it back to Africa.

"Here we go" lifting his hand from mine and pulling into a park. I look around unsure where we are, as I had not seen this park before.

"Alright lady, let's roll" Jake jumps out of the car, runs around, opens the door for me. What a gentleman, he is.

"Thank you."

"You are quite welcome." He replies smiling, his dashing looks accentuated in the sun.

@@@@@

He seats me on a bench facing a breath-taking garden, with the most gargantuan roses I'd ever laid my eyes on. He walks to the garden, picks up some of the yellow roses, quickly mixes them up with red and white roses and presents them to me.

"Oh my. Thank you. But can you do that though?"

"Can I do what?" finding his place by my side.

"Can you just go into that garden and pick those roses?"

"Oh that, I see," you need not worry about that.

"Oh?" Looking around, ensuring no one had seen him pick the roses for me.

"Relax Siberia. I know the owner. You don't have to worry about that."

"I'm not worried..." quickly switching gears.

"Oh really? You are an incurable worrier, aren't you" Jake adds.

"I know. It's a bad habit I have acquired since I returned to America from my last trip to Africa. I'm always waiting for something else to happen."

"That's no healthy way to live Siberia."

"Don't you think I know that? I am just exhausted about the chain of events in my life right now."

"Whenever I am going through tough times, I

talk to God and when there are too many noises around me, I find a quiet place where I feel it is just me and Him." A gentleman and a spiritual one at that. I am even more enthralled by Jake. His firm conviction and devotion to God and his strong sense of self was incredibly captivating. I find myself quickly drifting away into his world full of much needed tranquility. Most importantly, the feeling was great... The sudden calmness around me, his soothing voice and his comforting arms around me... all a recipe for a great romance.

"Can you do that for your sister?" his voice breaks into my stillness.

"Can I do what?" I ask, looking into his flashing eyes; eyes that had given away his feelings for me. "Can I do what?" I repeat.

"Can you just be still for a moment for your sister?" He repeats, his eyes locked into mine; there was no escaping his stare, nor did I want to.

"I will do anything for my sister." Replying, eyes still locked with his.

"Great! Then trust God to take care of your sister. Trust him and give it all to him."

"Wow! Such faith."

"Well, something I've had to rely on since dad and mom died."

"So sorry about your parents."

"Oh, it's nothing to be sorry about, but thank you. It was a great loss for Simon and I... Jennie too."

"I thought Jennie was your mom. I heard you call her mom."

"Well, she has taken the role of our mom since our parents died. So yes, we do call her mom."

"That's so sweet."

"Well, she's all we've got. Sometimes, I think Simon lost his way since their accident and he has never been the same." A little sorrow in his eyes.

"I understand your brother much better now."

"Well, I wish I could say that. I wish he would just stop messing around with his life and get his act together."

"All in good time, I guess." Consoling Jake.

"Well, he is not getting any younger, you know."

"And who is? I suppose we all have to grow up at some time. He will. You'll see."

"Look at me. I brought you here to comfort you and here you are comforting me." He reaches out and grabs me by my shoulders, pulling him even closer than before.

"That's okay. I don't mind." Smiling into his eyes. His next move was certainly unexpected yet gladly received. He plants a warm kiss on my lips! And I respond! Realizing what he had done, he quickly pulled back, stood up from the bench, embarrassed.

"I am so sorry. I didn't mean to do that. Will you forgive me?" He rambled on. "I will give you some privacy… just room to rest and meditate. It helps me." He continues, giving me no room to respond. "I will be waiting in the car for you when you are done."

"Jake? Jake?" I continue calling his name through his rambling spell.

"Yes… I will go now. Okay?"

"Jake? Will you stop for a second!" Finally getting his attention.

"It is okay. I am not upset." I reassure him.

"Really? It's not like me. It's just that I've been wanting to let you know how I feel since I met you."

"Now I know." Smiling at him.

"Alright then. I will take my leave now. I'll be in the car when you are done."

"Sure. Thank you."

"You're welcome." He rushes out of my presence before we could say more. I maintain my seat on the bench, now wondering what I was supposed to be mediating on. Is it the kiss he had just gave me? Or am I supposed to be reflecting on my sister's plight? Before this second, I had suspected Jake's intention and now, it is certain what his intentions are towards me. Suddenly, the wicked laughter of Yemoji comes crashing down my thoughts; her dark image... one all too familiar to me in my dreams flashes back and forth my vision; an instant reminder of my main focus. While scary, it was certainly what I needed to stay focused on my primary mission... to find the stone and return it back to Africa.

"Lord, please save my sister even without the stone, I know you can save her. I don't always understand what my tradition is all about. Sometimes, I am confused as to my culture. But you are always constant. I rest in that knowledge today." I glanced at my watch; I had been siting there for almost twenty minutes!

"Oh my God, I have to be in school in ten minutes!" I rush out of the garden and head straight for Jake's car.

16 YEMOJI'S SHATTERED COURSE

THE DISRUPTIVE ENCOUNTERS WITH YEMOJI IN
MY DREAMS HAVE INTENSIFIED. She is a nightmare I
have not been able to shake off, no matter how much I try.
Often, I would only see her boisterous image in my dreams,
then I would hear her voice echoing through the darkness yet
her mouth not moving, only when she is laughing out
wickedly. This time, something was different! Yemoji's mouth
begins to open. She starts speaking out loud to me, often
telepathically... all in my dream! The mysterious woman starts
to laugh loudly, echoing through the air. Since the appearance
of Yemoji in my dreams, I have mastered the act of escaping
the dream when it gets worse. This time is no different. I
jump out of bed with sweat pouring down my face, my heart
racing. I walk into my bathroom, gawking at my sweaty face
in the mirror and my bald head, a secret I'd not, as yet, shared
with anyone.   Suddenly, fear grips me! What would Jake
think if he knew I was bald? Alan who is obviously so
captivated by me... how would a high society guy like him
feel if he found out I was bald? As my fear deepens,
overshadowed by sadness and the realization that all of this

… the intense attraction… the emotions… between these men and myself are about to evaporate. I was not prepared to tell Jake about my dilemma with alopecia. I was ten years old when I started losing my hair. No one in the village knew what it meant. I secretly wondered if it was a punishment from the gods of my land for being disobedient; constantly sneaking out to sit underneath the tree in the village square. Children in the neighborhood called me baldy and I was forced to wrap my head in scarves… a practice I continue while living in America. Jessica and Josie, my nosy neighbors, assumed I was wearing these scarves because of my culture. I wondered how they would feel when they find out the truth. As my sorrow overtook my thoughts; mama's beautiful voice whispered courage…. "you are beautiful my daughter. Don't you let anyone tell you otherwise." Her voice reverberates in my ear.

"I am beautiful," speaking out loud, gently tricking my mind out of the gloomy feeling.

"And if they love you Siberia, they will accept you just the way you are." Spoken with conviction as I prepared to take my shower.

"Lord help me, I have to find this stone. Hang in there sis'. It's not over yet." My voice definitive, picking up my tooth brush, scouring my teeth. My final revelation occurs after 10 minutes of allowing the hot water to beat down on my body. I jump out of the shower into a steamy room, mirror fogged from the moisture. Wiping down the mirror, I gently apply my lipstick. More makeup for my eyelids and cheeks; then gently dabbing my apple spice perfume on my neck. I was on to something. Tonight, I was going to be the most beautiful woman in that room. I was going to work my African magic, as Jessica always says and see if it will get me anywhere with finding the stone. Perhaps this is the night I finally get to figure out all of these romances… That is, should it be Jake or Alan? When I am with Jake, I forget there is another world out there. Likewise, when I see Alan, something in me leaps and wants more of him. Could it be the elegant and powerful world he lives in that attracts me more to Alan? Or is it his rugged looks and firm, confident demeanor? It is often said that many women are attracted to the bad boys. Could I be suffering from such a fate when dealing with Alan? What's worse is that I am suddenly not moved by his situation with Fanta. Though I wasn't sure if he was indeed married or not, for some odd reason, it didn't seem to make a difference. Be that as it may, tonight I was going to also find out the truth where he is concerned. Until then, my intent is to keep him guessing and wanting more of me. Jake, on the other hand, though gentle, can hold his own too. He is strong, yet gentle-spirited, confident in who he is and content with running the consignment store that his parents had willed to them. Jake is definitely not one to bask in the lime night. Alan's glamorous lifestyle is so far removed from Jake's. Jake lives a quiet lie compared to Alan's multimillion dollar art world. I came out of my day dreaming with my radical face-lift complete! This was an art I had perfected to draw attention away from the wig I was wearing tonight. Mama always says to love on oneself if no one else does. Well, I followed her advice. Looking in the mirror, I blow myself a kiss.

@@@@@@

The two brothers are in my living room helping each other groom and dress appropriately for the party. Onye comes out on with mix-matched wear, his pants flying above his ankles showing the pair of Dunlop athletic shoes he's wearing. Onka's exaggerated and colorful bow-tie rules the day! Though his dressing is not any better, Onka sets out to correct Onye's attempt to dress properly.

"You this bush boy, look at you. Is this what they call elegant?" Onka's voice echoes down my short hallway to my bedroom.

"Hey, my friend, leave me alone. Let me wear what I want to wear!" Onye replies firmly.

"I have told you over and over again, you are not going to disgrace me in this America! Didn't you hear what that man Simon says?"

"So what did he say?" Onye asks cynically.

"This is an event of the year! This is an important event in America! You cannot dress like someone who was hijacked from a village and mistakenly dropped into the center of the party." Onka explains.

"Look, I won't bother you. So you don't bother me, okay? You are not looking that great yourself. Look in the mirror!" spoken out of sheer anger.

"These guys… what am I going to do with them? Always bickering about one thing or another." Murmuring to myself as their voices become louder and more annoying, I run out of my room to meet them at the living room.

"Guys, please tone down your voices. We are not in the village here!"

"Sorry cous', it is this pompous Onka causing trouble again."

"Don't mind him! He never listens to correction. I am telling him that he looks like a clown with short pants!" Onka speaks out.

"See… that is what I mean, always raining insults. Two can play the game oh! You say one more thing about my dressing and you will see what I will do" Onye replies angrily.

"Since when did you guys resort to threats? This is crazy! You are both crazy! Just don't let the neighbors call the cops on me. I have enough trouble with Mr. Babu as is! Do not compound my troubles please!" Yelling at both of them.

"What time is it?" Gazing at the wall clock in my living room. "And what are you two wearing. Did you go shopping when I wasn't home or something? Where did you get money to go shopping?" I continue my rain on their parade.

" Haba cous? You asking too many questions now. We are men, not children."

"You could have fooled me! Men don't bicker the way you two do! You might want to think about that!"

"That stings cous" Onka responds.

"The truth always stings!" Replying to him firmly.

"I am curious just looking at you two right now. You just got to America! You are already getting around? How? When?"

"Yes now cous'! Level don change now! We are doing it psychedelic way." Onye joins in the conversation.

"Besides cous, we must look the part for the party. Otherwise, that will be it for us."

"That's true but you don't want to be sticking out like a sore thumb either. Both of your outfits are very odd! But like you always say… your business not mine."

"Well, just so you know, Simon took us shopping." Onye replies.

"Simon? When did you guys link up with Simon? Are you talking about Simon, Jake's brother?"

"What other Simon do you know cous'?" Onka asks.

"You guys are scaring me! How did you connect with him? You know what? Never mind, we are running late. Let me go and get myself together."

"Better cous'. We don't want to be late." Onka agrees, relieved my piercing questions had stopped.

@@@@@@

Jake has insisted he wasn't going to the party. However, his heart is heavily set on me and determined to help me to retrieve the stone from Tee's mansion. Moreover, ever since I accepted Alan's invitation to be his date to the party, he has felt like the air was knocked out of him… call it jealousy or whatever. He is becoming even more miserable as the hour draws near. Regardless of the outcome, he will go and be the lookout guy for me; a gesture I do so appreciate. He glances at the time and notices he is running late. He finishes shaving, rushing to his room to inspect what he is wearing. Jake is ready to turn his charm to the maximum… a gesture all for my sake. At the other end of the hallway is Simon's bedroom. He is consumed with concealing his bruised face. He begins to cry a bit from the pain he is experiencing in touching his bruised face. He has not recovered from being ruffled up by Tee's guys.

"Shucks!" bawling out as pain shoots through

him.

@@@@@

Alan has his black tuxedo neatly laid out on the elegantly decorated bed. The rose colored silk caressing the bed frame alongside the barrage of succulent pillows on gold framed bed are all Fanta's handiwork. Though Alan is more of a rustic look guy, he has allowed Fanta to arrange the bedroom whichever way she chooses as well as pick the colors. Fanta plants herself in the middle of the bed, right next to Alan's tuxedo. Alan throws a side glance into the mirror at Fanta.

"Alright, spill it out. What's eating you up?" Alan asks with caution and quick remorse that he may have opened up a Pandora's box with the question. "You know what, let's forget I asked" quickly attempting to withdraw his question only it was already too late.

"I changed my mind baby. I want to go with you to Tee's party. I am cancelling my event tonight with Scott." Feeling the bottom dropping quickly from underneath him he turns abruptly towards Fanta.

"No need to cancel. Besides, this party is more of a business meeting to me" Alan promptly delivers his excuse.

"Oh really? Tell me about it. Tell me all about the business you will be wheeling and dealing at the event of the year." Fanta's sarcasm flows.

"It's no secret that Tee gets some of his most valuable paintings from me."

"Hun... hun... hun," she mocks, knowing deep down in her spirit what Alan is up to.

"Many of his business associates will be at the party. A perfect opportunity to get new clientele, don't you think?"

"Yeah sure, provided that was all you were doing, right?"

"And what is that supposed to mean? There you go with your smart remarks again! Please spare me that tonight. I am in a good mood! Do not ruin it for me woman!" picking up his shirt from the mahogany finished closet.

"Look, Roxie's friends will be there too. And the last I checked, I am her best friend."

"So what?" Alan lashes out. "I do not want you there period! Is that clear Fanta? I don't want your eyes all up in my business. By the way since when do you suddenly want to attend a party with me?"

"Granted I have been busy lately but I am available tonight." She walks up to him, stands in his way and looks straight into his eyes.

"Well, I am not ready for you to join me tonight, okay?"

"Is there something I should know Alan?" attempting to look into Alan's shifting gaze.

"Well?" taking over buttoning down his shirt for him.

"Well what Fanta! I don't know what you are talking about!" Stops her from further buttoning his white 100% cotton shirt.

"I am no baby. I can do that by myself!" Gently pushing her hands away.

"You use to like me doing that. What's changed?"

"Are you serious about that question or are you joking right now?"

"Do I look like I am kidding? What changed Alan?"

"Everything Fanta. You have chosen your career over our relationship even when I have more than enough to take care of you!"

"Oh... that?

"Is that all you have to say? Oh that?"

"I am not sure what I should be saying. You knew I was serious about my modeling career! This was everything to me before I met you!"

"That is the word right there... everything."

"You are twisting my words Alan! It is very selfish to expect me to quit my dream to stay home and pamper to your every needs. That is just plain selfish!"

"Well then, we are done here. I hope your career keeps you warm at night. I have got to really finish up here and leave in few minutes." He walks away from her towards the tuxedo on the bed.

17 THE FRIVOLUS HEIST

GUESTS ELEGANTLY DRESSED IN STUNNING
SHIMMERY DRESSES AND TUXEDOS GRACE TEE'S
ANNUAL VIP PARTY. One of Tee's henchmen, Jasper,
ushers the guests into the party area.
Jasper looks ahead of the rows of luxurious cars, from sporty
BMW, to the latest Benz, a Lamborghini ... All were
represented on the line up to Tee's well-lighted drive way.
Simon's Fiat seems out of place as he pulls in the driveway,
the two brothers, Onka and Onye, inside. They had decided
to all ride together, allowing me some quality time with
Alan, my date for the evening. Simon, Onka and Onye
intently watch the caliber of people being ushered from their
cars by the valet boys.
 "Bro', this is what you call life!" Onye
marveled.
 "Na wa oh. All these people... all this money
under one roof tonight, kai. In fact, I am blessed." Onka
replies.
 "What do you mean you are blessed? You see
all these rich people, you say you are blessed! What kind of

talk is that?"

"You will never understand. Have you ever seen such a view before in all of your illiterate life?" Onka continues.

"Precisely my point! How can that bless you?" Onye adds.

"I hope you guys know what you are doing," Simon interrupts the bickering. He is increasingly nervous about going into the mansion.

"Look, we are here now, either we know what we are doing or not. We are here! We must stick to the plan!" Onye replies Simon.

"You can't panic now oh. No turning back, right?" Onka asks Simon.

"Right. Guys, I don't have the money Tee's asked me to return and if I am caught, I will be in a lot of trouble with him! I can lose my life on this. We must make sure this plan works!" Simon states.

"Yo… yo… yo… what's up man" Onye practicing his lingo in a comical manner.

"Did you guys not hear what I just said?" Simon panics all the more.

"Chill out man" Onka adds to Simon's tension.

@@@@@

Tee is in one of the mansion kitchens that they seldom use. He takes off his jacket, throws it on one of the lounge chairs. Iridescent rays of light shoot from his jacket pocket, from the stone that he'd taken away from Simon. It catches his attention and he pulls it from his pocket and begins to examine the stone as it changes colors in his hands. He becomes distracted and places the stone on the counter and moves in the direction of the music playing in the party area. He looks into the mass of people moving around; they seem to be having a great time as they stand around in pairs, some drinking champagne, with others attempting to snatch a sparkling glass off the server trays. Tee sees a couple roaming around with no assistance.

"Hey you!" he howled at one of the party hostesses.

"Yes Mr. Tee," She replies right away.

"Will you help those guests find their way?"

"Yes Mr Tee... This way sir... ma'am." She ushers them into the party hall as Tee nods in their direction.

"Enjoy yourselves. Will be with you all in a minute." Tee smiling buoyantly in their direction and raising a glass of scotch, acknowledging their presence.

"Missed you pappy." Hailey says, tugging at her dad's pant leg.

"Hey, pappy misses his baby too. How is my main gal tonight? And what are you doing up or even out here sugar?"

"I'm fine pappy. Waiting for you to tuck me in tonight pappy. Did you bring me anything?"

"Hey sugar, this area is for grownups. Where is your nanny?"

"She is doing something with mami."

"Where are they?"

"Oh somewhere...."

"Where baby girl?"

"I don't know. So, did you bring me something tonight?"

"But I brought you something yesterday, didn't I? You want something else tonight?"

"Yes pappy. I want something else tonight."

"Oh sugar, you have to promise me you will stay in your room tonight. Pappy and mama have things to do tonight, okay?"

"Sure pappy. I came to say good night anyway once I get my gift from you."

"Oh come on sugar, pappy will get you another gift but not tonight." He watches his daughter pout around him.

"Don't be mad at pappy baby. You know pappy is good for it. I just have to attend to all of these people tonight dear. I promise you, I will get you another gift tomorrow. Anything you want baby. I promise." He reaches to hug her.

"Promise pappy?"

"You better believe it. Anything you want baby. I promise. Come here, give pappy a big fat hug." He pulls his daughter closer. "Good night doll." Her head on his shoulder, Hailey catches a glimpse of the sparkling stone across the room on the counter top.

"That's my girl" he hugs her even tighter.

"Pappy what is that over there?"

"What's what sugar?" He turns to look in the direction of Hailey's pointed finger.

"Oh? That?"

"Yes pappy. It's beautiful."

"It sure is, isn't it?" Tee glancing at the stone, pondering it.

"Can I play with it?" Hailey asks, jumping off Tee's shoulders and running towards the stone.

"Of course doll, you can have it if you promise pappy you will be off to bed now. Promise?"

"I promise. Off to bed I go pappy. Thank you pappy. Night, night."

"Night, night my sweet angel. And tell mummy I'm over here."

"Tell mami what? There you are, little rascal. What are you doing in this section of the house?"

"Hi mami, look at what pappy gave me."

"As usual, Tonya and I have been looking for this girl all over the house."

"And as usual, she is with her pappy," Tee smiling yet firm.

"Look mami, it glows. It's pretty."

"Yeah… sure, it's beautiful. Haven't I told you never to come to this section of the house by yourself?"

"Sorry mami, I had to come find pappy."

"Perhaps if Tonya had watched her closely, she wouldn't have snuck in here!"

"Yeah sure pappy. Perhaps if I wasn't married to you, I would have been taller than 5 feet! Being barely over 5 feet is the price I pay!" She whispers into Tee's ear in her thick Jamaican accent, planting kisses on his cheeks.

"Hey! Hey! Hey! Just saying dear."

"You've spoilt that kid rotten." Roxie laments.

"What am I supposed to do woman? Spank her for wanting to play with daddy?

"No, but at least say no sometimes."

"No dear," planting a light kiss on her lips.

"Hey pappy, what's up with that? Not to me. Her for crying out loud."

"Yes dear." Tee replies.

"I can see this is a battle I won't win." Roxie exclaims.

"Glad you know that already. Don't get between papa and his angel. No one does that." Smiling at his wife.

@@@@@

Jakes swings his car into Tee's driveway. He pulls up to Alan's Escalade, almost hitting the bumper. Jake is not dressed for the party as his goal is to drive the get-away car for Siberia once the stone is found. He looks in Alan's direction, jealousy rising up within him.

"Not sure why I agreed to this stupid plan." He watches me step out of the car, Alan swinging to my side to open the door. He bows as he swings the door open. With Jake's headlight almost blinding me, I looked in his direction for a split second, enough to feel his sunken heart watching me in another man's arms, game or no game. My heart dropped too but I instantly pick myself up as the goal is to focus... get the stone... stop all these mishaps around me... and save Naiya.

"You look ravishing tonight."

"You make me sound like a dish..."

"Well..." sighs, his eyes tilting from my head all the way to my dazzling shoes."

"Do you always speak to all your ladies like this? Ravishing?" she accuses Alan.

"Just those I find incredibly hot, like present company." Beaming with confidence, extending his arm in my direction.

"I see." My response tinged with sarcasm, as I gracefully place my hand in his. "Thank you."

"You are quite welcome, my lady."

"By the way, where is your girlfriend tonight?" Alan pulls back shocked at my comment.

"What did you say?"

"You heard me… your girlfriend, you know the one everyone's talking about around town." I repeat. Alan quickly composes himself, tucks my hand in his and begins walking towards the main entrance to the mansion.

"Well? Are you going to answer my question?" I repeat.

"My life is not what it may seem to many. Why? Are you concerned?" frowning.

"Perhaps, it's none of my business who you sleep with." Replying guardedly.

"I see. Perhaps, I will let you know the answer soon enough. In the meantime, can we just have a great time tonight? Yes?"

"Great time it is then." I continue walking next to him. As we approach the man guarding the entrance, my heart suddenly leaps right back to Jake. I glanced back, watching him drive off into the alley. Why am I feeling so sad? Why do I feel like someone had just cut off my life support as I watch him roll away? My feelings for him are more evident than ever before. I could hear my breathing and my heart pounding! Here I am with a handsome, rich hunk, an African at that, right next to me; yet my heart keeps yearning for Jake, a small business owner, a white American, everything my family or people would scream about if they knew what was going on in my head. Drowning in a sea of confusion, I quickly came back to reality at Alan's insistence.

"Are you alright?" His voice intrudes upon my deep thoughts. Alan had watched me as I glanced at Jake's car.

"Is there something I should know too?" He solemnly asked.

"Not sure what you mean." I quickly compose myself.

"I see. It seems it's not I alone who may have some explanations to do at the end of this night." I smile in response, tug my arm further in into his.

"Shall we?" I ask with a gentle voice.

As Tee's henchman opens the ornately decorated iron door in allowing us to enter, I hear a voice behind us. Jack Rubeau, Alan's friend, calls out.

"Wait up partner." He takes giant strides towards us… and here all I could think about was that we are almost into the mansion. I needed no distractions… nothing or no one to stop me from ransacking that house to find what I came for.

"Hey Jack. Glad you could make it." Alan comments while gently ushering me into the mansion.

"Well, well, well, small world. Fancy meeting you here mademoiselle…" He wittily declares, his eyes locking on mine. He quickly reaches out for my hand and before anyone could say anything, he plants a light kiss on it, turning to the side to wink at Alan who is looking quite embarrassed.

"I can't believe this man… you flirting with her in front of me?" Alan says, shaking his head at Jack. Jack's response to Alan's comment is a grin, his eyes still drilling into mine.

"Hello." Stuttering in my response.

"So, you do remember me, right?" Jack inquires of me.

"I believe so." Replying with squinted eyes.

"Don't look too hard. There is nothing there worth looking at," Alan comments.

"Ol' boy you don't want to go there. Two can play the game. Jealous perhaps?" Alan continues, his gaze not letting up.

"You are already there my friend," Alan whispers in Jack's ear.

"Anyway, great seeing you here, on better circumstances than last time. I see my friend here likes taking care of his victims," Jacks adds. All I could do was smile sheepishly in response. Alan quickly sidesteps him, pulling me away from Jack.

"You need to stay away from this one. He is dangerous." Alan laments.

"And what does that make you, a sly dog?" Jack comes back at Alan forcefully and cynical. As tense as the situation seemed to be, they suddenly burst out laughing and begin walking towards the entrance.

"Alright my friend, you win, ok?" Alan surrenders.

"Of course I know. I always win." Alan nods at the guard and we were let inside the foyer in the mansion. Jack follows.

@@@@@

All of the "who's who" in town... the mayor and his wife, the city council man with his 6 ft tall, slim and extremely gorgeous daughter gracing his arm, Tee's business partners... all strolled into the house in their sophisticated wear and their expensive cars. They are received at the door by the ever so graceful Roxie. With a light Jazz music blowing in the background, the mood was set to receive all of the VIP guests.

@@@@@

"Look man, why are you fidgeting?" Onka asks as they make their exit from the car.

"I still don't have Tee's money. That last time I had contact with him, it was either I brought the money or I get hurt badly."

"So, you be careful, right?" Onye joins in the conversation.

"I know he better not catch me in that mansion."

"You said it, we get the stone; we sell it and you collect your money. Then you can pay him!" Onka reminds him.

"Sure, it all sounds so easy. Anyway, let's do this before I change my mind." Onya pulls his pants up, his ankles exposed to the open air. They both practice their newly acquired lingo, making Simon laugh out loud.

"What's up man?" Onka says.

"Chill out man!" Onye replies in a comical manner.

"Game time folks. Let's do this in the least painful way as possible." Simon leading the way to the door.

@@@@@

Jack jumps in front of us and enters the party first.

"Hey my African padre. It's great to

see you again buddy!" Tee asks.

"Same here... same here.

"So how is South Africa treating you?"

"It's all good. Madam?" Jack acknowledging Roxie's presence while she gracefully nods in response.

"And the ladies?"

"You know how we roll out there..." Jack smiling.

"Oh please don't encourage him." Alan jumps in on the conversation from behind Jack.

"Look at this uptight fellow. Sometimes, I just wonder about you..." Jack replies.

"Get over yourself pal." Alan answers.

"You are the one tied down with one person at home and now trying to hook another fish in the pond. Me, I am a single soul, free to graze wherever I want to, whenever I feel like and however I choose." Turning quickly to Tee before Alan could respond.

"Let me take my leave... handle my business."

"Yes, you do that. But stay away from Siberia." I hear Alan warning Jack.

"Enjoy the party. " Tee speaks up as Jack walks away.

"That one is trouble." Alan says to me as he reaches for Roxie and hugs her.

"It's good to see you again Roxie." Alan seemingly buttering her up.

"Yeah, Alan. Flattering will get you everywhere. Please don't stop," hugging him back while scoping me. If only looks can kill, Roxie's wicked eye will send me straight to hell. I am not going to let her evil eye deter me from what I have to do tonight. Tonight is all about saving the ones I love… Naiya, my sister, and returning the stone where it belongs, with my family in Africa. I quickly summon courage and look beyond her cold stare.

"So Alan, who do we have here?" Tee inquires.

"Oh, forgive my manners. This is Siberia." Alan jumps in, cautiously watching Roxie's harsh look. I was still focused on Roxie when her husband gently grabs my hand and plants a kiss.

"It's a pleasure meeting you young lady. Welcome to our mansion and meet my queen, Roxie". Tee continues.

"Please call me Siberia. Hello ma'am, you have a beautiful home" accentuating my African accent. Roxie nods then ignores my compliments about her home.

"How is Fanta?" Roxie suddenly blurts out, disregarding my presence.

"Fanta is fine," Alan quickly replies, attempting to dismiss the question. I knew right there, it was time to remove myself from the tense situation.

"Can you show me where the ladies room is please?" I asked Roxie.

"Past the kitchen to your right." They all watch as I remove myself from their presence. Roxie excuses herself, nodding at Alan in total disapproval.

"My man, where did you find this fine broad?"

"It's a long story Tee."

"Well then, let me ask this…are you dating her?"

"I won't say we are dating."

"Oh really?" You could have fooled me. It looks like dating to me!" Tee replies.

"Tee, I am here to enjoy your party. Let's focus

on that. I am not dating her yet."

"A word of advice Alan, look I have my own dirt but when it comes to Roxie and my family, they are always on the front row! I cover my dirt real well and don't drag it home with me."

"Thanks for the advice friend." Alan looking in my direction.

"You know darn well that Roxie and Fanta are good friends. What happens if Fanta shows up tonight?"

"She won't! She has not been invited to this party."

"There is no telling what Roxie will do, particularly after seeing you with that broad. I don't need no problems here tonight. So you are gonna take care of the art work we discussed early today and you will take care of this Fanta business too, kapish?"

"Yeah sure."

I was relieved just walking away from Roxie. Little did I know that another troubled soul was gunning for me. Jack, Alan's friend rushes across the room and stops me in my tracks. Suddenly, it feels like things are not going the way I'd planned. While the attention I was receiving at the party would flatter some, this is not the case for me.

"Hi there," Jack jumps in front of me.

"Hi yourself… again" I reply, still moving towards the ladies' room.

"Enjoying the party yet?" he asks.

"We just got here, right Jack?" I respond with a dismissive grin. Jack soon steps in my way, deterring me from walking any further.

"I have a question for you." He continues.

"Oh?"

"Do you have a thing for my friend? I mean do you fancy him?"

"I beg your pardon? Jack, is it?"

"Yes, that's my name."

"Not sure your question is in the least appropriate."

"Alan is my friend. I need to know these things." Smiling sheepishly.

"Well then, here is my answer for you… whether I like your friend is not your business!" I glanced towards the entrance and look in Alan's direction, giving the signal for him to come save me from his friend. Jack soon catches me gaze in Alan's direction.

"I don't mean to upset you, just looking out for my pal, that's all."

"Well Jack, while I understand, your pal is a big boy… he can handle his own business, right?

"A woman after my own heart. You are one feisty broad. I see why my friend is attracted to you." Jack replies.

"Is he?" a perfect time to inquire.

"You should know that, right?" Jack says.

"I suppose, Now if you will excuse me, I need to be somewhere. Thank you." I quickly dismiss myself from his presence. I look around and finally see Simon and my cousins. Unfortunately, I was not the only one who saw Simon. Tee, his dreaded enemy, sees him too. I immediately attempt to catch my cousins' attention as Tee fixates on Simon.

"Well, well, well… who do we have here? It looks like someone's got a death wish! Friend, enjoy the party. I have some business to handle!" Tee makes an eye contact with his henchmen who are scattered around the party in dark suits. They instantly pick Simon up and take him to Tee's private chambers.

"Hold up guys." Simon attempting to explain.

"Sh-h-h-h! You will not disturb this party! You hear me?" one of the henchmen responds in a dark and threatening tone as they frog-march him towards Tee.

@@@@@

Onye looks around the beautiful party scene. He is enamored by the scores of ladies parading throughout the party. He really could get used to this scene and was ready to jump ship due to his proximity to these ladies.

"Bro' when God created these American women, he took extra special care. Just look at the whole room, full of beauties." Onye exclaims.

"I am ashamed of you right now! Aren't you the one with the crusade to stay focused? Now you see girls and your noise has been swallowed by your greedy eyes!" Onka replies.

"Oh I am focused. In fact, I am very focused. If I die with one of these babes in my arms and that will be a happy death. American paradise, here I come." Onye answers drenched in the scenery surrounding them. Onye starts to make funny gestures towards the ladies who walk past them.

"Remember, these girls are high class. Not for an illiterate village boy like you! I beg you to focus!" Onye insists as I jump into their discussion.

"Focus guys! This is not one of your games.

We need to do this right and do it fast before something goes wrong!" I speak up, ripping Onye from his fantasy.

"We are focusing… truly focusing, right Onka?" Onye looks past a young lady who walks right past them smiling in his direction.

"I sure hope so. Okay guys, run along. You take this floor and I'll handle the rooms upstairs. But for now, I've got to do something to help Simon. I see trouble brewing."

"What? What is wrong with him?" Onka asks.

"I just saw something I do not like but I won't bore you with the details now. We have to do this fast before we get caught too."

"What? Simon caught?" Onka yells out.

"Now run along… quick please!" answering him in haste as we disperse. Carefully ensuring that no one sees me, especially Roxie, I head straight for Tee's private study where I saw them enter with Simon.

@@@@@

Tee's henchmen firmly hold Simon down into a chair.

"Hi Tee," voice stuttering, fear gripping him.

"Surprised seeing you here… that must mean you have my money, right?" Tee asks with deadly intent.

"As I recall, you were not to step into my house or see me anywhere else until you bring me my money! Right punk!" Tee's voice fiercely escalating. He turns to his henchmen who instantly knew what to do. They begin to punch Simon repeatedly, which was enough to elicit moans and groans, as one of them tries to gag him, but then releases him allow him to talk. Tired of being their punching bag, he decides to fess up.

"I swear, there is a good reason to explain why I am here Tee" forcing the words out of his mouth as the pain from the several blows he'd received smothers him.

"Oh really? A great reason eh? Guys, this is going to be real good! Start talking! I'm listening!" Tee screams to his face. Just as soon as Simon was ready to let the cat out of the bag, I storm into the room looking lost. She instantly assesses the situation, seeing the henchmen slowly release their hands from Simon's shoulders.

"Oh, I am so sorry. I was looking for the ladies room… perhaps a place to just collect my thoughts," quickly providing an excuse to ease the tension in the room as well as the uncomfortable looks from across the room.

"Hey Siberia, no worries. Mistakes do happen. Right guys?" Adjusting his stance and moving towards me.

"Glad you understand." Looking in Simon's direction. Tee follows her stare.

"Mr. O'Connor and I were just handling some business. Right, Mr. O'Connor? Boys, help him up will you?" Tee attempting to cover what has transpired in the room.

"Oh yes … sure Tee." He quickly moves away from the henchmen. "I will take my leave now." Simon says, a great opportunity for him to make an exit without further injury.

"Oh sure. You my man! Don't forget what I told you!" Tee tells Simon. His unwillingness to let Simon leave the room was all so glaring. I look around to distract the henchmen and Tee. His exquisite antiques displayed in his study and the paintings hanging on his walls were great pieces and objects of distraction. With Simon's exit, it was time for me to make my own exit.

"I see you have exquisite taste." Tee walks up to me, as I stand in front of a medieval age painting I am admiring. He orders the guards to leave the room.

"You like that?" Tee asks in a solemn tone.

"It is spectacular! An incredible work of art." I reply.

"Thank you. I gather this is what brought you and Alan together, right?" inquisitive.

"Not really," I respond.

"Well, he always brings me unique things. Just like this one. Half the time I barely understand the paintings but I just love how they are canvassed." Tee continues.

"I have taken too much of your time already."

"No worries at all. You are a pleasant young lady to host." Tee smiles in my direction.

"Well then, I'll take my leave now. Sorry to barge in on your meeting." I begin walking slowly towards the door.

"No worries, it will be concluded at a later date." Hastening my pace to the door, Roxie storms in like a roaring African lion.

"Well, well, well, who do we have here?" cynical.

"Hey doll, come on in dear." Tee reacts to her arrival.

"Thanks for your understanding. I'll leave now," I curtsy a little and run toward the door, Roxie's cold stare following me to the door. I lock the study room behind me and begin hearing hurricane Roxie pounding down on Tee.

"Really Tee? Really? What is that woman doing here?" She storms down on Tee.

"I love it when you are jealous! It's very sexy on you mami." His laughter met by Roxie's serious tone.

"I am not kidding with you man!" Her husky Jamaican accent takes over.

"Of course, I know you are dead serious dear," I hear Tee's humorous response. I move out of the way, as I sense Roxie may come out anytime. If there was a time to ransack the house more, this was a perfect opportunity. Before I could move completely away, Roxie storms out of the room and into the hallway where I stand looking really stupid, trying to make excuse for leaning against the door. Roxie slams the door after her and proceeds to tackle what lies in front of her... an embarrassed me.

"Whatever your agenda is here, it won't work! You hear me, it won't work!" she screams at me.

"Ma'am?"

"Don't you dare ma'am me! People like you, I know you kind too well!" She continues.

"And what kind am I?"

"The kind that wants to reap where they did not sow!... Yes, that kind!" Roxie speaks even louder.

"I am not sure what you mean ma'am. Have I done anything to you? Have we met before?"

"I'll have you know that just because you came to my party with Alan, it doesn't mean I have to allow you do what you want to do here?" my stomach begins rumbling and wondered if she'd found out our scheme to retrieve the stone in the house. I start to stutter, stomach quivering profusely at the thought of Roxie knowing our plan. I was soon relieved when she finally says what she thought I was doing.

"My friend's man is not up for sale! Neither is

my husband!"

"Sorry?"

"Uh… uh! You heard me the first time. I won't repeat myself!" Roxie lashes out even more yet I find myself relieved. She walks out of my sight and into the crowd at the reception before I could respond to her last accusation. It was certainly a close call, one I would rather forget, get the job done and run out of the mansion never looking back.

@@@@@

Roxie moves through the party, greets her guests and finds herself heading toward the guest bathroom. She rushes to make a phone call, while watching me walk into the party scene.

"You know I've got your back right?" Speaking into her dazzling phone cell. "Look woman, you better come stake your claim here!" The voice on the other end echoes through the cell.

"What are you saying Roxie?" Fanta's loud voice streams through the phone.

"I know you said you are busy but you need to come out here… and do it quickly!"

"Are you saying that son of a gun came to your party with another girl?"

"Yes Fanta babe! He told you it's business not pleasure? You were here yesterday and you saw all the preparation. Does that look like business to you girl?" Roxie continues.

"I can't believe this! He's doing it again!" Fanta yelling through the phone.

"Well, he is here with some African girl. Just bring yourself down here!"

"I'll be right there. I am so done with this rubbish!" Fanta states.

"You've got that right! Handle your business girl! I want this chick out of my house! No one is going to disrespect my house!" Roxie rambles in a thick Jamaican accent, as Fanta hangs up the phone.

BRASH & SASSY FANTA PLAYED BY KIM DUKE IS NOT HAVING IT! NO MAN WILL CHEAT ON HER!..ALAN IS IN FOR A BIG SHOCK!

WHO SAYS WE CAN'T HAVE FUN ON SET?
CHECK OUT THE PRINCESS OF SUBURBIA &
FANTA…

18 FLUSTERED TEAM

MY FRUSTRATION REGARDING NOT FINDING THE STONE AT TEE'S HOUSE IS HEIGHTENED BY ROXIE'S HAWK EYES WATCHING MY EVERY MOVE AT THE MANSION. At this point, I can only hope my cousin, Onye and Onka find the stone before anything bad happens to any of us.

Onye joins Hailey, Tee's daughter in their kitchen. He had watched her go in earlier and tailed her sneakily, his dark glasses harboring nefarious intent, his ridiculous hat tilted. He sees Hailey playing with her set of well-dressed dolls on the kitchen island.

"Hello there," he whispers, attempting an American accent, quickly scanning the doorway with his eyes, ensuring no one sees him.

"Hello, are you pappy's friend?" Hailey asks, cautiously.

"Oh yes… yes. Do you mind if I stay here and play with you?"

"I don't know. Mamie said not to play with strangers." Hailey responds.

"That is a great lesson. But you just said I am your pappy's friend, right?"

"Right." Hailey replies, still guarded.

"Well then, that makes me a friend and not a stranger, right?"

"I guess so."

"What is your name?"

"Hailey."

"Beautiful name." Onye covering his motives, desperately trying to get Hailey to cooperate.

"And your name?" Realizing he could not provide his real name, Onye stutters through the question and provides the first name on his tongue.

"Michael. My name is Michael. Do you think you can help you pappy's friend?" he pushes further.

"Sure." This was the answer he'd been hoping for. Onye struggles with the android phone he had on him but finally retrieves a picture of the stone.

"Have you seen this?" He asks while closely watching Hailey's reaction to the picture in front of her. "Well, have you seen it around here?" he repeats, peeking in the direction of the party.

"Come with me." Hailey replies, jumping off the stool by the kitchen island, grabbing her toys and leading Onye away from the kitchen. Hailey walks Onye onto the backyard porch. She points to the stone, on the ledge. Onye rushes for it, grabs it as Hailey looks on suspiciously.

"Thank you. You have been a great help. Now run along, I am sure your Mami will be looking for you now." Attempting to shoo Hailey from the location.

"Well, are you coming back in too? I can take

you to Pappy or Mami." Hailey answers back.

"Oh yes… sure. I need to make a quick call. You go inside; I don't want your mami to be upset with me. Okay?" Onye watches Hailey walk back into the mansion; he grabs his cell phone and makes his quick call.

"Onka, come quick. I found the stone! Now please! Meet me on the back porch. Now, please!" Stuttering and panicking through his banter.

"On the way bro'," Onka voice echoes through the cell phone.

@@@@@

No sooner had Onye and Hailey left the kitchen when Roxie and Tee storm into the kitchen looking for Hailey. They see one of her toys on the countertop.

"Where did that girl go? Honey, please check the den while I look in the powder room." Roxie speaks up. "I don't know how many times I have told that girl to always stay put in her bed whenever we are entertaining people."

"Roxie, she's fine. Quit being melodramatic. Where would she have gone? She is right here in the mansion, so stop the panic." Tee storms at Roxie.

"I wouldn't have worried if there were not so many people in the house right now."

"Got it! We will find her." They walk out of the kitchen in different directions. Tee hears Hailey crying from afar. He runs into the den, picks Hailey up and grabs her tight.

" Hey angel, you mami and I have been looking for you." Hailey continues to cry even louder.

"Talk to pappy What's wrong angel?"

"They stole my new friend pappy! The one you gave me." She continues her sobbing.

"The stone?"

"Yes pappy." Tee looks into the darkness surrounding the lawn at the back of the mansion. He catches a glimpse of Onye and Onka with the stone glowing in Onye's hands. Tee drops Hailey, instructs her to quickly go back into the mansion.

"Your Mami needs to know you are alright. You have to stop walking around this mansion on your own, okay dear?"

"Okay Pappy." She replies as one of the maids walk in.

"Take her to her bedroom right away please. Stay with her till she falls asleep. And tell her mom we found her."

"Yes sir." Maid replies, grabbing Hailey's arm. "Come on... let's go Hailey."

"Two crazy dudes are on my property! They've got my daughter's stone! Don't let them off this property. And get me Simon as well... No one messes with my family and gets away! No one!" Tee yells into his cell phone as he rushes back into the mansion.

@@@@@

The danger heightened in the mansion. I begin feeling in my soul, it was time to up my game, find the stone and dash out of there. Then it dawned on me that I had not seen Simon... and neither had I seen my cousins. I dash out of the last bedroom feeling defeated, antsy and headed straight for the party yet again. No sooner had I landed my feet on the rug when the sound of a slammed front door interrupted the whole party. Suddenly, it seems like all who are having good time, sipping champagne pause for few seconds looking in the direction of the front door. Fanta bursts into the party, with everyone's eyes on her! Jack raises his head from speaking with a lady he'd just met at the party; he sees "hurricane" Fanta as he'd always called her. He swiftly scopes the room for Alan. He excuses himself from the group of ladies surrounding him and rushes towards Alan.

"Ol' boy, you'd better look up before hurricane Fanta hits you hard," he murmurs as he weaves his way to Alan's side.

"You are not the one to tell me how to run my life!" Alan raises his voice at Roxie.

"No one is telling you what to do… just do it somewhere else!" Roxie responds in an escalated tone. Jack ignoring their bickering, smashes into their conversation rudely.

"Ol' boy, whatever you both are yapping about, is not as important as what is about to hit you Alan!" Jack warns in parables.

"What are you talking about Jack?" Alan annoyed at his current discussion with Roxie.

"Excuse me," looking in Roxie's direction.

"Oh you are excused! After all, birds of a feather, flock together!" She proceeds to walk away.

"Excuse me?" Jack inquires then turns to Alan.

"Please ignore her." Alan speaks.

"Ol' boy, you are in deep 'sheet'. Turn around quick!" Jack whispers in Alan's ear, attempting to speak over the music in the background. They both turn around and see

Fanta charging towards Alan.

"Oh shucks!" Alan comments.

"You are so busted friend!" Jack adds. "Your Southern charm won't get you out of this. So you'd better figure something out real fast."

"Oh hush, what are you talking about?"

"I would hate to be you right about now. Well brother, it's been fun. I am outta here!" Jack excuses himself walks up to Fanta, hugs her.

"Hello Fanta, it's always great seeing you. You are looking fabulous as ever." Jacking smiling sheepishly, making his way across the room.

"Sure Jack. Glad seeing you in this playpen!" Flippantly dismissing Jack.

"I'll get outta' your way." Jack mumbles.

"Yes, do just that!" Fanta in Alan's direction. They meet in the middle and before Alan could say anything, he feels the effect of Fanta's tongue spewing out vile words in his direction, as she reaches out to slap him!

"You just slapped me!"

"And I'll do it again and again and again! You deceitful lying cheating bastard!" Alan grabs a hold of her arm in rage. "What are you going to do about it!"

"If you ever touch me again!"

"What? I ask you again, what are you going to do about it? Leave me for that bimbo you are here with?"

"I don't know what you are talking about." Roxie looks on, pretending she didn't see or hear what they were discussing.

"You did all of this Roxie! Why did you have to call her?"

"Just like you, I have no clue what you are

talking about!" She grabs her glass and walks out away.

"You want to dump me for that bimbo right Alan? Is that your plan? Where is the low life hustler?" If I was waiting for any clues to confirm that this plan was going wrong, this was it! I backed my way into the lady's room and gently waited to ensure Fanta and her rage had left, before exiting the bathroom. Suddenly, it seemed things had died down, it was time for me to move out of the bathroom and find my way out of the mansion. I opened the door, sneaked out and straight into the hallway. Only, Fanta and Roxie were there, waiting for me, with Alan at her side.

"You again? Alan? That? You want that thing you plucked from the streets over me?" Before I could take any step further, Fanta launches in my direction and grabs for me! This was certainly an unexpected change of events. She slams my body against the wall with Roxie on the sidelines cheering her. I managed to push her off me.

"Where do you think you are going?"

"Will you get off me?" I screamed from underneath her.

"We are going to settle this once and for all!" Fanta continues in her rage.

"I know your kind! You are a thief! A husband snatcher! I will teach you a lesson that will last you a lifetime!" She yells from behind Fanta.

"I didn't steal anything from you!"

"Who do you think you are fooling? I watched you go into my husband's study and a while back, one of my maids saw you upstairs! What were you doing upstairs?"

"Is that true Siberia?" Alan's stands horrified by the latest news.

"Talk to me. Tell me they are lying! What were

you doing upstairs?"

"It's not what you think!" Struggling to get out of Fanta's grip.

"This is what you want dear Alan? This is the nasty gal you have been running around town with behind my back?" Fanta continues.

"Will you just shut up for a second and let me think?" Alan shouts at Fanta.

"A common thief! That's what you are!" The struggle intensifies, with Fanta almost choking me. Alan finally intervenes and with Fanta's last push, I ended on the cold hard wooden floor. I was consumed with straightening the black dress I was wearing that I'd forgotten the wig on my head. The most horrifying thing happened, in front of everyone... Alan, Fanta, Roxie and few of the guests now beginning to gather. As I dropped to the ground, so did my wig! I was mortified! What I'd feared the most, finally came upon me. I began feeling all astonished eyes on me, as I struggled to get off the hard floor. Though he looked undeniably disillusioned and perturbed, he seem to be concerned for my wellbeing. He instantly rushed to my side.

"Siberia! Get up! Are you alright?" Alan screams on top of his lungs, enough to make a deaf man recover his hearing.

"Silly clown, yes get up and let me give you more of what you deserve! You filthy thing!" Fanta growls at me. With all eyes on me, many shocked by my baldness, Alan included; I quickly snatched my wig from the floor the minute I broke away from Fanta's grip. I ran from their presence.

"This is what you want Alan dear? Wonders will never cease," Fanta's evil and cynical voice trails as I run into Tee's henchman!

"Hold it right there before I shoot!" his cold and calculating voice echoes after me. Confused at the thought of being caught by Tee's henchman, I lunged ahead ignoring his warnings. My heart almost stops as I hear the gunshot and feel the bullet graze my left leg. This was my end... I stumble onto the lawn and try to move my left leg to no avail.

"Go get her... now Casper! And bring her and other fools to me!" I hear Tee's angry voice. Just when I thought it was over, Jake's car pulls into the drive way. I look ahead and the henchman was making his way towards me with his gun ready to shoot and this time, he might not miss.

"Come on girl, hop in!" Jake's urgent voice cries. I look at Jake, struggling to pull my wounded leg through the grass.

"You are almost there, push Siberia. Let's go girl, you are almost here." Jake repeats. I finally muscled the courage to drag myself up Tee's manicured lawn. I hop into the passenger seat and Jake zooms off, with the henchman in pursuit on foot. We lost him and Jake pulls over to the side of the road. He holds me, ignoring my sobbing. Jake turns my face toward him as I desperately try to hide my embarrassment.

"You are beautiful," he whispers passionately into my ear. "You are beautiful just the way you are Siberia, wig or no wig. Look at me," attempting to pull me close.

"It's just that I don't want you to see me this way," I sobbed harder.

"I love you Siberia... There you go, I finally said it! I love you. I've always known there was something special about you. I love you." Jake repeats his proclamation of love for me. I finally mustered the courage, raise my head, with teary eyes colliding with his.

"Just the way you are," he repeats. "Now I need to get you out of here. You can't return home tonight. That may be the first place they check."
"Then I have nowhere else to go. I wouldn't want to bother my neighbor, Jessica."

"You don't have to worry about that. I have an idea."

19 BE STILL MY HEART

JAKE HELPED ME UP THE STAIRS TO HIS CONDO. I looked around his well-lit sitting room. His books were neatly stacked on a study table, the warm beige colors on the walls were well coordinated with the browns of his leather sofas.

"You are safe here tonight." Holding on tightly to me as I lean on him.

"I need to go home. I want to sleep in my own bed."

"Don't you think if they are looking for you, that is the first place they will look?"

"I am exhausted and not comfortable sleeping in someone else' bed." An awkward pause emerges as he settles me into a couch in his sitting room. I quickly take inventory of his condo, with my roaming eyes.

"You are such a simple guy… down to earth."

"Is that how you see me, a simply guy? Too simple for you perhaps?"

"No, that is not what I said Jake."

"Well then, answer the question. Am I too simple for you?"

"Jake, I am tired and in pain right now. I just need to rest."

"Well then, perhaps we should take you to the hospital." Hiding the pain in his heart.

"And say exactly what Jake?" That I was shot while trying to rob someone? Because trying to take the stone will be stealing, even though it's mine."

"We'll think of something else. First let me take a look at your leg, then we will decide." Settling down by my leg.

"It is settled Jake. I can't go to the hospital. I am nobody and I don't want to get into any more trouble than I'm already in."

"You are somebody. I just told you a while ago that I'm in love with you. What do you think?"

"How do you Americans say it... argh, yes, I am flattered and honored."

"That does not sound good."

"It is a good thing, alright Jake. Let's just leave it at that for now." Smiling in his direction, soothing his ego.

"May I?" He says and I nod in response and watch him gently pull up my black dress above my bruised knees and my strained left ankle.

"I'll be right back." He runs out for a bowl of water and comes back, settling yet again by my side. "Let's take a look at this," softly landing his wet towel on my ankle. I sigh in pain, squinting my eyes and attempting to avoid him seeing my face.

"I'll try to be gentle okay?" he smiles in my direction; his firm grip on my leg with his gentle fingers caressing my ankle seems like heaven.

"I need to tell you something... it's been

bugging me for a while and I really didn't know how to say it."

"What is it Jake? You know you can tell me anything, right?" I pull myself up, sitting probably and awaiting the information.

"Is it bad news? Cuz' I can't take any more bad news tonight."

"You need to know this," his voice suddenly somber.

"Well then, I'm listening. What do you guys say, what doesn't kill you will only make you stronger, right?"

"Right," he agrees, his eyes now fixated on mine, yet holding my ankle.

"I am afraid your cousins and my brother cannot be trusted."

"Why would you say such a thing Jake?"

"Because it's the truth. My brother came to me with a proposition. They offered me money to find the stone, help them sell it and then we all split the money." Instantly, my heart dropped, and I pulled my leg away from him.

"What? What are you talking about Jake?"

"I am so sorry I didn't tell you sooner."

"I find this hard to believe. There must be some misunderstanding somewhere. My cousins would never do that."

"I will never lie to you either Siberia. It's the truth because I turned them down!"

"I am not saying you are lying but Jake you should have told me sooner. My cousins know the importance of getting that stone back."

"I am sorry I didn't tell you... I just wanted you to focus on your mission and I felt that was important... that if you ended up with the stone, then none of this would matter."

"Not sure if this will help but I did tell them to tell you their plans, otherwise I would let you know. They promised to scrap the idea and confess. By your reaction, they didn't!"

"I am so disappointed in them. How could they? Knowing someone's life is on the line! How could they betray me like that?" uncontrolled tears moistening my cheeks.

"Unfortunately I go through the same betrayal every single day with Simon. Nothing fazes him a bit!" sneaking a look at his wrist watch. "It's really late. We both need some rest. I am so sorry you couldn't get the stone back tonight."

"I will figure something out, you'll see." My response.

"He gently lowers my leg and heads for a pile of pillows and blanket placed on one of his sofas.

"You must entertain here a lot," I inquire of Jake. "Why?"

"Seems like your blankets and pillows are permanent fixtures in your living room."

"Well, I sleep here a lot, that's why. For some reason my bedroom just doesn't do the trick for me on days when I am so tired." He glances at me, my mischievous looks more glaring.

"Don't get any funny ideas. I can see the look on your face… No, I do not entertain ladies here a lot."

"Oh, my look is nothing… Just wanting to know, that's all," my eyes roaming around, looking for clues to perhaps the presence of a female touch in the condo. Alan had fooled me into thinking he was by himself; even though I had that feeling that his relationship with Fanta was deeper than he'd let on; I still developed some kind of attraction for him. This time, I was going to be very careful; I was going to listen to my heart; my instinct would guide me to the truth and when I find the truth, I will oblige! I watch as Jake pulls out the sofa, then lays the blankets on it. In few seconds, the sofa was ready for me.

"There you go. Let's get you tucked in here." Jake says.

"You mean I will be sleeping right here?"

"Unless you'd like to sleep in my bedroom. Don't worry, I am a gentleman." Grinning as he helps me to the sofa. He places a cover over me.

"Comfy?" he asks.

"Yes, thank you," my strained voice manages to speak up.

"You are quite welcome. Now, close your eyes and rest. We will deal with everything else after we have rested

"Jake?"

"Yes?"

"We need to go back for them, you know that, right?"

"No! I don't! Personally, I am tired of Simon getting himself in trouble and I always being there to bail him out. I don't want to do that this time. It's time he learns his lesson and that goes for your cousins too."

"Regardless, we can't leave them out there with Tee and his people!"

"Why not? You are way more generous than I am at this very minute. "

"What if something bad really happens to them; are you willing to live with that on your conscience? You will never forgive yourself Jake."

"I am so tired of running after my brother. I can't do it anymore!" I reached out gently caress Jake's face.

"We must go… okay Jake?"

@@@@@

"Bring them over here!" Tee's angry voice echoes through his living room. "I don't know you so who are you and what you are doing in my house? Start talking... right now!"

"Wait Onka, let me be the spokesperson" clearing his throat. "Big man, our names are Onka and Onye Tonka!"

"Yes? And I am still not getting you... who are you and how did you get into my party?" Tee snaps at them.

"A friend invited us to your party. By the way, you throw a great party." Onye jumps in.

"And who is this friend of yours. If I may ask?" he continues his interrogation as one of his guards walks in. "Yes Rollins?" in the guard's direction.

"Sir, Hailey told Casper that one of the men has her stone... sir."

"I see. Is that right?" he pauses for a second, then turns right back in Onye and Onka's direction.

"What stone? Do you know what they are saying Onka?"

"Oh no o, stone? What stone?" Onka begins to stutter through his speech.

"Perhaps you need your memory jogged. I will gladly offer that to you."

"And you!" Tee speaking to the guard.
Find out which guard was at the door when these goons crashed my party."

"Yes sir!" he walks out of the room leaving Tee and two of his henchmen with Onka and Onye.

"Brother, this is serious Hollywood scene o," Onye whispers in Onka's ear.

264

"Are you serious? You are facing death and you are talking about Hollywood scene." Onka nods his head.

"Na you sa be o! Isn't it?" Onye continues his distraction.

"It is obvious they are not ready to talk! And I am not ready to waste my time on time... you, deal with them!" Tee orders one of his henchmen. Onka begins to scream as the henchmen walk in their direction.

"Wait! Wait a second! I will tell you where the stone is!"

"You will?" Onye asks, unsure if Onka meant it or was just up to his famous tricks... tricks he often pulled at the village when he tries to get out of a sticky situation such as this.

"Yes, I don't want to die in America. Do you?"

"Oh no, but you will."

"Quit wasting my time and start talking!" Tee lashes out again.

"Our cousin has it."

"And who is your cousin?"

"Her name is Siberia... Siberia Tonka." Onka replies frightfully.

"You mean the girl who came here tonight with Alan?"

"Yes! That one." Onka responds.

"Where can my boys find her?" Onka and Onye begin shaking their heads.

"You will give my guys the address otherwise, the last beating you took will seem like nothing compared to what is waiting for you! You hear me?"

"Oh yes sir... We will show you where she lives."

"No! You will hand over the address. Kapish? You two are going nowhere until my guys retrieve the stone."

"It is just a stone sir… nothing to die for."

"You could have fooled me! Why in the world would you crash my party if this stone was just a stone?" Onye and Onke refuse to answer his question.

"You know what pisses me off the most, that people will come into my home and disrespect my family!"

"We are so sorry sir! We just came to have a good time."

"I will give you something to be sorry about!" Turning to his henchman, "I don't care where the girl runs to. If she goes under a rock, you go with her!"

"Yes sir," his henchman replies.

"Find her and bring her to me. Then bring the fool who drove her out of this compound. "In the meantime, you take care of these fools and if they give you any problems, you know exactly what to do with them. Waste them!"

"Start talking bro', I don't want to be wasted here in this obodo America." Onka speaks.

"Come on my friend, be quiet. There you go again! Wimp!" Onye whispers in his ear as they are dragged from Tee's presence.

@@@@@

It happens again! Another horrifying nightmare with Yemoji, my mystery woman right smack in the middle of my unrest. I wrestled violently with her images blasted in my subconscious and my sleep turns into another battle ground for Yemoji to exploit. I jump off of Jake's sofa in a cold sweat. Jake must have heard my screams during my dreams because I as jumped out off the sofa, he was standing over me, watching me with a worried look written all over his face.

"Are you alright?" His soothing voice caresses my tired soul. "Are you okay Siberia?" He repeats, watching me pull myself together. With my throat parched, I quickly nod to ease his mind. I began looking around for a wall clock.

"You need something?" Jakes continues, following my panning of room.

"What time is it now?" I inquire of him.

"It's almost 12 noon. Why?"

"Oh my gosh, I didn't realize I slept for so long."

"You've been through a great ordeal. You need your rest."

"I shouldn't be sleeping like this when chaos is out there with my name on it!" attempting to rise from the sofa.

"Look, whatever mess is out there, you didn't cause it and you most certainly must not beat yourself up over it. We all need to rest at some point in our lives. This is yours so take it!" His voice turns firm. Jake rushes closer.

"There you go. You need to take it easy when getting out of that sofa."

"Thanks. Can you turn on the television please?"

"Of course... no problem. Let's get you situated in a chair first. Okay?"

"I really appreciate you being here for me."

"I have to Siberia. I care deeply for you."

"I care for you too."

"Wow! Did you mean that?"

"I do not say what I don't mean." Giggling in his direction. His bubbling demeanor now accentuated. The Princess of Suburbia's daily show was just wrapping up when I caught a glimpse of its ending. The announcement I had been waiting for all of my life happened. The Princess of Suburbia announces where her next book signing would be! It was right at my neighborhood library! What are the odds of that happening!

"Alright friends and families, it's that time of the day when I say thank you for riding this journey with me on the Princess of Suburbia show. I have truly been blessed by you all being in my life." Her voice echoes through the television.

"I see you are completely engaged with this woman." Jake interrupts. I sigh in return, still fully engaged in what the princess of suburbia was sharing.

"I can't wait to meet you all today at the Springs library. It's going to be a great time people and bye for now" her voice trialed away as her show anthem music picks up the pace, then fades out.

"I have waited all these years to meet this woman. Here is my chance to meet her and I am taking it!" I continue my discussion with Jake.

"Call me crazy, I sometimes don't get you."

"What do you mean?"

"Here you are, all banged up and you are thinking about going to meet the woman… also saving your cousins … all at the same time. Can't you see that you can't go anywhere like this?"

"I'm afraid I just can't sit on my duff when Onka and Onye and your brother, Simon, are in grave danger being in Tee's custody."

"You are such a generous soul. "

"Don't be too quick to judge."

"Well then, I will go by myself if have I to."

"Okay make me understand why you want to expose yourself to yet another danger. Why do you feel the need to choose this time to meet the writer? Don't you get it, Tee's goons are probably looking for you now."

"She can help. I know she can!"

"Is she also in law enforcement? Isn't she just a

writer?"

"She is more than just a writer to me Jake."

"Then humor me, make me believe."

"This my chance to meet the woman I have adored her for so long... I am in America because of her."

"Sorry, I am not following you... I just don't get it."

"She gets it all... my culture... all I am going through now. She gets it. Perhaps she'll be able to help with my cousins too."

"I'm not sold in this idea of yours but if you are bent on following through, then I will take you to the library."

"Trust me, she will understand the importance of the stone and could perhaps explain better to Tee or anyone for that matter."

"That is such a long shot Siberia. I don't want you to be disappointed."

"If she is anywhere close to who I think she is, she will help."

"Okay Siberia. It's your decision."

"Don't get me wrong! I am so angry at my cousins! All their plots to steal the stone from underneath me... everything failed. That is a lesson in of itself! But I can't let Tee mistreat or kill them. I don't want them on my conscience." My agitation grew as I explain my reason for wanting to save my cousins and also meet the Princess of Suburbia. This provided the strength I needed to get up and walk towards Jake's front door.

"Are you coming?" I ask secretly hoping his answer would be a resounding yes.

"I am not going to let you face this alone. You should know that by now. Though it is really against my better judgment."

"Thank you." We dash out of his condo, reacting to every suspicious sounds I heard on the way out.

20 THE FRONTIER

THE PRINCESS OF SUBURBIA IS BEING HEAVILY
GUARDED BY HER ROBUST AND FIERCE
LOOKING SECURITY TEAM. They wear dark suits, dark
shades, ear wigs in place … kind of like what we see in the
movies. For a split second, I had the feeling that I was ~~of~~
crashing the US president's party. Her assistant stays
extremely close to her, carefully watching the crowd who
were waiting to have their book autographed by the princess.
After looking on for few minutes, I finally mustered up the
courage, slowly walk past those in line, hoping that no-one
would say a word. When her guards were busy persuading the
crowd to tone their voices down, I leap towards the princess.
It was my only chance at getting to her with no delays. I was
almost home free when a guard in a his commanding baritone
voice yells at me. In an attempt to ignore him, my eyes fixed
on the Princess of Suburbia, I increase my pace. No sooner
had I done that, when I see his 6ft 4in muscular frame
pushing through the crowds toward me.

"To the line ma'am! The line ma'am" he
continuously repeats, planting is full figure in front of me and

casting a dark shadow on me.

"I need to see the Princess of Suburbia please!"
I yell hoping she would eventually look my way.

"Look around ma'am, everyone wants to see
the princess. Your request is no exception. Now, please move
to the line." The murmurings of those in the line meant
nothing to me. I am in a desperate mood and this may be the
only chance I have to meet her and also seek her help with
my predicament.

"You don't understand. I must see her!" I
repeatedly yell above the murmuring voices in the
background.

@@@@@

The Princess of Suburbia hears the roaring and she watches
her guard walk me to the back for he line. She lifts her head
up, above the commotion in the crowd and our eyes meet as
I turned around in her direction. Suddenly, I felt my world
stop. At last, the Princess of Suburbia was looking at me. I
have finally gotten her attention. She signals for her assistant,
a young lady probably in her early twenties, her hair tightly
pulled to the back, her dark framed pair of glasses resting
comfortably over her eyes.

"Do you know what that is all about?" she
inquires of Amelia, her assistant, who shakes her head and
shrugs her shoulders in response.

"Can you find out for me please? Thanks" she
continues to look in my direction while juggling the process
of signing her fans purchased books.

"Yes ma'am," Amelia walks away. Amelia
signals to a bodyguard, instructing him to cover her spot

while she walks into the crowd. The Princess of Suburbia continues to sign her autographs, taking pictures with fans, while keeping her eyes alert ~~close~~ to the increased commotion. Amelia walks into the crowd, astonished eyes following her.

"Is there a problem here?" She whispers in the guard's direction.

"I've got this. It is nothing I can't handle." He whispers in response, ensuring that I did not hear his answer.

"Wonderful! Then let's try to keep it down a little so the princess can concentrate. The noise from this section is somewhat distracting!"

"Handling it," guard replies as Amelia makes her way back to the princess' side. In desperation and complete determination, I trailed her back into the princess' presence. She soon realizes I was trailing her, she abruptly turns back, facing me at close proximity.

"And what do you think you are doing? Ma'am, you've been warned to step back. Please comply." All eyes are on me, including Jake's, who is constantly butting in and attempting to persuade me from making a fool out of myself, yet I charged on.

"Look, I have to see her. It's urgent!" I scream, almost rupturing my throat. Jake steps up, puts his arms around me, attempting to pull me out of the situation.

"She just needs to speak with the princess for few seconds guys. That is all she needs."

"I am not leaving here until I speak with her! I have come too far!" "So have we!" a loud voice from the line blasts.

"Keep your voice down ma'am." Amelia regurgitates.

"I will when I am done seeing her." I respond, yelling.

"Alright dear, I think you have tried. Now, we need to figure another way out of this. You can always take her autograph some other time."

"Jake, this is not about her autograph and you know it!" I pull away pushing forward in the princess' direction. I look back at the incredibly long line, if I chose to join them; there is no telling what could happen to my cousins! If all I needed tonight was to see her, then it would make sense to join the line. This is not the case! I watch as the ticking wall clock makes a resounding noise, a reminder of the very slim chance I have of saving my cousins and Simon!

"Sorry! No can do! I have to see the Princess of Suburbia now! Sorry folks, I don't mean to jump the line. I just have an emergency situation right now!" the murmuring and rumbling form the crows begins to escalate. I quickly evade the guards, jumped in between them and Amelia, Princess' assistant and launched forward. This time, my quick move was effective! I attempt to drop a note in front of her when Amelia catches up and takes it from me.

"Please Princess. Please help me… please," all teary eyed. If there was ever a moment I knew I could reach anyone, it was this very moment. I see a glimpse of compassion in the Princess' eyes as Amelia barricades me away from her presence.

"Let her be." Her angelic, yet firm, voice breaking through the tensed atmosphere.

"But ma'am…" Amelia replies looking frustrated and confused.

"It's okay guys, you hear me? Let her be."

Amelia hands over the note as I make my way out of her presence, into Jakes arms and we rush out of the library.

"Are you satisfied now?" Jake asks, his arms securing my waists as I leap.

"If she is anything like what I believe she is… I know she will help." I smile in his arms.

"Now, we go to the mansion." Jake and I headed back to find my cousins. As papa and mama taught me, regardless of how family hurts you, they are still your family and you must act accordingly in time of crisis. This was a time of crisis and I was ready, willing and determined to risk it all, just to save them.

@@@@@

The Princess of Suburbia pauses from signing; she opens the letter handed over to her hesitantly by Amelia.

"What? You think there is a bomb in it?" smiling at a frowning Amelia.

"Ma'am?"

"Oh lighten up Amelia, I'm fine. See I am opening it and nothing has blown up yet."

.

PRINCESS OF SUBURBIA®, JAKE
O'CONNOR & FANTA.... WHAT ARE
THEY UP TO NOW? GRHHHHHH!

CAN SOMEONE TELL AMELIA (EMILY HAMBY), PRINCESS OF SUBURBIA'S® ASSISTANT TO CHILL A LITTLE?

IT'S FUN BEING OUT OF CHARACTER…
SMILE FLYING…

THERE GOES FANTA, JAKE AND THE
PRINCESS OF SUBURBIA®

21 THE LION'S DEN

AGAINST BETTER JUDGMENT, AS HE'D
REMINDED ME, JAKE ZOOMS ONTO TEE'S
ESTATE.

"I hope you know what you are doing Siberia. I
just have a bad feeling about this."

"We will be fine… I think" I reply trying to
hide my uncertainty. Here I am, in front of the very mansion
I'd escaped from; hoping that a woman I'd just met few
minutes ago will somehow show up to help. At this point, I
am not sure who is smarter, my cousins who got caught due
to their own greed or myself, who is now coming back to the
lion's den to save them! The thought of having to tell my
parents that the boys their sister had entrusted into their care
had died in America; the thought of them reaching to Onka
and Onye's parents with such bereaving news overwhelms
me. No one at the village will ever believe the story! It was
certainly the jolt I needed to conclude that I had no choice
but to go ahead with my plan to save them. I was deep in my
thoughts when I heard two baritone voices and a strong arm
pull open my passenger side door.

"You are either a fool or a martyr to come back here again!" A henchman murmurs, pulling me out of the car.

"Hey! Hey! Leave her alone. You don't have to push her!" Jake yells.

"It's okay Jake. We have to do this now! Please take me to Tee." I respond.

"Be glad to!" henchman cynical.

"Just me though"

"What?" Jake speaks up.

"Yes! Just me. This is my fight!" I remind Jake.

"Please do not listen to her. If you are taking her in, then you will take us both in."

"Yo man! You don't get to dictate who goes where on this ground! You hear me?" Jake and I suddenly are silent, watching to see what their decision will be.

"Stay with him here. Make sure he goes nowhere! I'll be right back!," one henchman pushes me toward the mansion leaving the other guy with Jake.

@@@@@

Onye and Onka are sitting off to the side of a room, their faces bruised and looking exhausted. Their clothes stained with dark streaks of their own dried blood.

"Bring the fool over here! You have the nerve to return to my house?" Tee's angered tone magnifies in my presence. My eyes welled up as the sight of my cousins. Suddenly, my anger towards them subsides as my determination to speak on their behalf took over.

"I'm not here to fight or argue with you. I just want to plead for my cousins, that's all." I continue sobbing uncontrollably.

"You mean those good for nothing misfits?"

"Call them whatever you want. Perhaps they deserve the name calling but please I need you to hear me out."

"Start talking and make it fast!" Tee shouts out, signaling his henchman to hold a gun right in my face.

"Your two seconds start now!" Tee's anger implodes.

"You need to believe me, we just want the stone back. We have to return it home to Africa where it belongs."

"Your time is up and I still don't know why I shouldn't waste you all!"

"I know the stone may be worth nothing to you but it is worth a life to us! We must return the stone home!"

"Look, that's all fine and good... the stone is of a sentimental value to you... I am a business man and when two or three of you starts getting desperate about a mere stone, my business side sticks out. I want to know the truth now!" unmoved by my sob story.

"You have few seconds left. I'll suggest you use it wisely!"

"Sir, she is telling the truth. Her sister is lying on her sick bed in Africa! We have to take the stone back home." restraining myself from kicking them both, just hearing Onka's plea for the retrieval of the stone.

"Since when did you grow conscience to return the stone?" I whispered in both their ears, standing in between them.

"You know?" Onka asks with a repentant stare.

"Every detail but now is not the time to handle

that. I will deal with you both myself!" quickly turning back in Tee's direction.

"Bro' we are in deep trouble, if she tells papa and mama." Onka reminds Onye.

"Look bro', you heard her… first things first. Let's get out of this mess. Then we will deal with the other issue. Right now, I don't know if we are even going to get out of here!" Onye adds.

"Hunnnnn…. Na real wa o. You and your brilliant idea got us into this mess!" Onka's voice bellows.

"Whoa… whoa… whoa! Do you guys realize where you are?" Tee interrupts.

"Seriously guys! You are going to start this here?" yelling at them with passion.

"I just want to plead for my cousins… as foolish as they are, they meant no harm to your family."

"Speak on sister, you talk true," Onye disrupts the conversation.

"Now, just how much is this stone worth?" Suddenly, I watched Onka and Onye's eyes shift and it became glaring that they had more secrets they were hiding.

"You said it yourself, it is of sentimental value… That's all, right Onye?" Onka stutters through his windy speech.

"Oh yes… no value at all… But, of course, to our culture." Onye picks up from where Onka ended. After what seemed like eternity, it was clear that Tee was not swayed by my expressed emotions. The only one who could rescue us now was the Princess of Suburbia. Jake was still outside and he could not get help. Perhaps Jake was right… we could have involved the police. I could have looked beyond all the stories I'd had about immigrants being harassed and just trusted the justice system to handle this. Instead, I have not only endangered my life but Jake's. Was I wrong in thinking that the Princess of Suburbia would find a way to rescue us? Have I been in a fantasy world all this time, thinking I could achieve my dream? With death staring me in the face, I quickly resolved I had been wrong!

"Yo, Casper! Do your thing!" Tee's voice echoing through the room. No sooner had Casper cocked his gun, ready to fire at me, when the Princess of Suburbia's security guards burst into the mansion. My first thought was that my mind was not conjuring up the princess to ease the pain. When I came out of my momentary lapse, Tee had somehow disappeared but some of his guards were apprehended, tied up, then seated on the floor. Shortly thereafter, we hear police sirens outside of the front door as the Princess of Suburbia strides into the mansion.

"Oh my God, you came! She came!" hysterical at the sight of the princess. Her genuine aura fills the atmosphere. Greatness had come looking for me! Jake is right behind her, following her to the mansion. He rushes straight to my side, holding me tight.

"Are you alright Siberia?" he keeps asking, feeling all parts of my body to make sure.

"I'm not hurt. I'm fine. See... I told you she'd come." Smiling and pulling slightly away from Jake.

"Thank you oh... Papa God, we dodged a bullet here o bro'? Onye frantic.

"I couldn't have ignored what you wrote, could I" her arms spread out awaiting my arrival. The princess opens my letter to her... "see," she continues, saying how could I ignore your plea to save your cousins and to get the stone."

"I have the stone! I just didn't want them to take it from me," Onye stands up from his knees and rushes towards me.

"Sis', I am so sorry! We were wrong," Onka joins them by the princess.

"Greed is an ugly poison to the soul. " The princess adds. Onye extends the stone to me, remorsefully as Onka and Jake looks ahead.

"No you hold on to it and get it home safe." I insists.

"I have heard so much of the Silleri stone when I was back home. Now I get to see it." The princess smiling as she takes a glimpse at the dazzling stone.

"Yes, my family owns it and I am so glad it's going back so my sister can get better."

"Allow me to share this with you. Our culture is our inheritance. So we must never do away with it. There is, however, a stronger message with Silleri. It is not the stone that harbors the power but those of us who value it. The stronger our faith is in bringing unity, in sharing love amongst us, the stronger we are." All captivated by the alluring Princess of Suburbia.

"It is how we value and treat each other that fuels all possibilities. The greater our love for mankind, the more the universe becomes open for us." The princess continues on.

"Thank you for your kind words princess. I pray one day, I can write a book about all of these adventures." I state.

"It is very possible. All things are possible. Our meeting is by no accident. Remember, there is always a gift of storytelling in a hard place like where you've been. Let's see how we can make this happen for you, shall we?"

"It is time to go back home with the stone Onye." Onka speaks up. "You won't tell papa and mama about all of this, or are you? We are really sorry sis'. We just got carried away."

"Your behavior was beyond being carried away. You both lost your minds! And don't you dare ask me not to tell them!"

"Forgiveness is a gift we must gladly offer," the princess interjects in a soft voice. There is silence as Onka and Onye look on to see what my reaction would be with the princess' last speech. Simon walks into the room from another part of the mansion.

"You don't have to worry about me telling them. All it's forgiven just as the princess says."

"I am so sorry Jake... Sorry... so incredibly sorry for all of the headaches I have caused you." Simon speaks genuinely.

"Where have you been Simon?"

"I was held in another part of this God forsaken place! The guard left me, hearing the sirens."

"Well, does that mean no more headaches from you... ever again?" Jake asks in a serious tone.

"You know what I am all about. This is your brother... Simon the infamous? Right?"

"I didn't think so!"

"Look... hear me out. I mean it when I say I will be on my best behavior from here on. This is the best I can offer for now."

"You promise to get help for your drug problem?" Jake cautious.

"Yes I will. I came close to being snuffed out

by Tee's men. It will never happen again!" Simon concurs as Jake pulls him and hugs him hard.

"It's good to see you in one piece!"

22. THE RESOLVE

IT'S BEEN ONE YEAR SINCE THE INCIDENT AT TEE'S PLACE. Tee and his people are still in court for charges of assault and kidnapping. My cousins have finally turned over a new leaf and her being productive at the village, helping others to read and study for their college entrance exams. From what I hear, they have set up a non profit organization devoted to educating children from the village, a debt they believe they owed to a society and culture they betrayed in America. The news that Naiya's illness is long past was so welcome. And finally, a young male teacher in the village has come seeking Naiya's hand in marriage and all plans are in motion for the long awaited wedding.

My relationship with Jake is going well and so is my relationship with my mentor, the Princess of Suburbia, who has since taken on my cause, helping me to get my first book published! Friends like Jessica keep wondering when Jake will pop the question; I know when the time is right, he will do what is right. In the meantime, we enjoy growing together and learning more about our different cultures.

You are probably wondering what happened to Yemoji, the mystery lady who disturbs my dream….Well, since my cousins returned the Silleri back to its' rightful place and owner, my papa and mama; the mystery woman showed up once again in my dream. Only this time I saw her in great turmoil, burning to ashes and screaming out of tremendous pain. Finally, her power over had been lifted!

"Siberia! Siberia!" Jake whispers into my ear, pointing at the line in from of me. I quickly staggered out of my thoughts of Yemoji, enjoying the captivated audience awaiting my signature on the book they'd purchased.
I look across the crowd once again with much content, Jake by my side and Jessica, my nosy neighbor cheering me on. As much as I believed I would someday become an established author, being a New York Bestselling author was just a dream. I repeatedly look into the cheering crowd, and familiar faces pop out… the face of my former landlord, Aashish Babu and his son, Sanje; Josie, Jessica's sister and Simon… all laughing out loud and screaming my name as loud as they can. How could this much success befall me, an African immigrant living in a countryside town in America? My heart is overwhelmed as I glance into the crowd yet again, signing one book at a time and responding to the cheers around me.

"Are you alright?" Jake bends down to check on me.

"I am just fine dear… Incredibly blessed to have you and to be here right now with you." I respond. Kairos Shopper, Lola, my newly found celebrity stylist… who was introduced to me by the Princess of Suburbia, walks into my presence carrying two oversized gift bags. She places the gift bags by my side, right next to my assistant, Jackee.

"Will take care of that ma'am," Jackee takes gift bags away. If there was anyone I needed to be at my very first event, it would be the Princess of Suburbia. Without her, I could never have had the platform or tell my story. If there was a lesson I learned throughout this process, it is that we all need each other to succeed. The Princess of Suburbia was certainly secure in herself... secure enough to help me publish my very first book and confident enough in herself to help push my book all the way into the bestseller list. I was deep in thought when I hear a still, small voice...

"Ma'am... ma'am?" It was the Princess of Suburbia's assistant and the princess herself coming to join the event. I look up and there she is... an epitome of beauty, love, and grace.

"Beautiful... This is just beautiful Siberia," she gently speaks into the crowd. If you wondered how the face of a content person looks like, it was mine! My mentor had finally arrived at my event! She grabs a copy of my book, Of Sentimental Value, and asks me to sign it for her. Another lesson learned during this journey is to never give up on our dreams, regardless of how stupid and impossible it may seem to others. Never allow the derogatory behaviors of your nay-sayers to put you down. You are fearfully and wonderfully made, with all the tools you need to succeed... lessons I have grown to share with my audience in all of my speaking engagements.

A Life Lesson from Siberia Tonka

A person who sows love reaps a harvest of good friends and family. It doesn't really matter where we come

291

from; we all have something of sentimental value. An this crazy chain of events has led me to my destiny....it has led me to fight for the people I love and this whole experience was just too good to not have its own book. And now, I get to share my story with the world~~~*Siberia Tonka.*

And all is well with the world...

AN EPIC EVENT!
AUTHOR'S SPECIAL NOTES &
EXTRA
SCENES FROM THE MOVIE

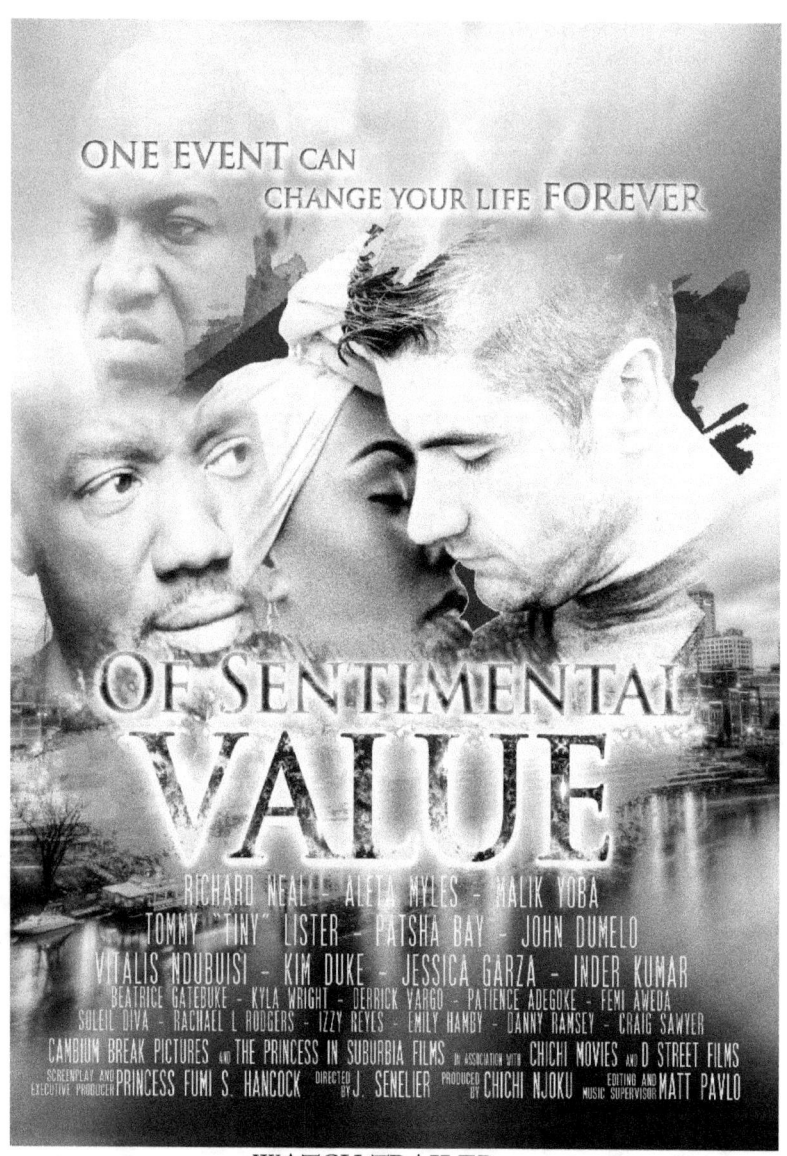

WATCH TRAILER:
WWW.OFSENTIMENTALVALUENOVEL.COM

ONE EVENT ELECTS WHO YOU ARE…

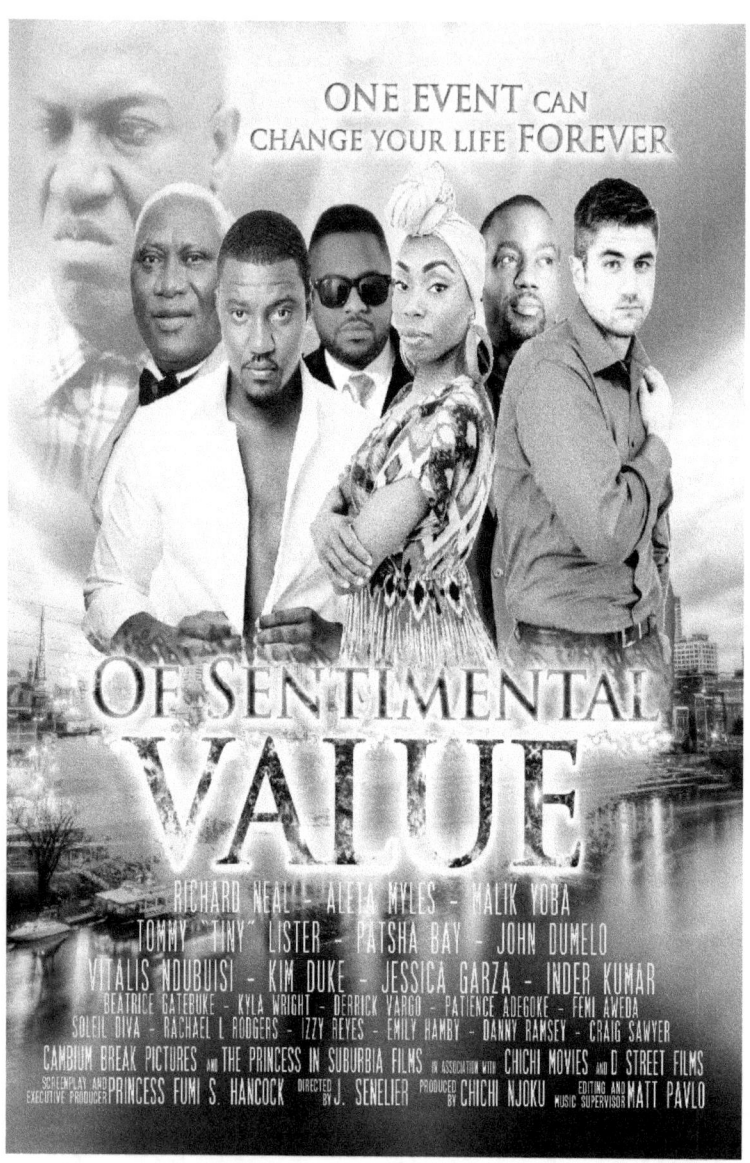

ONE EVENT MOLDS YOUR VALUES & BELIEVES...

ONE EVENT CHARTS THE COURSE OF YOUR JOURNEY.... GOOD, BAD OR INDIFFERENT....

EXECUTIVE PRODUCER & SCREENWRITER,
PRINCESS FUMI HANCOCK AND FRIENDS
ON SET

EXECUTIVE PRODUCER & SCREENWRITER
AND HUBBY, DR. DAVID HANCOCK

ONE EVENT DETERMINES YOUR DESTINY.... FOR LIFE!

ON SET WITH "JAKE O'CONNER" &
"SIBERIA TONKA"

"SIBERIA TONKA" & "THE PRINCESS OF
SUBURBIA" CLOWN AROUND ON SET

ONE EVENT WILL CHANGE YOUR LIFE….FOREVER!

DID "SIBERIA TONKA" BECOME A BESTSELLING AUTHOR TOO? FIND OUT IN THE BOOK, OF SENTIMENTAL VALUE AND THE MOVIE

"FANTA" & "THE PRINCESS OF SUBURBIA". GUESS WHO'S GOT THE BIG, BOLD, BAD MUSCLES TO SHOW OFF?

"AMELIA", THE PRINCESS OF SUBURBIA'S
ASST. ROCKS THE SET

DID "NAIYA" GET BETTER? ROCKING THE
SET WITH "SIBERIA'S MOTHER"

BLAZING "FANTA" & "THE PRINCESS OF
SUBURBIA ROCK THE SET

ABOUT THE AUTHOR

PRINCESS FUMI STEPHANIE HANCOCK, Ph.D.

BESTSELLING AUTHOR, NAFCA AFRICAN OSCAR PEOPLES" CHOICE WINNING FILMMAKER, AFRICAN OSCAR NOMINATED TV HOST, LIFE COACH & PHILANTHROPIST are just few accolades to describe this dynamic woman.

Born in the heart of Nigeria, Lagos State; Princess Fumi Hancock was raised to appreciate her royal roots from the South Western region of Nigeria, Emure Kingdom, where her family, the Adumori Nigeria Royal Household have ruled since the 1800s'.
After acquiring her first degree in English from one of the most prestigious colleges in Nigeria, Obafemi Awolowo University; she stormed the United States of America with a pen, a script and the dream to change the world. Little did she know that it would take her over thirty years to finally fulfill her dream of becoming a prolific writer and most importantly, one who would have the ability to translate her literary works into movies.

As an author, she has written several inspirational books for women, Beyond Idol Worship: A Diary of an African Warrior Princess; Starting Right Now to name a few! After writing these inspirational books and her return back to African after over 25 years absentia; she reaches out to help her community through her US based nonprofit organization, Adassa Adumori Foundation, Inc. (www.adassafoundation.org); she also decided to venture into the world of young adult fantasy. To her surprise, her very first young adult fantasy, The Adventures of Jewel Cardwell: Hydra's Nest became an amazon bestseller! There has been no stopping her since then.

Her new novel, Of Sentimental Value, a mystery & suspense drama is yet another landmark for her. The book was made into a feature film which is scheduled for release soon (www.ofsentimentalvaluemovie.com). In the advent of its release, it has garnered multiple award interest. It was nominated in the NAFCA African Oscar Peoples' Choice category for Favorite Trailer & Original Score while the Princess took home the winning trophy as Favorite Screenwriter. Since then, the movie itself has been nominated in the following categories: Best Diaspora Drama & Best Make-up. One of our supporting actors, Malik Yoba was also nominated as Actor in Foreign Film category.

Princess Fumi is one who truly believes that dreams do come true if we keep plugging away at it and never give up!

Her very first crack at writing, she will never forget her professor at a college in New York telling her, "you need to quit! You are a horrible writer!" "I was devastated," she said. But did not allow that to keep her down. With time, even the professor finally announced to the post graduate class that she was the best student he'd ever had. That screenplay, "The Royal Bird" ended up winning Best Screenplay of the year in 1988 in a New York festival. It was later auctioned to one of the largest television stations in Africa, Nigerian Television Authority (NTA). The rest of her time today is spent presenting her new empowerment program, Your Vision Torch, an Innovator's Prescription to Igniting Your Dreams & Harnessing Your Vision to leaders, business owners & women across Africa & the United States of America. More details on how to bring her to your event: www.worldoffumihancock.com

www.ingramcontent.com/pod-product-compliance
Lightning Source LLC
Chambersburg PA
CBHW072057020726
47501CB00003B/623